Enter Sandman

A Novel

Enter Sandman

Stephanie Williams

McWitty Press • New York

ISBN 0-9755618-0-4

Library of Congress Cataloging-In-Publication Data upon request

Author's note
This is a work of fiction. Names, characters, places, and incidents are either the product of the author's imagination or are used fictitiously. Any resemblance to actual persons, living or dead, is coincidental.

Address inquiries to McWitty Press, Inc.; 110 Riverside Dr.; New York, N.Y. 10024;

www.mcwittypress.com

Printed in the United States of America

First Edition

Jacket Art by Marion Spirn
Book design by Michael D. Keyes/Camden Printing, Inc.

A portion of profits from this book will go
to breast cancer research.

For Mums,
the best mother, caregiver, and friend
anyone could ask for

THE NEW YORK POST

WHO'S THAT MUSE?: Art tart has NYC guessing
MAY 22, 2010—*Who's that girl?*
The entire New York art scene—make that all of New
York—wants to know. Call this impassioned pretty woman
the "Moan-a Lisa." Not since Leonardo da Vinci's mystery
madam has a *femme* in a frame been the object of so much
speculation.

The question arises at the Museum of Modern Art's
blockbuster retrospective of James Morales, the "bad boy"
artist who thumbed his nose at the art establishment by
entering a self-imposed exile just after shooting to fame in
the late 1990's. For years, when curious collectors asked
after Morales's work, curators told them the hard-edged
Latino's brush had dried up (and, word had it, that the bald
bruiser himself had *cracked* up).

Now we find that his magic materials were flying across
the canvas the entire time. Along with *Junkyard*, the mixed-
media painting that won Morales his first kudos at 1997's
Promettente (as always, at the Galina Woodworth Gallery),
MoMA offers room after room of lush abstracts in lighter
flesh tones, browns, and reds—leading, chronologically, to
his final works, more straightforward paintings of what are
obviously half-body nudes featuring a porcelain-skinned
woman in repose. Many have compared the most tri-
umphant, *Untitled IV 2004*—a deeply textured, full-body
nude of a tortured and apparently scarred female form—to
the work of Expressionist Egon Schiele.

But the public has other associations in mind. "I think
the comparison to *Mona Lisa* is a valid one," observed Gresh
Martin, the self-admitted "George Plimpton of the art
world," who discovered Morales during his brief stint

curating the annual Promettente (Italian for "up-and-coming") group shows in their heyday. "The look on this woman's face…it's simply *exquisite*. It's impossible to tell if she's in agony or ecstasy. She could be dying—or having an orgasm!"

But the guessing game is complicated by the fact that so little is known about the personal life of Morales, who died in 2007 of an apparent overdose. And those who knew Morales, including current Oscar nominee Carly Croft, aren't talking. Some recall having seen former model Doreen Philbrick, who dabbled at the Woodworth Gallery before her marriage to Mick Jagger, with Morales at the time of his early success.

But others say the identity of the mystery woman is anybody's guess.

"Whoever she is, I can say this about her," Martin says, with a twinkle in his eye. "Morales owes her a great deal. But I think he's paid her back in spades. Thanks to him, she will live forever."

1997

Life

New York

⬚

Trisha sat down to a cold cheese-and-tomato sandwich at 4:45 p.m., an hour when most girl Fridays of the world cleared their desks and waited to be told they could go. But the Galina Woodworth Gallery operated on a different schedule—and 4:45 p.m. was lunchtime.

She stared at her computer monitor and, with one hand, absently reached for a baby carrot. With the other, she typed her e-mail password: PERSEVERE. She deleted several pieces of junk mail, which announced that she was "Winner #26310" and in need of "STEROIDS! Mexican grade Anabolics!" That left two queries about the upcoming Peter Saul exhibit and—what was this?

Yo Trishie!!

What up, babe? Nada here. Takin it easy and trying not to get into too much trouble. Met up with Glenn last week and he asked about you. Actually he asked if you broke into the porn biz yet but you know Glenn.

To answer your question, their still threatnin to offer me that NY job but no word yet so I'm not holdin my breath.

Take it easy.

M

Trisha hit REPLY and gnawed at the carrot, confronting the blank screen. In her last e-mail, a month and a half ago, she'd told Mitch all about her prestigious new job at SoHo's hottest gallery. Now that she'd settled in, she was far less eager to update him. What would she say—that she was working much harder, and commanding far less respect, than she ever had at the Museum of Modern Art? That she was low man on the totem pole, so low that she could sometimes taste the dirt?

And her love life was no less stunted. Her friends back at MoMA had been so sure Tom would propose on Valentine's Day that they'd reportedly held a pool about what time of day it would happen. Even Trisha was fooled; she'd hinted about it in the last e-mail to Mitch (who, thankfully, hadn't followed up with a congrats—the lousy bum). Maria, the office cynic, won the pot, having successfully predicted that it wouldn't happen at all.

Trisha cleared the blank form from her screen. Better to wait a week, and then apologize to Mitch for being too busy to respond earlier. It wouldn't hurt for her college boyfriend to think she had a life.

She overchewed her second-to-last carrot, savoring every last second of her lunch break. Rhonda—the plain-Jane assistant to notorious gadabout Gresh Martin, who managed the gallery—ducked her head into the office that Trisha shared with Doreen Philbrick and, humming a tune from *The Sound of Music,* dropped a memo into Doreen's inbox. Trisha noticed, as always, the beauty that yearned to break free from Rhonda's pudgy body, her drug-store makeup and Supercuts hair. According to what Trisha had heard, Gresh had hired Rhonda three years ago in a fit of pique with his previous assistant, a skeletal prima donna, who'd refused to answer his phone ("wet nails!") one too many times. He'd wanted the exact opposite of the usual gallery employee and had certainly gotten it. Rhonda was strictly bridge-and-tunnel, as Manhattanites referred to those who commuted from the outer boroughs (or, heaven forbid, New Jersey).

"Don't you look relaxed!" Rhonda chirped. "And I know you're crazy busy. What's your secret?" You could always count on Rhonda for a happiness injection. She was the office's unofficial mascot, the one person at the gallery who could get away with looking cheerful without getting slapped.

"Better have your vision checked," Trisha said. "I'm cranky as ever." But after Rhonda walked out, humming "Edelweiss," Trisha realized that the knots in her stomach were in fact looser than usual. And it wasn't just because Doreen was on a smoke break. Thank god Mitch was staying in Boston. She found her college boyfriend's innuendoes flattering in small doses whenever he visited on business trips, but the thought of running into him while jogging in Central Park was more than she could stomach.

The intercom on Trisha's desk buzzed. "Honey," rang a slightly accusatory, slightly baritone voice, "stop fondling yourself and get your cute little ass in here."

"Coming," Trisha called, and scrambled for her handheld blacklight. Halfway down the hall to the private viewing room, she slapped her forehead, imagining the chuckles her word choice had no doubt elicited down the hall. One of her duties as assistant registrar—her *favorite* duty—was filling out condition reports on paintings that entered the gallery or returned after going out on loan. She loved being the first person to see the works, relished coming to her own conclusions before her co-workers could overhype (or, far more likely, badmouth) them.

Corny as it sounded, Trisha had always liked to develop *relationships* with works of art. She felt protective of them.

Since childhood, she'd considered paintings to be practically...living entities that lay dormant, unable to breathe, until they interacted with the human eye. Viewing them, then, caused a process akin to photosynthesis in plants. It was a silly concept, a child's fancy, but one that Trisha had never particularly wanted to shake off. Just days before, when her blacklight revealed marinara spatterings covering a painting just back from a hedge-fund millionaire's dinner party, Trisha had almost cried.

"I thought we finished the Goodman stuff this morning," Trisha said now to Sebastian, the installer, who had positioned himself so as to frame the entrance to the viewing room like a trailing bougainvillea vine. (And he was just about that skinny.)

"We did," he said, rolling his eyes for the benefit of a fey young man he neglected to introduce. Giving him the once-over, Trisha couldn't help but be reminded of Dieter, Mike Myers's over-the-top, German talk show host on *Saturday Night Live.*

"So what have we got? How many pieces?"

Sebastian reluctantly held up a finger—the middle one.

"When did it come in?"

Sebastian threw forward his right hand to examine his nails, having apparently seen something in his manicure he didn't like. His sinewy shoulders bulged beneath an Armani sweater so tight that it rose as he breathed, revealing a taut abdomen. Trisha found herself wishing his stomach would bulge out to Homer Simpson size.

"So what is it? Where'd it come from?"

"I thought *you* knew."

Before Trisha could ask anything else, Sebastian sashayed halfway to the front of the gallery, Prada shoes clicking on the unbearably shiny white floor as his friend obediently followed like a pet poodle.

Come, Fifi, Trisha mouthed as she gazed after them. The animosity she felt toward Sebastian was nothing personal; half the time, in fact, the waifish junior installer claimed to idolize Trisha for her delicate skin and perfect, shoulder-length, honey-colored hair. But she knew as well as he did that her pastel cashmere twin sets, her pearls and her prim Upper East Side demeanor were all far too Pollyanna for Woodworth (or for any other SoHo gallery, for that matter), and when Sebastian felt catty he let her know it. Yes, Trisha might have been far better suited to the life of a curator at, say, the Frick, among dozens of Madonnas of the Italian Renaissance, but her heart irrevocably lay with what was *edgy, raw, new*. That's what made her heart race; go figure. She refused to change either her specialty or her wardrobe. This was perhaps her one rebellion.

At any rate, Sebastian was far from the moodiest of the junior staffers at Woodworth. Even back at MoMA, Trisha had found communicating with underlings to be no more personal, and no more satisfying, than interacting with computers. By design, they were capable of answering only the question at hand; they certainly couldn't be expected to *volunteer* information. Acting kindly toward them was not only irrational, but also completely inadvisable; they were likely to smell her weakness and piss on her to mark her as their territory.

Obviously, this gallery was exactly the wrong environment for Trisha's sweet—some would say saccharine—temperament. But, as Trisha reminded herself at least once a day, the proximity to the art made up for the bitchiness of some of the staff. And Trisha tolerated the support staff, reminding herself that they were just as passionate about art as she was, if not more so (if that were possible).

Sometimes to their detriment. They were frustrated artists who felt the need to trash every painter in the gallery to keep their own egos intact. Making believe that so-and-so was making it because of whom so-and-so was *making* allowed them to keep believing that their talent stacked up to what they hung on the walls. If they were getting nowhere simply because their work wasn't worthy, they'd have to, like, kill themselves.

Poor souls. Trisha sighed a deep breath, not for the first time thanking God and the fates for the clearly mediocre painting talent, and the perfect eye for others' work, that she'd been granted. She entered the small room and closed the door behind her. Immediately, she crossed to raise the shade, getting a glorious peek of afternoon sunlight. Only when she sat upon the black leather settee did she raise her eyes to the painting Sebastian had placed there for her.

Whoa.

The painting knocked her over with its violence. She could swear it had reached out and *punched* her. She recovered her breath and smiled. This was something else. Over the span of five by five feet, several media—acrylic, metal, clay, bits of…something—merged and separated. In the center of the work, the paint lay flat against the surface, but at the edges it bowed out by several tenths of an inch. Something about it reminded her of an alien landscape. A post-apocalyptic alien landscape: Parts of it were obliterated, and dips and craters fell where the canvas had apparently been beaten up and patched back together. It looked like a vast mistake that someone had trashed and then rescued. And yet the range of color—rusts and browns and creams and a bit of red, all within an earthy palette—was no accident. It was unsettling.

It was a mess. But a riveting one.

In the weeks since she'd joined the gallery, she could count on one hand the paintings that interested her. Galina's tastes were too cold and intellectual, too topical, even for Trisha (who'd never met a liberal cause she didn't like). Bill Clinton as Icarus, complete with wax and feathers? Get real. Galina, the absentee gallerist, favored gimmicky works that hit the viewer over the head.

Galina didn't want to work too hard to sound like the smartest person in the room at the openings and dinner parties that were, of course, the reason she lent her name to such a time-consuming endeavor in the first place. (And if she didn't understand it, she faked it. "It's so *relevant*," Trisha heard Galina say recently about a triptych of a cupcake, a banana and an unflushed toilet, by a flash in the pan who happened to have fought in the Persian Gulf.)

Galina picked up paintings like a kid picking out candy and left the real work to Gresh. Trisha couldn't fathom Galina requesting *this* raw slab of reality unless it had been painted by, say, a former stripper—or unless the paint contained metal from ground-up bullets salvaged from the conflict in Northern Ireland.

Trisha was up on Gresh's acquisitions—or so she thought. This had to be an unsolicited work that had inadvertently made its way to the big time, if Trisha's once-over qualified as that. Trisha's heart beat faster. Maybe this was fate at work. Maybe she was *meant* to discover this work, which would simultaneously change the artist's life and take her a step closer to fulfilling her fantasy of having her own gallery someday. That's why, difficult as it was, she'd left her dream job at MoMA two months ago. At least here, there weren't a dozen peers at her heels, all wanting the same thing.

But could this painting really be it—the work worth

hedging her fledgling reputation with the new bosses? ("Gresh," she would say, "got a minute? I wanted to show you something." Reeeeally casual.) Or was she too eager? Was she jumping the gun?

She cut the lights, closed the window, and turned the blacklight toward it, checking for surface damage. Nothing, aside from minor cracks around the edges, suggesting that the painting was not at all recent. Odd. She flicked the light. Nice.

She was just leaving when she got the distinct impression that someone was watching her. She pulled the tortoiseshell barrette from her hair and shook her head, like a puppy ridding itself of stress.

And there it was, just off-center, falling diagonally across the canvas: a close-up. It was subtle, something that might not have been there at all, like a hint of a face that you might see inside a house or in the front of a car. As soon as she saw it, the vision disappeared.

Trisha exited just as Gresh walked by, deep in conversation with his cigarette buddy, Doreen. All day long, they rolled imported Drum tobacco into tight little cigarillos; they might have smoked them constantly would this not have required relocating their desks to the street. Doreen's nicotine of choice had always struck Trisha as a bit contrived, but she had to hand it to Doreen: It was working for her. Doreen was hardly older than Trisha, but Gresh took her advice on what was happening, and what was worth being *made* to happen, in the art world.

Gresh was spelling out the implications of gallery hopping among club kids trolling for free beer; he was convinced that this would lead to future sales and future customers, which more than made up for the occasional drunken accident in the gallery. But for some reason, he stopped—without changing the subject or catching his breath—and ducked his head into the viewing room. Frowning, Doreen pivoted on one stiletto and followed.

Then Gresh did something remarkable. He stopped talking. Watching him, Trisha could hardly breathe.

"And what do we think of *this*?" Gresh asked.

Trisha would have answered, but Gresh had turned his body toward Doreen, who strained forward, stretching the translucent skin of her neck. Trisha took a wicked delight in imagining the eventual wrinkles. Doreen was only in her late twenties, but it was already obvious that she would not age well. Everything about her was too rigid: sheet-smooth black hair pulled back too tightly, affecting a makeshift face-lift; thin lips; and the tallest stilettos in SoHo.

Doreen took a long moment, then dismissed the work with a tiny upturn of her nose. "Moosecaca," she said in her signature staccato—a super-efficient, clipped Manhattanese that Trisha found unexpected in a girl purporting to be a Savannah blueblood. "Lookslikemoosecacatome." She turned to Gresh. "Whatabout*you*?"

"Re*fresh*ing!" he announced, nodding at Trisha. "Well," he said, turning to Doreen, "I do suppose it's back to the salt mines." His exaggerated nod toward the women approximated an old-fashioned bow as he departed for his corner office. Trisha's breath started at her sinuses, fell to her throat and then plummeted to her stomach. She'd been right, but a lot of good it did her. She hadn't stated an opinion. She *hadn't said a thing.*

Doreen peered down at Trisha. (A former print model, she was over six feet—closer to seven given her usual choice of footwear.) "What*is*it?" she demanded. For a moment, Trisha almost thought Doreen was asking her what was wrong. Then Doreen continued,

"Galina buy *that*?"

"Oh. I'm not sure," Trisha replied. "I can't find the packing slip."

"Figures," Doreen sniffed. "With *Rhonda* on the job."

"But if Galina *did* buy it," Trisha added, "good for her."

Doreen sniffed and walked away, and only then did Trisha relax. She wondered sometimes about the stress hormones that Doreen induced in her, and what they might be doing to her body.

She rummaged through the packing slips on the shipping table and was reduced to digging through the garbage—where, on a piece of plain brown wrapping paper, she found something. It was a shocker:

TRISHA PORTAM
MUSEUM OF MODERN ART
11 W. 53RD STREET
NEW YORK, NY 10019
PERSONAL!

Someone had crossed through MoMA's address and forwarded the package to the gallery. Trisha's eyes darted to the return label; it was from a "G. DOMINGUEZ" in a marginal area of Brooklyn.

Who in the world was G. DOMINGUEZ?

Trisha found it hard to draw a breath. Just as waitresses dreamt of $100 tips, young curators fantasized about the day an artist or a patron might bequeath them a masterpiece. Granted, G. DOMINGUEZ hardly hailed from a high-rent district—but neither did Basquiat, back in his day. And hadn't Gresh, a respected expert, expressed admiration for this very work?

Trisha flew back to her desk, dialed the MoMA operator, and asked to be connected to Marsha, the longtime shipping administrator. After the requisite pleasantries—which, for Trisha, went on far too long—Trisha questioned Marsha about the package. Ruefully, Marsha recounted that recently, the museum had discovered a stash of old mail in a back room, some of which had apparently sat there for several years—no doubt the product of some incompetent, short-lived mail guy who had no idea where to deliver the items…and had just given up.

"I hate to tell you, but I think your package, it sat there a *while*," Marsha said. "It got pretty beat up." Trisha could almost hear Marsha shaking her head through the phone lines. She knew how conscientious the older woman was about her work. "I did the best I could and just taped the note there on the back. I was going to look you up and call you to make sure you got it." She chuckled. "A little late."

"Did you say *note*?"

"Uh-huh, just on regular paper, that's what it was—"

Trisha got off the phone as quickly as possible and bolted back to the viewing room, bypassing Dieter giving Sebastian a foot massage. She quickly felt the back of the painting until she found half a sheet of lined notebook paper.

My dearest Patricia,
I think of you quite often since our meeting, and fear we not see each other again, despite our promises. This have a very special meaning, and I want you to have it. As I told you—

And that was it.

Defeated, Trisha stood and stared at the note for at least three or four minutes. She hardly noticed Sebastian gushing with curiosity in the background.

"You okay?" he asked.

"Yeah." Trisha sighed and shook her head, but resisted spilling the story. All of a sudden, she was exhausted. "Would you mind wrapping this to go out?"

"I'd love to help you, sweetie," Sebastian sniffed, "but it is after five. And I'm afraid I've got things to do." He wriggled his eyebrows at Dieter suggestively.

Trisha was just reinforcing the masking tape when Gresh passed, carrying his Yale mug. He prided himself on fetching his own coffee.

"Ah, Miss Portman," he sang out. "Am I to surmise that the refreshing moose caca is leaving us? So *soon*?" He smiled.

Trisha looked hard at him, wishing she knew him well enough to interpret the extent of his interest in the painting. A lot of good it would do her now. You couldn't get more unprofessional than to tout your personal property.

"Yes," she said, "but it's not going far. Turns out I've got a secret admirer, if you can believe it, who sent me the painting."

She held her breath, hoping against hope that Gresh would offer an analysis of the work, or a word of advice. Instead, he merely cocked an eyebrow.

"Intriguing!" he said. "Well, by all means, don't let that handsome attorney friend of yours know," he said with a wink. "Or—maybe you should. A little jealousy never killed anyone."

"Good god! What is *that*?"

Tom leaned forward to where *Junkyard,* as Trisha had dubbed the painting, was propped against the kitchen cabinets in the kitchen/dining nook, one of two rooms—make that *living areas*—in her entire apartment.

"It's …a gift."

"Whew!" Tom wiped invisible sweat from his brow. "Goodness, Trisha, I thought you actually *bought* the thing. It looks so…unsanitary." He chuckled. "I feel the urge to spray it with Lysol."

"It's not *that* bad."

"I don't guess the Salvation Army would want it." He cringed. "I guess you could take it as a tax write-off, but I wouldn't begin to know how to value it." Tom, a plaintiff's attorney who described what he did as "standing up for the little guy against big bad corporations," was always trying to fix Trisha's problems—whether she considered them problems or not.

He suddenly stepped back and snapped his fingers. "I know who'd like it." He cocked his thumb upstairs, toward where Nat, Trisha's best friend and college roommate, lived three floors up. (Once Trisha had signed her lease, Nat had *had* to live there—so Daddy had *bought* her the co-op.) Nat was a gorgeous, long-haired actress—and something of a wild child.

Trisha's hackles went up, as they always did whenever Tom mentioned Nat, or vice versa. "Why do you say that?" she asked.

Tom shrugged. "Just seems like something she'd like."

Trisha wanted to say, Yeah, because you think Nat's place is a pigsty, and this, a load of slop. But there was no use getting into it. Nat *was* a slob, and better that Trisha's boyfriend had reservations about her over-the-top friend than that he like her *too* much. The main thing was, Trisha and Tom got along. And *they* were both neatniks.

Tom absent-mindedly kissed her on the cheek and walked through an archway into area number two, the living room/bedroom. He pulled off his wingtips, sat on the couch, and, from the side table, picked up a *Times* folded back to the crossword puzzle. "It's Friday," he called, relishing the challenge, as the puzzles grew ever more difficult during the week. "Sure you don't want to help?"

Trisha wanted no such thing. "Helping" meant watching Tom breeze through the easy clues one step ahead of her and feeling useless once she'd filled in the pop culture references, of which Tom was stunningly ignorant. Instead, she squeezed the excess water from a sponge and began wiping down countertops. They always seemed dirtier when Tom came over.

"I got the idea Gresh thought it might be worth something," she called out in a moment.

"Mmm? Can't hear you over the dishwater," Tom answered.

"Never mind," Trisha shouted. "Tell you later."

Actually, Trisha thought, as she scrubbed Tom's famous shrimp scampi off a dish, she liked the painting all the more for the abuse it was taking. But if she kept it, she'd think of how much Tom loathed it every single time she laid eyes on it. And where was she going to hang it, anyway? Over the bed? *There* was a sure-fire mood killer—which, after two years of dating, was the last thing they needed.

Ironically, it was Nat's fault that they had met at all, an

accident that Nat never ceased to bemoan when she nee-
dled Trisha about her man (whom Nat had nicknamed
Potato, because he was "so damn starchy").

Nat had suckered Trisha into walking Baracus, a wily pit
bull Nat had adopted on a whim, the morning after Nat
spent the night at "a friend's house." Trisha was waiting for
Baracus to find a portion of concrete suitable for his purpos-
es when a squirrel landed on the sidewalk in front of him.
This sent Baracus (and behind him, Trisha) into a frenzied
gallop. The squirrel shimmied up a tree to safety, but
Baracus, hyped on adrenaline, jumped the nearest person—
in this case, Tom, in a three-piece Armani suit, holding a
steaming latte. He let out a manly scream as the steamed
milk bubbled onto his skin. "Goddammit!" he yelled.
"Watch your dog."

"Oh my god." Trisha's hand flew to her mouth. "I am so,
so, so, so sorry."

"Damn it!" Tom repeated. He quickly began to work on
his suit with a handkerchief. Baracus, having extracted
Tom's breakfast from a white paper bag, was chowing
down. "You should watch it," Tom said. "You can get into
serious trouble with a dog in this city. I should know; I'm an
attorney."

Trisha drew a ragged breath, praying she wouldn't get
sued, but finding the prospect of a repeat interaction
strangely appealing. "Believe me, I would never have such
an ill-behaved dog. Baracus belongs to my friend Nat.
Natalie," Trisha said, clarifying that Nat was no *Nathaniel*.

"What kind of name is 'Baracus'?" Apparently softening,
Tom squatted and felt for the nametag hanging from the pit
bull's collar, while Baracus licked what was left of the
steamed milk from Tom's hand.

"It's from *The A-Team*. You know, the Mr. T. character,"

Trisha said. "'I pity the fool,'" she added, doing her best Mr. T. impersonation.

"I don't watch television." Tom frowned. "Says here the dog's name is 'B.A.,' and it's owned by a 'Carly Croft.'"

"Right. Did I mention that Nat and I are dognappers?"

No response, save a suspicious stare. As Trisha would eventually discover, Tom was humorless when in cross-examination mode. "I'm sorry—Nat's an actress, and she just took 'Carly' as her stage name. I keep forgetting," Trisha said. "As for 'B.A.,' that was B.A. Baracus's first name." She cocked a suggestive eyebrow. "It actually stood for '*bad attitude.*'"

"Touché," Tom said. "I'm sorry. It's been a long week."

They introduced themselves. Baracus, having given up on the humans to work out their differences, laid down the biggest and smelliest poop Trisha had ever seen. She bent over with a plastic bag to clean up the mess just as Tom hailed a cab. He hesitated for just a split second after he slid into the seat.

Trisha had always believed in chance encounters, blind dates, and fate. (Or, when the Catholic schoolgirl reared up in her, God.) She was incapable of believing that the universe had presented her with this lawyer, with his wavy brown hair and intelligent brown eyes behind wire-rim glasses, for no reason. So conquering her shyness, she called out to him. "I really do feel bad about your suit," she said. "I'd like to pay for your dry cleaning. Or have Carly do it."

"Don't worry about it."

"At least let me get your card," Trisha said. Not watching what she was doing, she smeared excrement onto her left hand.

"Sure. You never know when this bruiser will get you

into trouble," Tom said, plucking a business card from his wallet. "See ya."

In a split second as he rode away, Trisha's mind raced through all that had happened to bring them together. Maybe she had gone to Penn in order to meet Nat so that she would be walking Baracus at that very moment. Maybe having met Tom, the two of them would go on to have a child that would prevent nuclear war or cure cancer or paint like Michelangelo.

She beamed at Baracus, who was too busy spraying a fire hydrant to notice.

Trisha, determined not to stand in the way of fate, e-mailed Tom almost immediately—although not quite as herself.

> Arf!
> I'm sorry bout the stainz I got on
> your funny-looking fur.
> Please let me help lick them off.
> I promise I will not be ruff.
> Baracus

For the next several days, her empty e-mail box taunted her. Trisha wanted to reach inside the computer and yank back her stupid message. But, just after she'd given up, Tom wrote Baracus back, explaining that he'd been tied up in court ("where bad people go when they kick doggies"). After several days of man-dog correspondence, Tom had Baracus deliver a message to his non-furry friend: Would she dine with him on dried liver and pigs' ears?

They compromised on Italian.

When he wasn't being menaced by a hyperactive pit

bull, Tom was actually a very nice person—and a liberal to boot. A good conversationalist, he, as a bonus, had a working knowledge of some rather obscure artists. (Tom later admitted that he'd prepped for the date just a little.) He was fully evolved, a *man*. In fact, after he described some of his *pro bono* work, Trisha cheekily asked if he were the *perfect* man.

"Hardly." He looked down at his wine glass. "I might as well tell you I have a fatal flaw. I'm married—to my work."

"Me too," Trisha exclaimed. "That's a relief. It's so hard to date someone short of ambition."

But Tom was not exaggerating. It took a month to pull off another two dates. They were always starting again, awkwardly, as almost-strangers; at the beginning of each date, the sexual momentum was nil. Before they really got going, Trisha was already resenting his work, and him for not making her a priority.

Reluctantly, she turned to Nat (as she still insisted on calling her friend) for advice; she had long since realized that their dating styles conflicted so dramatically as to render this almost useless, but she missed the heart-to-hearts of their college days. They curled up against Trisha's headboard, sipping tea and enjoying the view from the full-length window beside Trisha's queen-sized bed.

"It's obviously time to—you know, Do It," Trisha said. At age 27, she still couldn't discuss sex, not even with Nat, without euphemisms and hesitations. "And what does it say that we haven't? Is he not into it? Is he gay?"

Nat shook her head. "Based on everything you've told me, I think the problem is, he's *just like you*. So go for it already. Take him out for a test drive." She wiggled her toes happily on the patchwork quilt. "You'll find out soon enough if it's there or not."

"That's the problem. What if I...do it, and then figure out too late he's not right for me?"

"Define 'too late.'"

Trisha rolled her eyes. She knew better than to get into a conversation about sexual morality. "We both know that if I have sex I'll feel attached," Trisha said.

"Here's my answer to that: don't," Nat said.

"But—"

"I'm serious. I don't want you to see you end up with someone again just because he's the one who happened to come along. I know in this case you made the first move, and that's great—I'm proud of you—but look at you now! You're settling! You're holding onto some romantic dream in your head that it's 'meant to be' because of how you met. I want to see you date someone that *you want*."

Trisha sat cross-armed for a minute, taking this in. Then she leaned over and opened a drawer in her side table. She flipped through a pad of paper, shoved it in Nat's face, and pointed at it. "But look at this."

Nat gave a bemused grin, looking at Trisha's wish list for guys, which she'd concocted back in college.

"That's got to mean something," Trisha said. "He's everything I ever wanted."

"Oh, this is something, all right," Nat said, with a laugh. "But listen." She looked Trisha straight in the eye. "It takes more than what's on this list. It takes *fire*. Like, like—you know what old movie I watched the other day? *Romancing the Stone*, with Kathleen Turner and Michael Douglas. Man, *they* had fire. Or—*Fatal Attraction*. Whew." Nat was up for a bit part in a Michael Douglas movie. "I'm not saying you and Tom won't have fire," she said, "but if it ain't there, don't let yourself stay out in the cold, know what I mean?"

Not only did Tom fit the bill, his apartment did too. It was straight off Trisha's wish-list: a huge two-bedroom with a working fireplace, exposed brick walls, loft ceilings, big armchairs, and a multitude of books.

His bedroom housed only a scrupulously-made, queen-sized bed with a burgundy velvet duvet and a dark wood headboard, along with a matching side table. A Japanese print hung over the bed. The minute Trisha entered, on "the grand tour," her mind went entirely blank, in a good way. She was calm. But she had no idea what to say. Neither did he, apparently, which might be how they ended up sitting on the bed, him wearing a nervous grin. He sat closer. Awkwardly, jerking, he leaned in to kiss her.

It soon became obvious that she was in good hands.

But afterward, luxuriating in the most comfortable bed she'd ever encountered, she wondered what had gone wrong. Not enough spontaneity? Too much love, not enough...well...fuck?

Not enough desperate fumbling? Too much perfection? Not enough *fire*?

People always said that "when it's right, you just *know* it," leading her to expect a click as things fell into place. Instead, she felt a microscopic sinking feeling in her gut. She wished it would go away. Why wouldn't her animal instincts fall in line with her intellectual choice?

Because when it was over, instead of slapping his gut, belching, and making a beeline for the bathroom to ditch the condom, Tom leaned over, looked Trisha in the eyes and kissed her, softly and lovingly, on the mouth.

And instead of smiling with relief at finding a kindred spirit in this world, Trisha wanted to shout, "*Be a man!*"

But it was too late: She was attached. As the relationship

coalesced, Nat knew that Trisha wasn't happy, but also that she could do nothing about it.

And so Trisha and Tom became a couple, a gold-plated ring masquerading as solid gold, serious from the start by nature of their no-nonsense personalities, formal with each other because they might as well have been strangers, as little as they saw each other. Trisha was Tom's girlfriend, and then his long-time girlfriend, and then it was time for her to be something else, but unfortunately that required action, and each waited to see if the other would make a move.

⊠

Nat, as expected, adored the painting.

"*Divine!*" she said the moment she spied the painting, still propped up against the kitchen cabinets. "It's like—poop on parade!" She was referring to the light chocolate flecks swirled throughout the piece, which might well have been confetti. Now that Trisha had had more time to examine the work, it was obvious to her that the artist had torn up tiny pieces of paper—or fabric, or, most intriguing, other canvases—to create a jarring impressionistic feel.

"Ugh. I can't deal with that right now," Trisha grunted, thinking of Tom.

She threw on her winter coat and shooed Nat out the door; they were headed for dinner. But Nat insisted on getting the scoop, and once Trisha mentioned the painting's shadowy past—while they were still inside the elevator—Nat began to squeal and jump up and down. "It could be a Picasso! You could be a millionaire!" she exclaimed, both hands over her mouth.

"We both could be *dead* if you don't watch it!" Trisha answered her. She'd told Nat upteen times that she had qualms about the tiny elevator, which bounced when under too much weight. Sometimes, Trisha was reminded of why Tom had a problem with Nat.

"Okay, okay—isn't it *exciting*? You have a secret admirer!"

Trisha had to admit that it was.

"Who do you think it is? Oooo—Monsieur Lemon?!"

Trisha laughed, recalling the sexy French patron, wearing a yellow leather motorcycle jacket, who'd *insisted* on having Trisha show him around the gallery.

"Well? Are you going to *find* him?!"

"Or her," Trisha pointed out. "I don't know."

Nat glared at her.

"I called information, and there's no DOMINGUEZ on that street in Brooklyn. And I ran the name through the artists' and owners' database and—"

"And *nada*," Nat said, getting into the spirit. "You got to go *find* him, homegirl! And I'm going with you."

Perhaps Trisha's fates really *were* suddenly aligning: Strangely enough, Gresh had similar ideas. Later, Trisha would wonder why she hadn't just reminded her boss how little she knew about the painting's provenance. No doubt he would have gotten a kick out of the story and then gone on in search of a more likely Promettente candidate.

On second thought, maybe that's why she *hadn't* reminded him.

She was heading to her office when he caught her gently by the elbow. "Oh Miss Portman!" Her mouth curled into a bemused smile. There was something so comforting about talking to Gresh. He could recite the phone book, and you'd feel honored that he would share it with you. "Miss Portman. I wondered if I might have a word."

"A whole paragraph for *you*, Gresh."

He settled her into a leather armchair in his office and patted her on the shoulder. As usual, Trisha felt a strong bond with this mentor, who had plucked her from obscurity—well, the crowded back office at MoMA, full of aspiring art historians—after serving with her on the judging panel of an amateur art competition in Harlem. (Trisha, having noticed the invitation in her boss's trashcan, had plucked it out and volunteered to represent the museum. She'd almost gasped when she'd gotten the go-ahead.)

"I don't know if you're aware, but we always have a little"—Gresh's hands churned the air as he searched for the correct word—"*sub*theme to our little Promettente" (the "little" event that the entire New York art world awaited all year). "Certainly, we choose artists we believe will be important, *will* have something to say. But to *focus* the exhibit we choose a theme, and many times—unless the artists have *existing* works that we and they deem *appropriate*—we commission, as it were, *new* works *solely* for our event. It's *quite* remarkable that the artists do this for us and *rather* exciting."

Trisha nodded eagerly. Of course she was aware. Anyone worth her salt in the art world knew the details of Promettente, which fell annually on the first day of spring. In the few short years since Galina and Gresh had opened the gallery, it had become to art what the swimsuit issue was to modeling: the one event of the season that defines who *is*.

"At any rate, one of the risks we run, given this rather *exciting* scen*ah*rio—which adds, as it were, great energy to the proceedings—is that *occasionally*, we have an artist who either *refuses*—well, I hesitate to use that word, let us just say is not *comfortable* with the year's theme, or with the concept of being quote-unquote *told* what to contribute, believing, justifiably I might add, that it may *compromise* their artistic integrity, or, alternatively—let me say first of all that Galina and I choose *quite* carefully, but unfortunately one of the downsides to attaining the *edginess* that this show strives for is, as I said, an element of *risk*, and at times the artists just *aren't up to* the theme at hand.

"And *that*"—he pointed with his index finger—"is where we find ourselves this year, with artists I hesitate to name *unable*, for one *reason* or another, to *participate*, only we find ourselves '*there*' much more than in other years, and *at a later date. Which is where you come in.*" He now focused entirely on Trisha, leaning in and flashing her a Gresh Martin smile. "You will recall, I'm sure, the painting I admired in the hall. '*Moose Caca*,' I believe it was called." His eyes sparkled, signifying that he knew good and well this was not the name of the painting.

Trisha gulped. "Sure."

"I say, Miss Portman, we're in a bit of a jam, and I think '*Moose Caca*' would fit rather *well* with this year's theme, which I am *utterly appalled* to realize that I have not yet mentioned to you. It is 'Urban Detritus.' What do you think?" He smiled again, with the net result that Trisha didn't mind not being given a chance to register an opinion. "Now tell me this, is the artist—what is his or her name, again?"

"Um…right…G. Dominguez, I believe."

"Right. Now, do you believe the artist would loan it to us?" He had forgotten it was hers, if he'd ever fully absorbed that fact in the first place.

"Well"—her voice shook—"I don't suppose it matters, because '*Moose Caca*,' um, happens to be in my personal collection."

"Ah! How *fortuitous*! Well *done*, I say! Well done." He viewed Trisha with newfound respect. "And would I be remiss in inviting *you*, Miss Portman, to loan us the painting? We would pay for the honor, naturally, and I *do* believe that the value of the work is most likely to rise. What is it the painting *called*, by the way?"

"Oh. Um. '*Junkyard*.'"

"Splendid! Although perhaps rather *obvious*, given the theme. Perhaps we could speak to the artist about changing it to something with perhaps a bit more mystique?" He leaned in, his silver hair flopping into his blue-green eyes. "Between you and me, I do *rather prefer 'Moose Caca!'* Ah-ha-ha. Now—what was I going to say? Oh, *yes!*...Now. To be a Promettente artist, it is not *imperative* to be of a certain age, although we would have a bit of proverbial egg on our face if every single one of our up-and-comers were over the age of, say, *eighty*. Ah-ha-ha. What do we know about him or her?"

"He—she—the *artist*—likes to cultivate...an air of mystery."

"Ooooh, yes." Gresh rubbed his hands together. "We like that. Yes indeed."

"But let me see what I can do about—"

"Yes. Rather. Gathering the *minimal* biographical data." Gresh put his arm around her and walked her back toward the viewing room. Trisha didn't bother to point out that she had been headed in the opposite direction. "If you could do that, Miss Portman," he said, "I would be *most* appreciative."

"I'll see what I can do."

"Jolly good."

Unbelievable.

Thank you, secret admirer, Trisha murmured. She had half a mind to give the mystery person a fat, wet, deep kiss on the lips. Just as soon as she found him. Or her.

"N—Carly. I need a favor," Trisha told Nat's answering machine, as usual forgetting her best friend's new name until she'd half said the old one. "If you don't hear from me by five o'clock tonight, send the cops to Two-Three-Five—"

"Wha?"

Trisha almost dropped the phone, she was so shocked at

achieving live contact. For Nat to be at home on a Saturday morning was surprising enough. And to inspire Nat to wake up, crawl out of bed, and walk ten feet to the phone—well. Trisha didn't know who in the world could manage that, short of Martin Scorsese.

"You're going, aren't you?" Nat panted into the phone. "Take me! Take me!"

Even on non-red-letter days, Nat loved tagging along on Trisha's work excursions, and Trisha usually let her. And although there was never any danger of Nat's being left behind—Trisha wouldn't call if she didn't want company—Trisha always let her pal do a little begging.

The trips normally consisted of gallery hopping, which meant rubbing elbows (and shoulders and hipbones) with beautiful young people, all sipping Molsons while they squinted at the walls. Although Trisha would never admit it, Nat came in handy. When one of Trisha's friends was the artist behind a guaranteed dud—and this happened far more often than Trisha liked—it did a lot to assuage the pain when a sexpot with legs up to *here* showed up to compliment the aesthetic. Nat was equally helpful when they had a hot ticket; not only did she photograph well, she also had a way of charming the powers that be into letting their guard down. What wasn't safe to talk about around a dumb actress? Trisha had been the star of many a morning meeting at work when she passed along what "she" had heard. And it never hurt to have company when you wanted to keep up with what was happening at dozens, if not hundreds, of out-of-the-way shows in the area. Nat was tough; she knew no fear. That came in handy when Trisha needed to troll the galleries in Brooklyn's seedier (read: hotter) sections on the weekends. But this was a whole new animal: Bedford-Stuyvesant.

"You sure?" Trisha asked. "This is hard-core Crooklyn. And I'm leaving in an hour. Is that enough time for the Chronic Hangover Tonic to take effect?"

"You kidding? I'm there," Nat said. "I wouldn't miss this for anything. And besides, it's great research. Kerouac wants me to practice my 'ethnic.'" Kerouac, was Nat's—Carly's—dialect coach.

"But if you come with me, who'll call the cops?" Trisha was only half-joking.

"No worries! I'll be your trusty bodyguard. . . uh...*Raquel*," Nat said, rolling the "r." "But we'll tell them I'm your assistant, *chica*."

"Okay. Just remember: I'm working."

An hour later, a rusted-out Town Car pulled up to the front door. Trisha figured that's what they sent you when you were heading to Bed-Stuy.

For better or worse, "Raquel" looked the part. "Oh my *gawd*," Trisha had said when she entered the elevator and seen Nat-Carly-Rrrraquel. "In the immortal words of Marisa Tomei in *My Cousin Vinny*: 'You blend!'" Nat had pulled her long hair into a ponytail and used a curling iron to create wispy, curled-under ghetto bangs. Huge gold hoops dangled from her ears. She wore an acid-washed jeans jacket over an orange FUBU tee and a navy miniskirt, beneath which black tights and heeled knee-high boots were the only protection from the bitter March sleet. She was the height of MTV fashion, circa 1983—far better suited for the trip than Trisha, in her pink cashmere twin set.

The Town Car driver, a skinny Asian with a wispy mustache named I.M. POON, according to the nametag on the sun visor, smiled when he got a good look at them. "You relate?" he asked, smiling. Once Trisha figured out what he meant, she shook her head. She wondered: Did he think Nat was her younger sister? Her daughter? Here was Nat, jamming out to "No Doubt" on her Discman while Trisha skimmed the *New York Times*.

The sleet picked up as they neared their destination, and POON grew increasingly agitated. Trisha, who never left the apartment ill-prepared, offered him a printed map she'd downloaded from the Internet; he waved it off and instead called his dispatcher via a squawk box on the front seat. After what sounded like a Chinese screaming match, POON turned around and sucked in his breath. "I get you there," he said, "but no good fo' you." He shook his head and pointed out the window, repeating himself: "No good fo' you."

Trisha nodded. Normally, she would have agreed that going to Bedford-Stuy was an *awful* thing for her, but in this case, she was increasingly excited. She was going to meet her secret admirer. She felt a like a cross between Nancy Drew and Meg Ryan in *Sleepless in Seattle*.

As POON had apparently attempted to tell them, he could not deliver them all the way to the front door; thwarted by roadwork, he had to stop several blocks away and leave them to make their way through the storm. He shrugged, palms up, to apologize. "You use. Good fo' you," he said, pointing at Trisha's map. Trisha, ever the softie, gave him a 35 percent tip on the car service voucher.

They emerged into an acute wind that blasted wet needles into their faces and, within just moments, rendered their umbrellas useless. Flyers and muddy leaves covered the streets. They passed a GROSSERIES store and a pizzeria with a windowed façade; burly men in leather jackets and dark-haired women sporting high ponytails peeked out and stared at Trisha for several seconds longer than neces-

sary. They moved on, and the crowded downtrodden gave
way to a lone, crazy-eyed panhandler who greeted Nat
with a huge, toothless smile and a "hello," then trailed
them for several blocks.

They finally arrived, soaked, on a surprisingly tidy res-
idential street. Trisha calmed at the evidence of neighborhood improvement: Scraggly trees came up through peri-
odic breaks in the sidewalk, and although they looked as if
they might not survive the night, they had obviously been
planted with hope. Trisha saw nothing resembling a crack
house, but rather, liveable two-family homes, similar to the
sort near her own high school, albeit built with the types of
materials that were always on sale at Home Depot: muted
multi-colored brick, gaudy awnings, plastic house numbers. All too often a frumpy exterior boasted a mini-satellite
dish as proud decoration. The only signs of life were two
wiry teens, sitting on a stoop partially protected by a green
awning, sipping from a paper bag. They catcalled in
Spanish as the women passed, and Nat yelled something in
return.

"What'd you say?" Trisha said under her breath. She
didn't need Nat to translate the hand symbol.

"Nothing they didn't deserve," Nat said. "Anyway,
which house are we heading for?"

Trisha consulted a soggy piece of paper and then looked
behind her. "The one they're sitting in front of." For a split
second, she considered nixing the mission—going back and
telling Gresh that his young superstar was a juvenile delin-
quent. Then she realized that Gresh would eat that up.
"Let's go."

They turned and approached the sweathogs. The more
talkative guy had shorn black hair, a black goatee, and a
New York Jets jacket. The other sported a do-it-yourself

orange bleach job poking out from under a Knicks cap.

"You come back for more, hon?" Jets asked, using his fingers and his tongue to show Nat what he wanted to do to her.

Nat opened her mouth to rebut, but Trisha broke in. "Actually, no," she said. "We're looking for the Dominguez residence."

This caught the guys by surprise. They frowned and looked at each other. "Yo, girlie," Jets asked Nat. "Who you be lookin' for?"

"Dominguez? That you?" Trisha reminded herself that it was wise, in such situations, to act as if you knew what you were doing. Having already blown it, she tried again. "Dominguez," she said authoritatively.

"Mamacita, mamacita, keep your panties on." He pulled his eyes from their lock on Nat. "But like, *who*? Jimmy or Miss Grace?"

Trisha remembered the G on the return label. "Grace."

The boys shared another sideways glance. "You a friend of hers?"

"Sort of," Trisha said. Then she owned up to the truth. "Not really."

The boys sighed with relief. "Oh, okay. 'Cause you, like, three-four years too late," Jets said.

"Excuse me?"

"Miss Grace, she's like, *dead*," orange hair said. "Her son live here now."

"Oh," Trisha said. Then her eyes grew wide. "*Ooooh*." Her breathing grew shallow. "This Jimmy, would his last name be *Morales*?"

As she stood frozen, unbelieving, the guys continued their banter. "Yeah, *James*," Jets scoffed. "You lemme know if *James* gives you any trouble, a'it?"

"Yeah, James, you got to watch him."

"Don't worry, mama," Jets said. "We got your back." Before Trisha could stop him, he cocked his head toward the open second-floor window. "Yo *James!*" he screamed. "You oughta see what be down here f'*you!*"

Trisha started to shake. She wasn't ready for this; she was. . . flustered. Jets didn't notice; to the contrary, he was obviously enormously pleased with himself. "Happy I could help," he said, holding a hand out to shake Nat's. "I'm Chick, and this here's Fat." He nodded at his friend.

"*Oh.*" Trisha's eyes widened. "The infamous Chick and Fat! And what have you done with Puppy?" She smiled wryly.

The guys' jaws dropped so precipitously that Nat broke into giggles.

"Aw, *shit!*" Chick said. "How you know dat?"

"I'm Jimmy's parole agent. We've had lots of talks about you boys. You better watch it."

The stoop went silent. Then Chick broke into pleased laugher. "Aw, you messin' with me!" he whooped. "You just messin'!"

Trisha nodded. "I'm just messin'," she agreed.

The front door opened a crack. "Yeah?" came a growl.

"Yo *James*, you know these lovely ladies?" Chick yelled, way too loud, as if James had problems with his ears instead of his eyes.

"Hi," Trisha said to the voice. "It's Trisha. Portman? We went to college together?"

"Huh. Oh. Yeah." He failed to open the door any wider. No one said a word; Chick and Fat stood in open-mouthed wonder and waited for their boy to ask the ladies in. It struck Trisha that this might be the biggest event of their year so far. Or they might be involved in activities far beyond her wildest dreams.

"And this is—do you remember my roommate Nat, now known as Carly?" Trisha continued. "Glenn's, um, girl-friend?"

"Fuckbuddy," Nat offered.

"Your name's *Nat*? Or is it *Carly*? Yo, they both sexy." Chick stared up at her in awe.

Nat shook him off.

"So, what you selling, ladies?" James finally asked through the door. "I keep telling those dickweeds who call on the phone: I ain't got no money to donate to the school. They done got it all. And if I did, I wouldn't give it to *them*." He sounded fiercely, unimaginably bitter, although in this case, given the callousness and persistence of Penn's fundraising efforts, Trisha was inclined to empathize.

"We don't want your money," Trisha said. "We're here to talk about *you*."

She knew better than to say *your painting*. One of the first things Trisha had learned about James, going on seven years ago, was that you *don't* ask about his painting, not ever. In fact, if he was the artist behind *Junkyard*—as she now assumed he must be—she might as well get I.M. POON on the horn right now for a return trip to Manhattan.

Trisha held out her hand and Nat handed over the cell phone she'd acquired so her "people" could always get in touch with her about auditions; Trisha tapped it, hoping to bring on a signal. But just then, James opened a slightly larger crack in the door, and a hard, scraped, paint-encrusted hand signaled them in.

As Trisha squeezed through the door, she flashed back to the first time she had reluctantly entered James's lair, near the beginning of her senior year at Penn. She felt no more welcome than before. As always, she concentrated on not staring at James, not gawking at his face, as so many people must have done. Instead, she listened to Nat's heels sinking into the carpeted stairs behind her, and to the guys, out on the stoop, beat-boxing to Billy Joel's "Uptown Girl." The hallway smelled of dog, kasha, and tomato soup. The cool railing beneath her left hand must have been a veneer, given the scratchiness of the wood-colored paint. Twice, Trisha bumped into the thin, popcorned wall on her right; the stairway, if not the house itself, was too narrow.

She hated herself for thinking it, but this hardly seemed the place for a girl from the Main Line, much less an Ivy League grad—although of course James was one too. To put it the politically correct way: This felt like such an invasion of privacy. It was just too surreal, seeing James at all, much less in his *real world*. It felt *wrong*, overly personal, like running into your therapist buying tampons at the grocery store or walking in on your friend's boyfriend as he leaves the shower. What do you say?

But…underneath the wish to make excuses and leave, Trisha was amazed at how once again, through the strangest set of circumstances, she and her polar opposite had been thrown together. The last time she saw James, she'd been certain she'd never lay eyes on him again—and been glad for it. He was like a case of herpes; just when she thought he'd disappeared forever, he would flare up.

And given her pseudo-philosophical belief that everything happened for a reason, she couldn't shake this off. Maybe there was a reason that James's mother had sent his painting to Trisha—if that was indeed what had happened. And that it had gotten misplaced until now, when Trisha could actually do something about it. Maybe there was a reason that the painting had reached her just as she was starting a new job at the Woodward Gallery. Perhaps there was a cosmic plan: to give James the big break his mother had never gotten.

Nat, having passed Trisha in the stairwell, was sizing up James's muscular frame, bulging beneath a ribbed tank and a pair of khaki shorts. Leave it to Nat. James had always reminded Trisha of Sylvester Stallone from the early *Rocky* days, had *Rocky* been bald.

And then Trisha noticed something. His clothes were covered with redness. Something that, judging from its brightness, was still wet.

And then, as the body in James's living room came into sight, Trisha stopped and screamed, so loudly that she didn't even hear Nat join her.

1991

College

Philadelphia

⊠

Purple blotches spread like fingers, tearing through her white silk nightgown. Trisha stared at the debacle in her hands, blinking back tears. What a way to start her senior year. Her boyfriend would be arriving within the hour from his own college for the weekend, and this gown was Trisha's secret weapon for counteracting the recent malaise in their relationship.

She didn't even look good in purple!

Trisha glanced at the hand-lettered sign above the washing machine. IN LAUNDRY ROOMS, AS IN LIFE, it read, A LITTLE KINDNESS GOES A LONG WAY. The sign was covered with graffiti ("Penn is a slumlord," "Clean this fucking shit-hole!!" "Fuck you!!!"), but Trisha, for one, took what it said seriously. She did unto others. She followed rules. And she did her best to follow laundry etiquette, confusing as it could sometimes be.

Apparently, one of her new hall mates did not. Due to his ignorance of the laws of laundry—after three years of practice! on a senior floor!—purple soap suds oozed all over Trisha's unmentionables, dripping down from a just-washed purple shag rug. Trisha had left her wet things in the open dryer for less than three minutes, the time it took to run down the hall and fetch some quarters, and that's all it had taken for this laundry demon to throw his rug on top of her clothes.

With a resigned sigh, Trisha tossed her nightie back into the washer. She reached to tighten the scrunchie holding her strawberry-blonde hair, the way she always did when she was overwhelmed. Gingerly, she hoisted the rug with thumb and forefinger and carried it to the sink on the far side of the room, in the process dripping purple liquid onto the dusty linoleum floor. She dropped the rug into the sink and absent-mindedly wiped her hands on her khakis, only then noticing that she'd just ruined them, too.

"*God*," she spat out. As an afterthought, she added, "Please let the purple come out," to transform this blasphemous curse into a prayer. She always tried to be nice to God, in case He existed.

She walked back down the hall to her new dorm room, defeated. She returned a few minutes later—having changed into a pair of sweatpants—with detergent, Windex, and a roll of paper towels. She believed in good karma. After massaging detergent into the purple, which was everywhere, she slammed another five quarters in the proper slots, in the process breaking a fingernail. She drew a ragged breath. "Damn," she said mournfully.

But then she closed her eyes and counted, the way she'd learned in yoga this summer, and when she opened them, things were better. How bad could things be? *David* was coming.

Trisha went to fetch her cleaning supplies, and smiled as she bent to wipe the purple trail from the floor. The campus chapter of Greenpeace, of which Trisha was treasurer, had finally convinced a local polluter that had once dumped chemicals in the Schuylkill River to undertake a clean-up. That was good, too. The river would run clean again, just like the laundry-room floor. It made her happy, thinking about it.

But just then, someone burst through the door, rocking it so far forward, it screamed on its hinges. A dark-complexioned guy, a Latino, with a shaved head and pitch-black sunglasses, nodded his head to the heavy metal music blasting from his yellow Walkman. As he barreled past Trisha, who stared at him from her Cinderella pose on the floor, one of his Doc Martens landed on her right ring finger with a *crrruuunch*. Thank god for the promise ring David had given Trisha years ago—he might have broken her finger. Nevertheless, it hurt. Bad.

Trisha looked up and saw only the backside of his black t-shirt, covered in concert dates. A tinny scream erupted from his headset: *"Eeeeee-xit light! Eeeeennn-ter niiiiiight! Taaaaaake my hand! We're off to never-neverland!"* Trisha wanted to knock the sunglasses off this guy's stupid big square head.

But the sign, which she could *just* see from the corner of her eye, spoke to her. KINDNESS! it screamed. KINDNESS! KINDNESS!

And so she did her best to be…kind. "Well, excuse you!" she said playfully. The guy didn't even look at her. The only reply was another wail from his Walkman.

She cleared her throat and rose to her knees. Arms stretched out, she waved her hands in an exaggerated windshield wiper motion. "Hello!" she yelled. Continuing to ignore her, the guy shoved his clothes into a duffel bag too small for the task at hand. "*Hey.*" Trisha rose to her feet. This was getting ridiculous. She reached to tap him on the shoulder, but didn't anticipate his sudden pivot as he walked away. What happened as a result was worthy of vaudeville. Having missed his arm, Trisha, stepping hard in an attempt to regain her balance, instead landed *directly on a big purple streak of Windex*. She slid and fell flat on her face.

When she opened her eyes, the first thing she saw was purple, absorbed in the balled mass of paper towels that had kept her chin from directly hitting the floor. Now her chin was purple (and, as she was soon to find out, purple dye didn't come out easily). "Shit!" she yelled. Trisha never swore. She threw the paper towels at the trash can—and missed.

Never in her life had such a thing happened to Trisha, and never in her life had she felt such a visceral hatred for a person she had never met. The only thing that kept her sane was the thought that David, her David, was on his way for a weekend visit.

⊠

The next day, Saturday, after Trisha had touched upon denial, anger, bargaining, and depression, and momentarily settled into a somber, red-eyed acceptance, Nat sat her down with some take-out pizza for the first of a great many morale-boosting talks. This is the First Day of the Rest of Your Life, it might have been titled. Or, There Are Plenty of Fish in the Sea. In other words, Nat shared nothing revolutionary, but rather employed words that time immemorial had proven useful when a friend got dumped.

"The great news," Nat concluded, "is that *finally*, after all these years, you can come scamming for men with me!"

Through her tears, Trisha looked skeptical. "Nat, there's a reason that we have remained friends all these years," she said, "and that is that I *don't* go scamming for men with you." Trisha was accustomed to playing second fiddle to her untamed roommate. Nat had two cup sizes and a foot of hair on Trisha, plus a seeming indifference that drew guys like a magnet. She was sensual, whereas Trisha was...straightforward. Nat was Sophia Loren to Trisha's Meryl Streep.

And Nat had another claim to fame. Sophomore year, she had co-starred in a short-lived campus soap opera, "Nights of Love," that Penn's public access station still re-ran at least twice a day. During episode #4B, "Laying it Down," Nat even had a love scene with a guy named Julian Marcus, and it was urban legend that one of Nat's nipples had been exposed briefly. The station never re-ran that particular episode, lending credence to the claim, but every year, a new crop of freshman men watched the show obsessively for a time, hoping against hope that 4B would turn up—say, some Tuesday night at 4 a.m.

"I'm not saying you have to go to frat parties with me..." Nat was saying.

"*No* frat parties."

"...but take it from me: There are a lot of guys on this campus. You'll be over Dudley Do-Right in no time. It's been, what, six years since you were out there on the market?" Nat peered at her roommate through sympathetic, heavily mascara'd eyelashes.

"Seven."

"Wow." Nat shook her head, tossing her fluid sheet of hair. "Let's look at this as an opportunity." Nat tossed Trisha the Domino's menu. "Here. Order up a guy."

"What?"

"Just do it."

Trisha scowled and held her left hand to her ear. "Hello?" she said, speaking into her pinkie. "I'd like one guy, please—tall, dark, and handsome."

"With a big sausage," Nat added.

Instead of making Trisha laugh, this only depressed her. She picked up a slice from her half of the pizza—the veggie half—and absently nibbled it. She wished she *could* custom-order up some men: ideally, a clean-cut Catholic boy for her, a tattooed sex-and-Sex Pistols fan for Nat. More likely, they'd end up with meatheads, or, worse, with nice guys hopelessly devoted to Nat...who liked her guys not so nice.

"Seriously," Nat was saying. "You've got to order up what you want. Make a list. I'll help." She fumbled for a pen and pad of notebook paper beneath the books and folders on the coffee table, and wrote ARTISTIC atop a piece of lined notebook paper.

Trisha sighed. "Good luck finding *that* again," she said.

"My classes are four-fifths women, and the other fifth is gay." She and David had met in sophomore art class back in high school in Pennsylvania. One day, on a field trip to the Philadelphia Museum of Art, they hung back in the room that housed Brancusi's *The Kiss*, and took the hint. In the succeeding years, David had opened Trisha's eyes to so much. When they met, she'd liked "pretty" paintings, like Degas dancers and Cezanne pastels. Seven years later, Trisha had acquired not merely an appreciation but a love for abstract modernists; she saw patterns in paintings that once seemed too chaotic for a self-confessed control freak. It never occurred to her that this education might have taken place without David, as a natural result of growing older.

"What else?" Nat prodded.

"*Okay*," Trisha groaned. "How about serious?"

Nat threw her a look over the top edge of the smart-girl glasses she'd just put on, which, truth be told, contained plain old glass. "No sense of humor?" A man without humor, to Nat, was anathema.

"I hate jokes."

"Hmm," Nat said, making the notation. "I never realized that about you."

Over the next fifteen minutes, they came up with a decent list, which included AESTHETIC, KIND, EDUCATED, PRINCIPLED, and PASSIONATE ABOUT SOMETHING.

"You're sure you don't want to specify hair or eye color?" Nat asked. "You'll never get what you want if you don't ask for it."

"Nope," Trisha said, happy to finish the task. "I'm flexible on looks."

"So you're telling me if Mr. Wonderful walked in right now with a hump on his back, that would be okay with you?"

"C'mon," Trisha said, and hit Nat atop the head with a pillow from the couch.

"I'll let that go by," Nat said, "only because it's good to see you smile. So tell me," she continued, "who's the last guy you had any interaction with? Besides Dudley."

Trisha, who had returned to the pizza, chewed carefully and swallowed before answering. "The dick in the laundry room." She'd given Nat the blow-by-blow when she recounted the horror that was the previous day.

"Well, look it," Nat said. "You've called this guy a 'dog' and a 'dick.' I like dogs. I like dicks." She raised her eyebrows. "What does he look like?"

"Uh-uh. No way," Trisha said. "I don't want this guy, nor do I want him hanging around here. He's a cretin. I fucking—*hate* him." As Trisha stood to go, Nat's eyes widened. Trisha never cursed, and she'd never hated a fly. She made excuses for everyone, save Hitler.

"Anyway, I didn't get a good look at him, but he seemed kind of…bulky to me," Trisha continued as she headed for her oasis.

It was on the tip of Nat's tongue to suggest to Trisha that maybe she was protesting a bit too much, but Nat decided against it. No use making Trisha that much more touchy about one of the only twelve males with which they cohabited the sixth floor. (On move-in day, Nat had counted.)

The moment Trisha walked into the oasis she'd put together in her sizeable private bedroom within their two-bedroom suite, the tension in her shoulders dissipated, and the few stretches she performed caused popcorn-like pops in her back and neck. It felt good to relax.

No matter how bad things got during Trisha's senior year—and already, things could hardly be worse—she took comfort from her new home. It was a particular godsend considering the chaotic circumstances in which she'd lived in the past three years at Penn. Freshman year, she and Nat had been placed together randomly in Hill House (a.k.a. Hell House), perhaps the dreariest of all dormitories on campus. The only thing that kept them sane within their cell—somehow, they shared a *six by nine foot* area—was each other.

From the beginning, Trisha and Nat made sense in a Felix Unger/Oscar Madison way. Trisha held Nat's hair when she threw up and brought her chicken soup, while Nat took care of Trisha's style deficiencies, forcing her to wear a bit of makeup and to vary her look occasionally from the Capri pants and twin sets that were, to this day, Trisha's standards. Nat was thrilled enough with the arrangement to want to repeat it her sophomore and junior years, but as much as Trisha loved Nat, she had another plan: to return to Hell as a resident advisor. It certainly wasn't the accommodations that lured her. RAs got the same types of rooms as their charges, only they didn't have to share. But what space Trisha gained by Nat's absence, she immediately lost: Homesick, lovesick, or just plain *sick* freshmen were always plopping themselves down on her twin-sized bed and dumping their problems on her.

By the end of junior year, Nat had had enough of watching her friend's martyr act. "You owe me," she whined. "Since you abandoned me, I've been stuck living with a pyromaniac, a kleptomaniac who stole my underwear *and wore it*, and a Christian Scientist who doesn't believe in deodorant."

Trisha had long since tired of hearing from freshman girls about the abhorrent behavior of freshman boys. She let Nat keep talking, painting a picture of the high rises as a land of luxury—a picture few residents would recognize, as it failed to mention insects, vermin, mildewed bathrooms and crumbly walls. "I'll even keep my dirty laundry out of the living room," Nat promised. "I won't leave my finger-nail clippings lying around."

"Will you give the main room a break from the television every once in a while?"

Nat swallowed. Hard. "I'll try," she pledged.

Upon moving in, Trisha pretty much left the common room to Nat, and concentrated on her inner sanctum. It was three times as big as the room she and Nat had *shared* three years before. Thanks to tips she'd culled from design books and magazines, it hardly resembled a dorm room. Because the university forbade students to paint their walls, Trisha had painstakingly tacked up extra-wide strips of sun-flower-hued poster paper, "wrapping" the room with color. She covered the particle-board desk with a leather-bound desk set and added a sterling silver lamp and a photo of Gus, the late, great, three-legged mutt she'd rescued from the pound as a child. She scattered around the room $20 candles with names such as "citrus orchard" and "burning leaves," and filled her stereo with the best of Billie Holiday, John Coltrane, and Chopin.

On the Sunday night after David left, Trisha pulled back the peach-colored sheets on her twin bed, climbed in, and surveyed her domain.

Given that this was one of the worst weekends of her life, she felt cozy, safe. This room would be her reward for three years of Hell. Literal Hell.

She sighed and ripped the cellophane from *Artful Women: A History of Unsung Female Modernists*, which had sat on her bedside table. Halfway through chapter two, at the uncollegiate bedtime of 10:30 p.m., she dozed off.

And then, a little after 2 a.m., a bomb exploded.

Well, not a bomb. But heavy metal flew through the air and hit Trisha like shrapnel, ripping her from her dreams with an almost physical force. It was the same exact song that had echoed from the Walkman of her nemesis: *"Eeeexit light! Enter niiiiight!"*

"No kidding," Trisha spat out.

She nestled deeper into her Egyptian cotton sheets and shut her eyes even more tightly, with the irrational hope that this would neutralize the noise. Meanwhile, the singer moaned about *holding my breath* and *wishing for death* and called upon God to help him.

"I wish," Trisha muttered. She stared at the ceiling, beseeching God to silence this aural violence and even offering a helpful solution: Maybe he could drain the batteries in this guy's boom box? When God didn't respond, an unwelcome thought crossed her mind: There *is* no God.

As if in direct response to her lack of faith, the music segued into a ballad of sorts. Trisha closed her eyes and atoned for the blasphemy, just in case. But truth be told, she was still angry—and, by now, entirely awake.

Trisha stared at the ceiling. She was a firm believer that everything happened for a reason. So what was so god-awful important about her being awake at 2:15 a.m., *the night before classes were to begin*?

Maybe the dorm was burning down? Or she had set her alarm clock wrong? (She checked; nope.)

Nat was passed out, choking on her own vomit? Nope. She wasn't even home yet.

Okay then. Maybe Mr. Right was, for some reason, loitering in the sixth-floor lounge, waiting for her to wander in and say that she, too, was so juiced about the next day that she had insomnia. She could almost buy that.

Trisha slid into her slippers and performed, in double-time, all the yoga moves she knew that didn't involve touching the carpet with her hands. (She made a mental note: BUY RUG ASAP.) She peeked in the mirror; not bad for someone who'd gotten a mere four hours of beauty sleep. Pajamas? Cute enough for prime time. Trisha took a deep breath, walked over and opened the door, half expecting to see the man of her dreams standing there with a bouquet of flowers.

She was sorely disappointed.

Instead, she encountered a wall of sagging cardboard boxes stretching to the ceiling. She darted one way, then the other, but even someone who, like Trisha, carried only 110 pounds on her 5'6" frame had no hope of squeezing through to the hallway. "Hi! Anybody there?" she called toward 6H's open door. She struggled to right the wobbling pillar of boxes, which were threatening to topple now that Trisha's door had knocked it. "Excuse me!" She waited for a quiet moment between songs and then repeated at top volume: "Excuse me! I don't know if you can hear me, but I think this is a fire hazard!"

In response, something that sounded like a fifty-pound barbell slammed into the wall.

The next song kicked in.

Trisha stepped back inside, letting the door slam behind her, and made an obscene gesture at the wall shared with 6H. Then she walked to her bedroom, climbed into bed and put her pillow over her head. Even long after the music stopped, she stayed tense, knowing that sooner or later, given her luck, it would come back.

"Well, there's Beauty and the Beast, of course," Nat was saying. "And Harry and Sally. And let's not forget Luke and Laura."

"Would you shut up? Please," Trisha added, realizing she was being harsh. "My head is killing me."

"Come on, Trisha, help me: OPPOSITES WHO ATTRACT. Act like you're on *The $100,000 Pyramid*."

"You're nuts. Besides, I don't think you get it. So far this guy has ruined my negligee, nearly broken my hand, trapped me inside my room, and kept me from getting any sleep whatsoever with his awful head-banging music. I'm ready to *kill* him, not get involved with him."

"First of all, I happen to *like* heavy metal," Nat said. "I can't help it if I have a thing for long-haired guys with cucumbers in their pants. Second: killing a defenseless animal? What would your colleagues at PETA think?" Nat cracked. "Anyway, is that what we're here for? You haven't done a very good job of arranging this hit."

"No," Trisha said. "I just want to let him know the pain and suffering he's—"

A hoarse voice echoed down the hallway: "God, what a stupid bitch. I mean, that's what I get for signing up to take a woman teacher, right?" The sound faded into the distance as the voice headed for the elevators at an impressive clip. "Jesus Christ, I shoulda known."

"It's him!" Trisha hissed. She cautiously opened the door, tiptoed out into the hallway, and signaled for Nat to follow.

"The thing is, I knew better. I *knew* better." By now, the

words were barely discernable. Trisha began to run, but Nat's heels slowed her down.

Finally, they made the corner, looking entirely composed. The first thing Trisha saw was a wildebeest plunging a sword into the side of a naked woman, the scene playing out on the back of the jerk's t-shirt. Trisha fought the urge to run back to her apartment, lock the door behind her, and never come out.

"So," he said to his friend (standard college male, ball cap pulled low). "I didn't want to have to take Corcoran, 'cause I heard he only gives three A's a semester," he said. "I'd probably get one of them, but who wants to take a chance—"

Trisha cleared her throat.

"Uh-huh," the friend murmured.

Trisha opened her mouth to speak—but instead, her jaw dropped. Forgetting her manners, she stood, mouth agape, utterly taken aback.

His face. Something was very wrong with the jerk's face.

It had been ravaged by—what, acne? Flesh-eating bacteria? Whatever it was, it had carved crags into him from the middle of his forehead to where his neck disappeared into his black t-shirt. His flesh had—what, melted?—and hardened in a new and certainly imperfect configuration. Once again, he was wearing dark sunglasses. No wonder.

The elevator arrived. Nat had to elbow Trisha to get her to move. They got into the back of the car. Trisha took a new interest in the silver rings she'd worn since adolescence. Meanwhile, the guy planted himself in front of her, oblivious to her personal space, boxing her into the corner.

And he continued to rant. "Jobs are at stake, know what I'm sayin'?" Brooklynese barraged them from all sides, ricocheting off the metal walls. He shifted from foot to foot.

Trisha feared he would lean back and crush her.

"So then I went to go talk to her and you can imagine how well *that* went. Cunts. You can't reason with 'em." He laughed hoarsely. The elevator crept past the fourth floor. Behind him, Trisha cringed. "I swear, I wish this school never let 'em in."

"They're good to look at though."

The guy let out a *sheesh* sound. "Yeah." He obviously agreed wholeheartedly. "But still."

After hesitating a beat too long, the elevator door opened to reveal High Rise North's musty, disheveled lobby. Trisha and Nat loitered in the space in front of the elevators, pretending to read an Army flyer urging them to BE ALL YOU CAN BE, until the guys exited the revolving doors.

Immediately, Nat draped her hand over Trisha's forearm and peered at her with concern. "You all right?" she asked.

"Yeah. But, wow, I feel bad. If I'd have known he had a— well, a disfigurement...." She sighed and shook her head. "I feel so bad," she repeated. "I bet he couldn't even *see* me in the laundry room. I mean, what the heck happened to his face? Has he never seen a plastic surgeon? Maybe I can help. My mom's friends with the wife of that guy who. . . *What*?"

Nat was staring at her, puzzled. "Yeah, dude needs an IV hookup to Retin-A," she said very slowly. "But I'm sure that's not what's on your mind right now."

"Well, yeah, the misogyny is troubling. But I don't know that now is the time to discuss it."

"Sweetie, you okay?" Nat turned to face Trisha dead-on. "Is it *possible* that you just occupied an elevator with David's identical twin and you didn't even notice?"

"*What*?"

"The *other* guy. He looks *exactly* like David."

"Oh my god. Oh my god." Trisha's hand flew to her mouth. She stumbled to the benches in the lobby, ignoring Rhett at the front desk, who tried to hand her a magenta flyer advertising a mixer for GLAAD, the Gay & Lesbian Alliance Against Defamation. "Oh my god."

Ironically, it was in the laundry room where Trisha laid eyes upon the second coming of David. By that time she'd had over a week to daydream that they would have all the glories and none of the problems that she and David had shared. Things started out rather well; when she looked at him, she realized that Nat was wrong. He wasn't a dead ringer for her ex. Yes, he had the same boyish Matthew Broderick-style cuteness, but he was far better looking: taller and fitter, with better skin and hair. Like a redesign that this time, they had gotten right. He nodded when he caught Trisha looking at him.

Given the previous debacle at that very locale, Trisha had taken up residence atop her washing machine, guarding it cross-legged. She tried to concentrate on the art history book in her lap, but she couldn't help but notice the nice-looking t-shirts he dropped into the machine, or the dark-hued jeans (just the way Trisha liked them). After the guy deposited his clothes into the washer next to hers, he, too, jumped atop a machine. Then he turned and introduced himself: Mitch Robertson. "I haven't seen you around before," he said. "You new here?"

"To the high rises," she said. "Not to Penn."

"And how are you liking good old High Rise North? I've been here for years."

"It's a really nice face," she said, and then turned deep crimson. "I mean, *place*." To cover her Freudian slip, she quickly added that she was in room 6J, by the way, leading him to volunteer, more happily than was necessary, that they were neighbors.

"I hate to do it," Mitch then said, "but I guess the question must be asked: What's your major?"

"Art history."

"Art!" Mitch said. "I love art. My screensaver's that Salvador Dali painting—the one with the, um, melting clocks?"

Trisha nodded and tried to smile.

"*Okay*." Mitch winced. "Wrong answer. Let's try this another way: Who's *your* favorite artist?"

"An abstract expressionist you've never heard of."

"Try me."

"Joan Mitchell."

Mitch made his thumb and forefinger into a gun and shot it at Trisha. "Sure," he said. "Love her music. I heard she painted too, but I haven't seen her stuff. What's it like?"

"Actually, it's *Joan* Mitchell. Not Joni."

Mitch cradled his head in mock shame. "Try me again?" he said in a small voice.

"Gerhard Richter? Josiana Soder?" She hesitated. "Jackson Pollack?"

"Now, there's a winner!" he said. "But can I ask you a question? Do you really and truly like all those squiggles? I mean, I can see how that cr—that *stuff* would be fun to paint, but it's not much to look at. Give me the good old *Mona Lisa* any day."

The washing machine buzzer rang with great dissonance.

"You're up," Mitch said.

"No, *you* are." Trisha took the opportunity to avoid the Pollack question, which really got on her nerves. "What's *your* major?"

"Well, I'm afraid I'm your garden-variety Whartonite." He held up his hands to block his face. "Please don't hate me." The Wharton School of Business was one of the most prestigious in the country, and the undergraduates walked around campus like so many navy blazer-clad princes.

"Look at it this way," Trisha said. "I'm sure I know even less about business than you do about art."

"Sounds like that's by choice."

Now it was Mitch's buzzer that sounded. Meanwhile, having safely delivered her clothes to a dryer, Trisha closed up her book and prepared to go.

"Listen," Mitch said. "I'm sure you think I'm a conceited know-it-all who's about to get paid ridiculous sums of money to tell middle managers twice my age what to do. But I'm not all bad. I want to go into consulting because I like to figure out people's problems and solve them."

"Like what? 'Lay off half your workforce and you'll make more money?'"

"Fair enough. But I hope I can be a bit more creative than that." Trisha walked to the door; Mitch followed. "Tell me," he said. "What's your biggest problem right now?"

She considered. "The noise that comes out of your room at random hours of the night."

The confidence on Mitch's face dimmed ever so slightly. "Done."

"'Done?'"

"Say no more. It's taken care of."

Trisha, wearing a puzzled frown, thanked him and disappeared into the hallway. Upon encountering Nat in her usual place on the couch, she told her the latest; she was convinced Nat would be happy she was "out there." But Nat's face gave away nothing. She rifled through the papers on the coffee table until she came up with Trisha's list.

"Hmm. Well, he's not exactly AESTHETIC or an ARTIST, is he?" she said. "And we don't really know yet about PRINCIPLED or PASSIONATE."

"I think he gets points for being KIND."

"Why? Because he's trying to lure you into bed?"

Trisha sighed.

"Not that there's anything wrong with that," Nat said. "I just don't want my little Trishie to get hurt out in the big bad world."

Twenty minutes later, when Trisha returned to the laundry room, Mitch was there, stuffing a last pair of jeans into a black trash bag.

"I know this is kind of forward of me," Mitch said, "but do you want to go back to my room and help me fold all this?" He caught himself. "I mean, hang out while *I* fold this stuff."

"I don't know." Trisha raised her eyebrows. "You could fold them here." She absently picked up a pair of his boxer shorts and folded them into a perfect square until she realized with a jolt what they were. Trisha was being coy; she was on the rebound, and Mitch was cute; she would have accompanied him to a bris, an NRA meeting, or a root canal.

Mitch stuck out his lip in a mock pout. "You wouldn't leave the clothes in the lurch, would you? What if they never make it back home? Wouldn't you feel guilty you abandoned them?"

"I guess I could come," she said, biting her lip. "For the sake of the clothes."

She accompanied Mitch to 6H. He insisted on carrying her laundry as well as his. At the door, he put the clothes down and flung open the door, then held it open for her with his foot. "Welcome to the Rump!" he proclaimed.

"Sorry for the mess," he added. "Maid's day off."

The living room mirrored Trisha's and Nat's save three things: Almost every surface held an article of clothing, textbook, or dirtied plate; the left wall sported a strange extra refrigerator with a spigot on the front; and the guy who had occupied so many of Trisha's recent thoughts lay sprawled, open-legged, on the couch.

"And here's Señor Rumpy himself: my roommate, James," Mitch said. At first, James appeared to be staring at a thick textbook with utter loathing, but on second glance, Trisha realized he'd fallen asleep. Mitch reached into his bag for a pair of socks and, with a major league wind-up, threw them hard. James jolted awake. Frantically, he picked up the remote control lying on his stomach and tried to click his textbook off.

Mitch cackled. "Dude," he said, "you've either been watching too much TV or drinking too much beer—or both."

The Rumpster burped. He tossed the remote onto the floor and removed his feet from the coffee table, where multi-colored candles puddled in various stages of melt-down. He blinked like a newborn chick. Trisha, having never seen him without sunglasses, saw that the skin around his eyes was wrinkled and pink. Scar tissue covered one eye entirely; fragile, milky skin surrounded the other.

"So man," Mitch said. "You know Trish?" He waved an arm her way. "From next door?"

"I've seen you around," Trisha offered.

James closed his eyes as if pained and shook his head. "What time is it?" he grunted.

"I don't know, man. Eight-thirty?"

James emitted another apelike grunt and slammed his book shut. He stood and stomped toward the bathroom.

The game of musical chairs continued; Mitch tossed his garbage bag onto the ramshackle plaid couch James had just vacated, and went to sit there, and Trisha followed. She picked up some jeans that had fallen from his bag and began to fold them.

"Let's worry about that later," Mitch said, taking them and holding his hand on hers a second too long.

"But—okay."

"Let me give you the grand tour." Mitch displayed the room with outstretched arms. "This is the couch, but, of course, you two have already met."

Trisha smiled and rolled her eyes.

"Yeah, I know. Pretty rank." Mitch chuckled. He leaned back, folding his arms behind his head. "And that"—he nodded with his head at the extra fridge—"is the world-famous Kegerator."

"Excuse me?"

"The Kegerator." Mitch beamed. "My buddy Glenn found this old fridge on the street, and we ordered all this stuff you use to alter it, like, y'know, a Transformer. Now it's like, uh, a special keg—it holds one just perfectly. We get a new keg delivered every week. Beer?" He licked his lips and stood.

It was a rhetorical question. He removed two mugs from the freezer and, one by one, tilted them under the spigot. Walking back to the couch, he took a long sip and then sighed, content, as he licked the foam from his upper lip. He handed Trisha her mug. She scraped white frost from it and forced herself to take a sip.

They sat in awkward silence. The sole wall decoration, a plastic Coors clock, ticked more loudly than any clock had ever ticked, crying out desperately for the new couple to make out or say something or *turn on the television*, for god's

sake. Trisha wished Mitch would kiss her yet simultaneously wanted to leave. A voice in the back of her head clearly
informed her that she would be bored and/or fed up with
this fellow by now if she were in her right mind, but Trisha
thought of David and turned the voice off once and for all.
She was due a rebound, complete with sex, and for that,
this guy was as good as they came.

She stood and approached the real refrigerator. She
turned her attention to the photograph stuck on front with
magnets. "Is this your family?" She pointed toward a standard vacation shot.

"Yep, them's the folks, at the Grand Canyon."

"And…your sister?"

"Uh-huh."

Trisha examined the potential in-laws: jolly dad, subur-
ban-flavored mom, slight but pretty sister. Then she scruti-
nized Mitch more carefully than she would dare in person:
six feet in stature; carved from smooth, tan marble, with
gold details on the head, arms, and chin; wavy brown hair;
ideally proportioned.

She turned away, but as she did, a close-up of a brunette
caught her eye. She plucked it from the fridge for a better
look. Make that: *stunning* brunette.

"Your girlfriend?"

"Nah. That's Cindy, James's fantasy girl. They grew up
together."

"She's *his* girlfriend?"

"God no." Mitch said. Then, in a quieter voice: "He wish-
es."

Trisha frowned. "Don't be mean."

"Oh, don't get me wrong," Mitch said. "I love the guy
like a brother. But…." He hesitated, and then beckoned her
over with an index finger. As she turned to rejoin him on

the couch, Trisha saw James walk from the bathroom to his bedroom wearing only a gray towel. His scars covered his stomach. When he slammed his bedroom door, she heard him turn a deadbolt. The bedroom doors didn't come with locks.

"*Anyway*," Mitch whispered once she'd sat back down beside him, "James has never had a girlfriend, as far as I know. I think he's a *virgin*."

"Wow." Trisha wasn't far from one herself. "It must be hard being…him. What happened?" She gestured vaguely toward her face.

"He was in a fire when he was a kid. Crazy." Mitch pursed his lips, and then let them go slack, as if to accentuate their kissability. "He was in the hospital, like, in elementary school. They were able to do a lot to help him, but he's still legally blind."

"He can't see?"

"He doesn't seem to bump into too many walls." At Trisha's horrified look, Mitch quickly clarified. "I know he has trouble seeing the TV. But he'll never admit to having any trouble. I know sometimes he has to go back to New York to see doctors and stuff. I'll wake up and he'll be, like, gone."

"And here you are opening up to *me* about it just"—she checked her watch—"four hours after you met me. Nice of you."

"Well," Mitch said, "I can tell you're a trustworthy person." He leaned over to caress her hair, then her face. He shifted toward her. As if on cue, heavy metal kicked in on the other side of the wall. Trisha pulled away.

"What do you say we go someplace quieter? Like…your room?" Mitch said with a wink.

⊠

True to his word, Mitch solved Trisha's sleeping problem; the heavy metal stopped immediately. But as Trisha had feared, this only opened up a new set of problems. Now, whenever Trisha passed James in the hall, he threw out a menacing glare—as a warning to her, or so she imagined. And whenever she showed up at 6H, which was often, he retreated to his bedroom and locked the door.

One evening, after she and Mitch had been … carrying on … for about a week, she raised her hand to knock but stopped short at the sound of male voices.

"—new piece of ass?" a guy with a Texas accent was asking.

Trisha froze. Could he be talking about her? She pressed her ear against the cold red paint, but missed Mitch's mumbled reply. "But I'd rather hear about N'arlins," he was saying by the time she got her bearings. "You guys. Driving all that way to party for, like, three hours."

"Have you *seen* those sexy little swamp mamas?" Tex asked.

"Yeah—and they're about thirteen years old!"

"You know what old Glenn say," said old Glenn: "Old enough to pee, old enough for me."

Trisha was preparing to leave when the door swung open. She fell forward—onto James.

"Gosh. Sorry." Trisha stood and brushed off her palms. "Is Mitch here?"

James motioned her in and passed her, departing for parts unknown. Trisha walked in. A handful of hyperkinetic guys encircled the television like electrons, sitting, standing, moving from couch to chair and back again. Trisha spotted Mitch in the center of the couch, glued to the TV screen, manipulating a video game controller. His eyes remained riveted on the tiny green man on the TV screen.

Suddenly he screamed, "Fuck! Fuck! Fuck!" and then fell back on the couch in disgust. He raised the generic blue football jersey he was wearing and rubbed his belly with one hand.

"Mariotard," said a fleshy, frizzy-haired redhead, bald at the crown—the one with the thick Texas drawl. "That's fifty more you owe me." He high-fived a string bean of a guy who sat huddled over a huge bong. He was wearing a yellow t-shirt that read JESUS '88. "Unless, course, you wanna make it double or nothing. *Again*." He chuckled.

Suddenly shifting gears like someone pogoing between multiple personalities, Tex offered Trisha his hand. "Glenn Boshanks at your service." Under his breath, he added, "They're damn *good* services, too." He took a sip of beer. What he didn't wipe from his face dripped from his chin.

"Well, who have we here?" asked Mitch, as if just now noticing her presence. "Trish*ie*!" He stood and toppled toward her, and ended up hugging her midsection as he walk-slash-dragged her down the hall to his room. "Just be a second, guys!" he yelled over his shoulder.

And so Trisha met Glenn and Phil.

"Typical." Nat said after Trisha had described Mitch's crew. "This Glenn guy, he have a pot-belly? Not so tall? Balding?"

Trisha nodded.

"I know that guy. Did him sophomore year. He's got a pencil dick." Nat folded her arms over her generous chest. "And to compensate for it," she added, "he strutted 'round the dorm like a bantam rooster, telling everybody I shaved my pubes into a heart. At least, that's what Rhett said, and he sure as hell wasn't going to make up something like that." Rhett, who manned the High Rise's front desk, was the hub of dorm gossip, as well as the secretary of the campus gay and lesbian organization. "You know, T-bone," Nat added, "I must say that compared to Mitch's other friends, good old James sounds positively charming."

"Well, at least with them, you know what you're getting," Trisha replied. "James gives me the heebie-jeebies, big time. The boy needs help. Mark my words: One day, you'll hear about his killing spree."

When Mitch's birthday approached, just weeks after Trisha met him, Trisha chose to broach the subject with his friend Glenn instead of James. She waited until Mitch went to the bathroom—he'd been known to read a whole issue of *Mad* magazine on the toilet—and addressed Glenn in between games of Mario Bros. "It's Mitch's 21st birthday next Wednesday," she whispered. "Anybody got any ideas?"

"Beer bash!" Glenn shouted. He thought *everything* merited a beer bash, including the last day of winter and the first day of TV sweeps.

"Isn't that a little...typical?" Trisha asked.

"We'll make it a surprise." He pointed a finger around the room. "And whoever lets the cat out of the bag will have to suck my fat dick." He stood, lifted the front of his shirt and did a belly dance, jiggling his fat and using his wiggling forearms to mimic his alleged penis.

Trisha grinned, recalling Nat's take on the actual dimensions of Glenn's apparatus.

"Oh, you like that?" Glenn's eyebrows flickered up in surprise at the feedback from such an unlikely source. "I bet you do." He gave her a come-here signal with his index finger. "Guess what I'm getting him as a perzint?"

"A perzint?"

"You know, a *perzint*!"

"I don't want to know."

"A hooker! No offense, but one woman ain't enough for a young buck like Mitchie."

It was determined that Trisha would take Mitch for a lavish dinner at the Palladium, the one formal restaurant on campus, and deliver him to the rooftop lounge, a floor-wide space on the eighteenth floor, at ten-thirty. The guys would supply the kegs and chocolate ice cream and make sure everybody got invited.

As if on cue, the toilet flushed.

Of course, the approaching event called for a clothing consultation with Nat. "If ever a time called for the Fuck-Me Dress," Nat opined, "it's now." The Fuck-Me Dress was Nat's property, but it miraculously fit Trisha, who was smaller in the bust but taller (and therefore heavier) than her knockout roommate.

The Fuck-Me Dress could make *any* woman a knockout. It was black, although the primary color you saw when you looked at a woman wearing the Fuck-Me Dress was flesh. It had two straps, one of which wound in and down and around itself; only Nat understood the workings, and it took her approximately fifteen minutes to get everything attached exactly right. Nat swore up and down, on the other hand, that it took a man only *one* minute to get a woman *out* of the Fuck-Me Dress.

Nat had worn it three times. The first time, she was asked to dance by Johnny Depp in an upscale New York City bar. The second, a representative from a renowned

modeling agency's "petite" division (anything under 6')
handed her his card. The third, she'd had her picture taken
for *Philadelphia Magazine*'s society pages.

It goes without saying that all three times she wore the
Fuck-Me Dress, she'd gotten fucked.

Now it was Trisha's turn.

At seven forty-five, she knocked on Mitch's door, bearing the bag that accompanied the Fuck-Me Dress as well as
a sack of small presents (including Sixers/Knicks tickets).

No one answered.

Trisha put her ear to the door; the place was uncharacter-
istically quiet. She shifted from foot to foot, debating, and
finally returned to her room. Trisha called the restaurant to
say they'd be late for their reservation.

At nine, she called the front desk to ask if Rhett had seen
Mitch. "Sure thing," Rhett said. "Took off a while ago? The
whole gang?" He sometimes spoke in questions.

"Know where they were headed?"

"I really don't know? But, they were having a good time,
like, celebrating, I guess? I know I'll be there later—with
bells on!"

"Cool," Trisha said, and hung up.

At nine-thirty, she made herself a peanut butter and jelly
sandwich and spilled a dab of jelly on the Fuck-Me Dress.

At ten, Trisha went upstairs. The group was too wild and
thirsty to notice that all but one of their hosts were AWOL,
and that the one in attendance had proverbial steam coming out of her ears. They just wanted beer.

At ten-thirty, the guys blew off the elevator, stinking
drunk and laughing. Mitch carried a blow-up balloon of a
sheep with holes at its mouth and crotch and a Santa hat on
its head; someone had scrawled LOVE EWE across its belly in
black marker. The motley group of guests half-heartedly

yelled, "Surprise!"—although given Mitch's advanced state of inebriation, Trisha wasn't sure he recognized what the word meant.

"Hey!" Mitch said. The crowd swarmed around him.

Trisha, dull-eyed, waited until it dissipated a bit. Then she pushed her way through to him, like a subway commuter determined to make her way to the one vacant seat. "Where have you been?" she asked, too calmly. People nearby signaled the rest to fall silent.

Mitch looked helplessly at James, who happened to be standing between them. As Mitch's roommate and best friend, a role akin to best man at a wedding, James understood his role: Front man. Point person. Heat taker. So he acted as proxy. "Hooters," James replied.

"*Hooters?*"

"Hooters."

There were women—Nat among them—who would excuse a trip there, possibly even go along for the hell of it. Trisha wanted to be one of those women. But the thought of Mitch ogling another woman's breasts terrified Trisha, because it made her feel insecure. The combination of fear and shame made her mean.

"Well fuck you then," she said to James. In her mouth the f-word sounded prudish, and she knew it, and that just made her more furious. "You're an asshole," she said. She looked up to address the group at large: "You're all assholes."

Spittle flew from her mouth and happened to land on James's chin. Two dozen eyes watched them square off, chins and chests jutted out, like mismatched boxers. He towered above her.

James blinked quickly—and then struck: "No, fuck *you*, Trisha. You're the asshole." His voice was clipped; his face, impassive as always. "It's not like we *kidnapped* Mitch. Did you ever stop to think he might *want* to go to Hooters?" He moved toward her. "No," he continued. "Just like you don't ever stop to think about whether or not you're wanted in our apartment. You waltz in every day like you have a right to be there." He drew closer. "You use my television and VCR and never ask my permission, then have the balls to get annoyed with *me* if I accidentally tape over your *Masterpiece Theater*. You make my living room your study hall, so I've got to go someplace else if I don't want to see lovey-dovey lovebirds. And you don't have the balls to ask me to turn down my music in the middle of the night, so you get your pussy-whipped boy-toy to do it for you. You act like you're the center of the universe. Guess what: You're not.

"Yeah, it's not ideal that we screwed up. So sue us. Mitch said he wanted to grab a drink for his birthday. Somebody suggested Hooters, and it sounded like fun. We got hungry, so we ate. We lost track of time. You don't have to be such a *bitch* about it." James crossed his arms, signaling that he was done.

Glenn stepped forward and clapped, slowly and loudly. Everyone else shifted uneasily on the balls of their feet and eyed the carpet.

Trisha opened her mouth like a dying fish gasping for air. "I *am* sorry," she finally got out. "I didn't realize I did that," she said, lowering her head in remorse. "I had no intention of—"

"Save it." James dismissed her with his hand. "I don't need your apologies. I just need your absence." He turned around. "Sorry, Mitch."

If there was one thing that Trisha couldn't forgive, it was lack of mercy. She looked around, as if trapped, then moved toward the long metal table. She grabbed a chunk of melting ice cream cake and drew up her hand. "Hey," she said, to get James's attention.

He turned back toward her just as a glob of chocolate came toward him. It hit him square on his one good eye. Trisha gasped and stepped backwards, onto the foot of a mousy girl from 6F. *You okay, man?*s and *Dude, you all right?*s rung out from the perimeter of the room.

"I'm fine," James said firmly. "Fine."

Trisha, hand over her face, backed out of the room and then turned to run into the stairwell.

When Mitch left for his 9 a.m. class the next morning, he asked Rhett, who'd worked a double shift, if he'd seen Trisha come home. "At, like, 4 a.m.?" Rhett said in his characteristic sing-song voice. "She said she'd gone to the movies. Down at that theater that's open all night."

"Did she seem upset?"

"I'd say," Rhett replied. "When I asked why she was up at that hour, she said, 'Because Mitch and his friends are penises.'"

"Jeez."

"I know." Rhett shook his head. "I tried to tell her the correct term is *peni*? But she wouldn't listen."

⊠

The next day, Mitch entered Trisha's room and apologized, sort of, by hugging her from behind and fondling her breasts. She wriggled away. His caresses always seemed so needy, like a hungry baby's.

"I was looking forward to our dinner; I only meant to go for a quick drink," he murmured, kissing her ear with too much saliva. "Let me make it up to you."

That he did. The only time her relationship was *good* was when they were making up. This time, Mitch even spent the energy to bring her to orgasm.

In fact, thanks to the amount of tongue wrestling she did with her virile young stud, Trisha woke up one morning with a new problem on her hands—or, well, her face: The delicate porcelain skin around her lips, as well as her lips themselves, were red and painful.

Mortified, Trisha ran to the dermatologist, with a scarf tied around her neck in case anyone saw her. She didn't usually consider herself a vain person, but when she developed fever blisters, she went a little crazy. Way back in first grade, kids had teased her about her sensitive skin, asking had she gotten into a fight? And was she contagious? Granted, Penn students were theoretically well acquainted with cold sores, but Trisha still felt dirty, ugly, and unclean whenever this happened. Worse, everyone stared at her. She'd be having a conversation and realize that the other person was focused on her *lips*.

The doctor had no problem writing Trisha a prescription for a pill that would clear things up within a matter of days; in the meantime, Trisha would enlist Nat to lie for her, telling everyone she had a virulent flu. Then Trisha noticed the doctor frowning as he looked at her shoulder.

"Is something the matter?" Trisha asked, a little unnerved. Did she have a hickey she hadn't noticed?

The doctor pointed to a large brown mole and asked, "Have you ever had this biopsied?"

Trisha shook her head.

"I don't like the looks of it. I'd like to take this off right now," he said.

"Can't it wait?" Trisha said. "I'm supposed to meet someone to pick up some class notes."

"It really can't," the doctor said. "This is the sort of thing you really should stay on top of."

That didn't sound good. "Because?" The doctor explained that the mole had all four telltale signs for melanoma: It was asymmetrical and irregular in color, for starters.

"So this could be...*cancer*?" Trisha choked out. The doctor nodded. "What's best case scenario?"

"It could be *pre*cancerous," came the reply. "We'll know after the weekend."

Trisha retired to her room when she got home, feeling as if she really did have the flu. After a while, Nat came in to say hello. "How's the fake invalid?" she cracked.

"Fine...except—turns out I had this mole...."

Nat sat down on the bed, somber. "Wow," she said. "Scary."

That's all she had to say on the subject, but Trisha could tell it didn't entirely leave her roommate's mind. Later that day, Nat even brought her a pint of Ben & Jerry's (although that might have been so she could steal several bites of it).

Even Trisha got a little spooked. In bed that night, she

wondered what it would be like to be told she had cancer. The idea was preposterous, especially since she had no family history. Or did she? Her mom, a Main Line Philadelphian, stayed as far away from doctors as she could. And her father, well, he was out of the picture. But she couldn't forget the concerned look on her doctor's face. Tentatively, she allowed herself to ask the obvious questions: If the news were bad, would she have to undergo chemotherapy? Lose her hair? Would she be able to finish school? Would Mitch stick around?

What she needed was a hug. Finally, after doing her best to camouflage her cracked lips, she went to find Mitch.

They sat on his bed. All the lights in Mitch's room were out, save a tiny desk lamp. Trisha stopped him from kissing her by holding up a hand and saying she was contagious. "I'm still not well," she said, "but I wanted to tell you something." She knew this was a terrible time to tell him, but she felt so emotional; she really did need that hug. "I went to the doctor and he, um, found something."

Mitch jumped up off the bed and held up his hands. "Wait," he said defensively. "We always used condoms...."

"It's not that," she said. "It's a mole. But there's a chance it might be...cancer. Melanoma."

"*Shit*," Mitch said. He gingerly sat back down on the bed, but farther away from her this time, as if she really were contagious. "Shit, man, I'm sorry."

It felt like a *nice knowing you*.

They sat there for several minutes, neither of them knowing what to say. Then Mitch got a brainstorm.

"I know!" he said, suddenly excited. "You ought to talk to James. His mom has melanoma. Or lymphoma. Some noma. Hold on."

Trisha opened her mouth to stop him, but realized that

James wasn't home; she'd seen him leave. A moment later, however, Mitch returned and signaled for her, and then pointed her toward James's room. "Go ahead," he said. "He's waiting for you."

Trisha knocked quietly, half-hoping James wouldn't hear. It took a minute, but then he opened the door, sweeping his arm back in an exaggerated welcome that negated the gesture. He sat at his rolling desk chair; Trisha tiptoed through a mess of men's magazines (she was afraid to examine them too closely), stale-smelling clothes, and CDs, and balanced herself on the front of his navy comforter.

Not wanting to look James in the eye, Trisha bypassed him for the items on his desk: an old desktop computer, dusty bottles of hard alcohol, and an overturned earthenware crock spilling over with loose change.

There was no possibility here of small talk. "So," James began. "Mitch says you got a bad diagnosis?"

Trisha felt like a fraud. "Not exactly," she said. "It's a suspicious mole. It's either precancer or cancer." She shrugged. "Actually, I'm sure it's nothing."

"Yeah, that's how my mom's started."

To Trisha's surprise, James seemed somewhat interested, more so, at least, than she'd ever seen him. She'd pictured him a blank slate, pigeonholed him as a crass brute with a take-no-prisoners philosophy. Having never taken such a dislike to anyone in her life, she wondered if she'd been unable to look beyond the pain to the person within. That he couldn't relate to her in the slightest until now, when she exhibited the capacity for pain, made her suspect this might be his only currency.

As she opened her mouth to speak again, her periphery caught X-rated images of swords, tongues, blood and breasts, assaulting her from black posters all over the walls, which certainly backed up her new theory. Above his bed hung a red cloth imprinted with a pentagram. "How long has she been sick?" Trisha asked. "Your mom, I mean?"

He thought for a minute. "Two years. But she was lucky. It had barely metastasized when they first found it."

"Metasta—?"

"Oh, right. Spread."

"How is she now?"

He sighed and closed his arms. "Dying," he said bluntly. "But that's the thing with cancer. Pretty much, you get it, you die. They play with the numbers to keep the patient optimistic, but that's pretty much the way it is, sooner or later. I study statistics. I know these things."

"Jeez, that's harsh."

"That's life," he said. Then he swiveled his chair and took on steam, as if he was behind on an agenda. "So here's the thing. They'll want to rush you to have surgery and start chemo right away. Don't let them. Take a few days. It doesn't really matter, but you want to make sure you end up somewhere good. If I was you, I'd go to Sloan-Kettering." He then proceeded to lay out tips on getting through chemotherapy ("lots of ice chips for the mouth sores") and radiation, if necessary—going so far as to cover the health care proxy and living will—all as if Trisha had already gotten bad news. "Let me know if I can do anything to help," he said to wrap up. "I stay up late. *Real* late."

"*Thanks*," Trisha said. His words hung in the air. She wanted to say something else, but really, she was stunned in equal parts by James's barrage and by the very real possibility that she might *need* this kind of information. She looked around for—she didn't know what, but something to say.

And that's when she saw it. *Them.*

Two portraits hung in the midst of the posters, very different but equally stunning works. One was a straightforward portrait of a soulful, elderly Latino man in a blue suit, who struck Trisha as hard-working and humble.

"Wow," she said. "Who painted that?"

"My mother."

"Is it your father?" she guessed. James nodded curtly.

The other painting—the other caused Trisha to start playing with her scrunchie. It was at first an abstraction, then a portrait of a blondish brunette, but painted so as to hardly leave her human.

"Did you do this?" Trisha asked James.

James shrugged.

If she were to write a critique of this work, she would have said the painter had worked through a filter of *disease*, had mutated his subject, perhaps so as to have her join him in his world.

In fact, maybe this was the girl on the refrigerator.

She noticed, then, the easel crammed up against the wall, behind a curtain of clothes, and the spare brushes and pastels and clays in the area in front of his closet. "So do you take classes? Or ever work in any of the studio rooms?"

James scoffed. "What kind of putz comes to the most expensive school in the country to study shit like art?" he said.

"I guess. . . I do," Trisha confessed. James just stared at her. "I'm an art history major, and I can tell you: You're really amazing. But I guess you know that. Your mom is too."

"My mom's okay," he said. "I suck." He had stood and was now opening the door for her. Trisha left and turned to thank him again, but he had already closed the door.

When Trisha got the word that all was A-O.K., she sent

up the briefest of thank-you prayers, and then immediately put the experience out of her mind. No sense dwelling on bad outcomes, especially those that hadn't happened. So she was taken aback when she saw James in the Rump later that day and was greeted with a concerned "how are you?"

"Turns out I'm fine," she said. "False alarm."

So were the signs that she and James could be friends. It would take quite some time for her to regain any rapport with him; in the meantime, he was back to being as aloof as ever.

⊠

Melinda Portman was a lonely, middle-aged socialite who would never recover from having thrown away her debutante youth on Trisha's father—who had left shortly after Trisha's birth. Spending any holiday with Melinda was a lousy prospect, which was why Trisha didn't mind when, this year, her mother had decided to take a cruise over Thanksgiving, leaving Trisha to spend Turkey Day on campus. Actually, it was more than okay by her: She didn't eat meat, hated football games, and took offense at the holiday's historical ramifications. She'd heard that the local homeless shelter was short of volunteers, plus she had a thesis to write.

But Trisha never thought she'd end up alone, working on an art history paper about martyrs. Depressing. She stretched her arms over her head and closed her eyes, meditating on the color Xerox in front of her, of her favorite figurative painting—of a dead man in a bathtub.

Of course, Trisha wouldn't have minded if Mitch had invited her to spend the holiday in White Plains. But that hadn't happened, even if by now, they were boyfriend and girlfriend. Things had been shaky between them just after Trisha's melanoma scare; even after he'd discovered that she was cancer-free, he'd kept his distance, and Trisha didn't appreciate the lack of support. But that had been a month ago. When Trisha allowed herself to think about the relationship, which was seldom, she felt pessimistic.

By Wednesday night of the break, Trisha felt like the Burgess Meredith character in that *Twilight Zone* episode about the bookworm with all the time in the world to read—and broken glasses. After bitching all semester about the noise, it was too damn quiet. She turned on the white noise machine to *create* sound. Then she pulled out the Xerox of Jacques-Louis David's 1793 painting, *The Death of Marat*, the springboard for her examination of the artistic depiction of martyrs.

The painting was dark, in blacks and greens, except for the figure that took over the left third: the spotlighted upper body of an angelic-looking young man in repose, who had just been slain in his bath. It was one of her favorites. That had little to do with who was pictured or why; Marat might as well have been a dead California surfer as a French Revolutionary. Long after the politics had faded, Trisha could take one glance and somehow still care that this person had died. Why—when everybody dies? That's what Trisha hoped to figure out. Put another way: What makes a martyr?

Beauty had something to do with it. Trisha twirled an unsharpened pencil around her thumb. She peered at Marat's face, and at the right arm draping over the edge of the bathtub, his skin as smooth and translucent as mother-of-pearl. She recalled something she'd read in *Art for the Ages*, an art history primer that Nat had borrowed and used as a doorstop: Marat had had some disfiguring disease that marred his complexion and caused him to take frequent baths, and even conduct business in the tub. The artist knew this; the two were friends. And the painter had been granted permission to view his friend's decomposing body. Knowing the gory truth didn't stop David from finding a beauty within—even if it was a beauty tinged by evil—and bringing it to life in such a manner that two hundred years later, people a world away would still mourn.

Trisha sketched the painting on her pad of paper, taking

special care with Marat's sculpted arms. When she reached the Frenchman's turbaned pate, she paused and on an impulse she didn't understand substituted James's bald skull; in an attempt to recreate what he really looked like, she added veined crevices to the cheeks. Not bad. She drew the crate in front of the tub; on it, she drew a maiden surrounded by fire—one of James's favorite images, judging by how often he wore that particular t-shirt. James would probably love *The Death of Marat*, since it featured blood and murder. She smiled. It was the heavy metal t-shirt of its day.

Trisha spent a long day at the shelter and returned with bits of yam smeared on her clothing. She was exhausted. She flashed her ID card and walked through the turnstile. The lobby was deserted except for an older Latino woman in a flowing ensemble that swallowed her body and a paisley scarf that covered what little hair she had left. Trisha stared at her, before realizing that the woman was the one looking over with compassion. Trisha waited a moment and then headed for the stairwell to avoid being observed. The moment the door shut behind her, she began to cry; by the time she exited onto the sixth floor, she was out-and-out sobbing. Blame it on PMS, but she felt so alone.

But she was not really alone. The woman had just stepped out of the elevator and was walking down the hall toward her.

The woman smiled; she approached and laid a surprisingly soft, manicured hand on Trisha's forearm. "Do you want to talk about it? I am Graciella."

As if in a trance, Trisha nodded. "I'm all alone…my boyfriend, he's off for the holiday. My mother took a cruise. I can't start my thesis…." She hated the whine in her voice.

Trisha could tell that this woman would never whine. But neither did she judge. She took Trisha's hand in two of her own and began to rub. "I know, I know," the woman muttered, her gaze urging Trisha to continue.

Once Trisha was done, the woman patted Trisha's arm. "Come," she said. "I make tea."

Trisha nodded, and followed Graciella—to 6H. When Graciella knocked, Trisha backed away in confusion. James answered before she could make an escape.

"Jimmy. I just talk to this lovely young lady. Ah—." She turned to Trisha, questioning.

"Trisha. James and I are neighbors." She pointed at her own door.

"Wonderful. I Jimmy's mother." She peered at Trisha. "You are ...artist?"

Trisha glanced in surprise at James.

"Jimmy tell me. Only, he no mention how *lovely*." James closed his one good eye, as if in excruciating pain. But Graciella's eyes sparkled. She turned to the kitchen—which now smelled of lemon and pine—and filled a sparkling new silver kettle with water.

Trisha shook her head in wonder. Could this woman really be James's mother? Maybe he was adopted.

⊠

"So Patricia. What bring you to U. Penn?"

Graciella had just finished a fifteen-minute reminiscence of her childhood in Nicaragua. ("Ay-yi-yi, I talk and talk. When I get on my pain pills…." She shook her head.) James slouched on the couch with one thumb down his pants, listening, mostly with his eyes closed. He joined the conversation only to add a wisecrack when Graciella mentioned her eccentric brother, James's Uncle Raul. Every year, Raul threw a huge Thanksgiving bash at his house in West Philadelphia, got drunk and threw everyone out by early afternoon. "He hates it when other people drink his beer," James cracked. They had just come from there.

In response to Graciella's question about where she grew up, Trisha replied, "Near here. In beautiful country, like something out of a Wyeth painting, you know the Wyeths? I was very lucky. I loved coming to Philly as a child. It was my childhood dream to live in the city and be a great artist." She paused. "I used to pray that one day, one of my paintings would hang in the Museum of Art. Now it seems silly."

"*Tu madre*, she give you this love of art?"

Trisha laughed ruefully, shaking her blond hair. "Not so much," she said. "She did bring me to the museums; I'll give her that. But she didn't come to look at the paintings; she'd come to fundraisers. She sat me on the benches and left me there to look at the paintings for hours."

Graciella shook her head in dismay. "It was actually the highlight of my childhood," Trisha added. As Melinda lunched with former Main Line debutantes, the young

Trisha lolled on cushioned benches surrounded by colors and shapes that her young mind struggled to make sense of. Melinda had just enough maternal instinct to plant her daughter in front of soothing works—Manets, Monets and the like—because Goya and Brunel, even Caravaggio and dark-toned Rembrandts, gave the little girl nightmares.

As Graciella made tea and listened (and James brooded), Trisha spoke of how her mother allowed her to buy one postcard of a painting every time they went. "I still have the box of them somewhere," Trisha said. In lieu of a diary or a scrapbook, Trisha scribbled thoughts and chronicled events on the backs of these postcards. "I really should do something with them, put them in an album, but you know how it goes," Trisha said. "Procrastination."

"So this why you study not the *making* of art, but the *history*?"

Trisha thought for a minute. "I guess so," she said. "That's definitely what my passion was: looking." Trisha blew on her mint tea to cool it; she took a small sip. She smiled and shook her head at Graciella's sidelong look, which attempted to call Trisha's bluff. "Believe me: The world is better off without my contribution to landfills."

Graciella looked confused.

"I'm not good. At painting," Trisha clarified.

"Who says?"

Trisha shook her head. "I was blessed with an eye, not a hand, but with a perfect eye. I know what has potential. What is a diamond in the rough, what is a rhinestone in a gorgeous setting. And it didn't take me long to characterize my own work."

"I don't know," Graciella said. She pointed her index finger at Trisha and shook it from side to side. "I will not take your word for this. I think every person is her own harsh critic. I, too, am artist, and think my own work is—" She made a face showing her distaste. "Who else has seen this work?"

Trisha looked up. "Oh, right! You paint!"

"Answer the question first." Graciella smiled.

Trisha laughed. "My middle school teacher remains a true believer. *But,* my high school teacher agrees with *me.*" She blew a raspberry. "Tell me about *your* work."

"We are not through with *you,*" Graciella said. "Maybe you just not *ready* to paint before. Try again. Try forever." Graciella began to cough. When she was finished, she shook her head. "What will you do with your degree?"

James snorted. Trisha ignored him.

"That's the question, isn't it?" Trisha said. She paused, and then said, "If things go well, I'll get to spend my life looking at beautiful things." But Graciella didn't reply, and Trisha sensed that she wouldn't take that as an answer. "Seriously," she continued, "if you paint, you know that what ends up on the canvas is *nothing* like what's in your head."

"Yes, yes." Graciella nodded eagerly.

"I don't have to feel that disappointment any more, just the joy of seeing what others have done and, if I'm lucky, the pride of knowing that I did *my* part to ensure that the paintings are seen. Appreciated. Not lost. What if the next Picasso or Pollack gave up their art and became a supermarket cashier because I wasn't around to champion him?"

"Ah, but you can't save everyone," Graciella interjected. "You could never prevent this. Try, and you set up to fail. It must be enough that the artist get joy out of the work itself. That the artist draw *strength* from it." Graciella hit her open palm with a fist. "And sometimes, others will, too."

"Enough about me," Trisha said. "Your turn." She

glanced at James, sitting stone-faced on the couch. Given the lack of elasticity of his face, Trisha could never read his expressions, but she suspected he was long past bored—impatient for her to go, and, as always, angry.

"I am creature of the past. I paint portraits, from time I am small girl. But that was before. Now, landscapes of Nicaragua." She dramatically trilled the "r" and ignored the "g." As she spoke, she brought her hand to her heart. "I come to Brooklyn as a young woman, but still in my mind, dream of that land."

"Why portraits?"

Graciella paused. "I once believe the face is secret to soul." Her eyes shifted to James, who by now appeared to be dozing. "I do portraits for—*everyone* in Nicaragua. Actors, officials, all." She smiled. "It is so...strange. You must judge if this person wants to see himself as is. I have many paintings that the subject see and not want." She shook her head. "I have others that look nothing like the subject, but I know what they want. These," she dismissed them with a sweeping gesture of her hand, "just for money."

She continued. "Of course, there are some other things portraits are good for. If I paint portrait to be shown *here* of any person in my homeland, it shows sadness, which is the history of my people. But those in *this* country, they believe photographs to be enough. Photographs do not judge as portraits do. Portraits bring out the truth; many photographs do not. While I am here," she shrugged, "I paint landscape."

"Did you go to art school?"

Graciella shook her head. "I work to support Jimmy. And there are medical bills. I had shows but never success." Graciella lapsed into a coughing fit, and Trisha refilled her water glass. "Very difficult, to be a painter and a woman," she finally choked out.

"How did you support yourself?"

"James did a lot for such a young boy. He always had jobs. I was secretary. I was receptionist, cleaned houses—oh, many things. Him, too." She smiled at her son. "I am so proud," Graciella beamed. "Jimmy did so well in school. He had four-oh *gee pee ay*. He got scholarship to school, the, what do you say, fiscal—"

"Financial aid," he growled, eyes still closed.

"Financial aid," she repeated. "'Ma,' he said, 'it not *worth* it if you have to sacrifice.' But I know he dream of coming here, and I dream for him too." She glanced at him again. "My Jimmy, he have what it take, too."

"*Ma*." James sat upright and glared at her.

"He could be *great* artist." Graciella leaned toward Trisha conspiratorially. "Oh, Patricia, you should *see* his palette. From an early age he had great sense of color. His favorite thing was to come to my studio and play."

"*Ma*."

Graciella shook her head ever so slightly. She was obviously tiring. "Barely a day goes by that I do not—be—*sad* that—we lost so much," she said, looking Trisha in the eye, "in the fire."

"I heard. I'm so sorry."

Graciella acknowledged this with a tiny nod. "I had his very young paintings—from back when he, you know, *finger-paint*." She laughed. "Once, he was seven, just seven! I convince a place in Brooklyn to show his work with mine. Just as a little joke, really, just to say, artists come in all shapes and sizes." She spoke more slowly now. "The people at the tiny gallery, they forgot to put up the *display copy*. Anyway: Two people want to buy it! And of course *I* sell not a thing. I said then that he would be *great artist*."

"Ma, I will *not* be a great artist." He looked at his watch. "And it's time for your nap." Trisha knew that this cue was meant for her.

"And we lose more than the physical. In the fire." Graciella shook her head. "James, no painting after that. *None* at all. For long time." She peered at Trisha.

"I don't know about that," Trisha said. She looked over at James. "Maybe he will surprise you and paint again."

"Ma, c'mon," James said, standing now. "Time for rest."

James's concern for his mother was impressive. Trisha wondered how much of it was sincere, and how much stemmed from a desire to get rid of her. Then she cursed herself for being so cynical.

"You should see Jimmy as a boy," she said, as she allowed James to help her to her feet. Trisha, too, rose to go. "He smile *all* the time."

Trisha laughed heartily. "That I find a little hard to believe."

"I know." Graciella grinned back at her. "He was *so* sweet tempered. We need to get that back on his face. You and me, together." Trisha blushed at being mistaken for a potential girlfriend. "He *always* been my sensitive Jimmy. Even as a very young child, things got to him, *touched* him in a way *unusual* for a child. I take him to see *Bambi*, and he cry and cry!" She smiled and her eyes glittered. "But he *never* let you see it. At least, he don't *think* he let you. It come out eventually other ways. You know what I mean. I can tell you do."

Trisha looked down. She felt embarrassed for James— Bambi!—and guilty. She had been no fan of James's; she'd been hard on him. Though he wouldn't let her in unless she pushed herself on him forcibly, she still blamed herself now for not trying hard enough.

"It's been such a pleasure," Graciella said. "You must come to Brooklyn and see the studio. You must! You *will*." She took Trisha by the arm for a startlingly strong hug. "We paint there, and I will *show* you that you have the heart of a great painter. You see what is *here*"—she simulated a canvas—"does not matter. It's what is *here* that counts." She pounded on her chest.

"I've got the heart, maybe, but not the hands," Trisha said, laughing. "I'll do my very best to get there. It was an honor to meet you. And you never know," she added. "Maybe someday, I'll display your paintings in my very own gallery."

"Oh, none of that. It's too late for me. But—you must help me out with this one." She nodded toward James. "He's destined for great things." She smiled wistfully and pinched Trisha's cheek. "You too."

1997

Life

New York

The high-pitched screams terrified the blood red guy in James's living room, and then *he* screamed, which made the women scream all the louder—until everyone came to their senses and realized that the guy was only Phil (Penn's friendly neighborhood pothead) and he was only painting. Unfortunately, in all the uproar, Phil had flung his hands up, and a roller brush full of paint had spattered all over Carly-slash-Nat's acid-washed jacket—and Trisha's Burberry camel's-hair coat.

"That is…*red*," Trisha croaked when she regained her voice.

"Not to mention…*rad*," Nat contributed. She nodded approvingly at the spontaneous new contribution to her jacket.

"We're painting," James explained. He disappeared for a second and returned with a roll of paper towels for Trisha.

What I wouldn't do for art, she mused.

James nodded at the walls. "What do you think?" He picked up a second roller and prepared for the task at hand.

"Um… striking. How exactly did you decide on this color?"

"It's part of a theme," he said. "I'm constructing a torture room. Goes along with my swords and shit. It works, right? Like, you could torture and kill somebody in here, and the cop's 'd never even be able to tell." (He didn't tell them the truth—that he'd expected Rustic Red to be more *rustic*—for several hours.)

Nat laughed. "You're funny. I forgot how funny you are."

James gave her an entirely blank look. Nat, eyes widened, abruptly began hiccupping.

Trisha took her first real look at James. She realized that she was so long accustomed to his scars that she could now look beyond them. The real changes in him were the new definition in his always-large muscles, particularly in his chest.

James, meanwhile, apparently thought he would somehow lose face by asking why Trisha and Nat had turned up out of the blue and refused to make small talk. Nonetheless, the vibe was loose; James spent a good forty minutes trying to convince Nat that he worked at a morgue and performed hits for the Latino mob on the side. Finally Trisha had had enough, but even she felt sad when he finally admitted that he worked "a totally stupid job" at the back end of a multinational bank. "I freakin' *hate* it, and all the bastards I work for," he said. He shrugged. "I want to apply to business school next fall, but whatever."

"So, yo, what do you think?" James asked, obviously to change the subject. "Will the chicks dig the Torture Room?"

Trisha stifled a chortle but Nat, somehow realizing it was a serious question, threw her a nasty look.

"It depends on the rest of the stuff in here," Nat said. "Pretty soon we'll be able to move everything back in and see, don't you think?"

"'The rest of the stuff?'"

"Chairs, bookcases, you know. *Furniture*?"

James scoffed. "This is it. I gave Ma's stuff to the Salvation Army. I'm about to buy some kick-ass shit. A leather couch, leather chair—cool shit."

"You might want to go with neutral colors, to round out the room," Trisha said. "I could help you if you like."

"I like black."

The girls shared a look. Getting the drift, James sheepishly agreed to let Trisha help him—"just for a second pair of eyes," he said.

By now the paint was beginning to clot. James lit a cigarette and sat on the edge of his window, exhaling outside and occasionally waving at a passing neighbor, while Nat flirted with Phil in the background.

"Aren't you going to ask me why I'm here?" Trisha said.

He shrugged, but she answered the question anyway. "I actually came to talk to your mom, and take her up on that invitation she gave me such a long time ago," she said. "But I heard I'm too late for that. I'm so, so sorry, James."

He took a last deep drag and threw the butt out the window. "I hate when people say they're sorry. You got nothing to do with it."

She opened her mouth to apologize for *that* and had to bite her tongue. "So listen," she said. "While I'm here, do you mind if I see her studio? It would mean a lot to me."

He thought about it through the course of cigarette number two, and then nodded brusquely as he tossed it out, half-smoked. He pulled a thick jangle of keys from his right khaki pocket and began to twirl them around his index finger.

"I didn't mean it had to be right now."

"Now's as good as anytime."

They left Phil and Nat downing beer. Downstairs, Chick and Fat stood guard in the twilight, perhaps waiting for another Nat sighting. James bummed a Marlboro Red from Chick and balanced it between his lips while he juggled the key in the downstairs door. "So," he managed to say without the cigarette falling, "you never told me how you found the place."

"Your mom sent something to me at MoMA. There was

a return address. I guess you told her I got a job there?"

James shrugged.

"I wish you would have come to visit me at the museum," Trisha said. "I could have shown you some great stuff that isn't on display."

"This is it," James said, ignoring her, when the gated door swung open. He strode to the center of the room and pulled on a chain to give them some light.

It was a dungeon, a perfect milieu for committing murder, or, for that matter, cutting off your ear in despair. "Jeez," Trisha said. "I think you've already *got* a torture room." Light from the outdoors tried to squeeze in through two long grilled windows at eye level, but the glass was too old and frosted with dirt. "Hardly the best light—especially for a studio," she muttered.

"Better than nothin'," James snapped. He walked over to a green-topped metal stool at the edge of a huge butcher-block table in the center of the room. "Ma never complained."

Trisha turned to get the lay of the land, then stood opposite James at the thick wooden table, covered with layer upon layer of paint. This was the center of the action. At one end of it stood an easel; two naked bulbs dangled overhead. Despite herself, and for the first time in years, Trisha felt the itch to paint. She ran her hand over the table's surface. "I love everything about painting—the feel and the smell of it, even the accidental taste of the turpentine," she said, more to Graciella than to the flesh-and-blood human before her. "I used to think it was the great tragedy of my life that I wasn't any good."

James grunted humorlessly.

"What?"

"It's the great tragedy of *my* life that I am," he said.

Trisha was shocked he'd opened up that much.

She could have stood soaking in atmosphere all day, but got the feeling James might shut down shop at any moment. She gave the edge of the table one last pat, and a brownish-blue smear of fresh paint came off on her hand. Aha. So he *was* painting.

She turned to survey the room's perimeter, where deep wooden shelves held thick canvases, often a dozen deep. Trisha approached the paintings with care, like a nurse in a preemie ward. When she pulled out the first stack, from a shelf at waist level, dust stirred. She stood back and took in an earthy panorama with too much sky.

But after a few mediocre landscapes, Trisha came to Graciella's true métier: dozens and dozens of portraits, of proud winners and lost souls. Without knowing these people—aristocrats and regular folks with the desire to be immortalized—Trisha's heart reached out to each one of them. Some might be contemporaries, people who lived and breathed today, but thanks to Graciella's masterful use of shadow, the portraits were both hyper-real and ageless. And in their simple, earth-toned clothing, these might have been either medieval princes or faithful servants.

"Your mother was so very good," Trisha said, breathing reverently. "I mean, this is top-notch stuff."

"I know," James said. "Lot of good it did her." Trisha didn't blame him for sounding bitter.

She replaced what she'd seen and took down more. By now she ached to break these works out of their prison, to let them breathe and live again. Even if it hadn't been for the sad circumstances of where they had ended up, Trisha knew she would have felt emotional; a good portrait could break your heart. Each one confronted her with her own and her loved ones' mortality, which was, after all, the tragedy of every human life.

"Did she ever paint you?" Trisha asked.

"Huh?" James had been circling back and forth on the stool, which issued cold metallic noises. "Uh-uh."

"I'm surprised."

The painting that struck Trisha hardest was that of an impassioned young woman in an uncharacteristic pose, head back at a dramatic angle, eyes mostly closed, neck elongated. Trisha allowed several minutes to tick away as she stared at this olive-skinned beauty. Was she experiencing great pain, or perfect joy?

"James," Trisha said. "Do you know who these people are? Why did your mom paint *these* people—and why did she end up with their pictures? Like, this girl, for instance—do you know who this is?"

He hardly looked at the picture Trisha held up. "No clue," he said. "I think sometimes she'd see somebody on the street. Or she'd take a picture of some stranger…. Who knows."

So she'd never know. Trisha could hardly take her eyes off it.

"Did she paint a lot at the end?"

James scoffed. "You kidding? She could barely go to the bathroom." He walked over to a dartboard that Trisha hadn't noticed, and threw three darts all at once, hard. Only one hit the board; it dangled and then dropped to the floor. "Fuckin' cancer, man." He shook his head. "They say it's a blessing when you go, but that's bullshit. She didn't want to go." He shook his head and his voice dropped. "Even though she was in a shitload of pain. I got to hand it to her, right to the end she thought she was going to make it."

He retrieved the darts, went to his mark, and aimed one carefully. "She cared so much about her work. 'The work,' 'the work'—she'd go *on and on* about it. Now it all seems like a big pile of shit. A fucking waste. One of these days when I have the time I'm going to burn it all."

"No!" Trisha felt as if he'd just stabbed her. "James, promise me you won't do that. You know she wouldn't have wanted that." Her breathing turned shallow. "If you don't have a place to keep everything, get it to me. I'll figure something out. Look how much happiness it brings me. It can bring that happiness to other people, too. Just trust me."

He leaned back into one corner of the room and, sliding to the ground, folded his arms like a petulant child. "It *kills* me. I came to see her one day and caught her sitting outside on the stoop, in the total fucking cold, trying to sell this stuff for, like, fifteen bucks apiece. The shittiest thing is, nobody was smart enough to buy it! She would have given it away if they showed interest! I think it broke her heart to leave all this here." He breathed in deeply. "I bet part of *her* wanted to burn it. It's a hell of a lot better than leaving it to rot."

Trisha could understand that. He didn't want to watch his mother die again before his eyes. She sighed and walked back over to the portrait of the girl, which she'd left on the table.

On the other hand, he had a point, one that Trisha wasn't yet willing to concede. "You know, portraits are a really hard sell. Incredibly hard," she said, "unless they have some gimmick—I mean, some *twist*, like yours do. But especially if you could help me figure out who these people are—the ones who are actual historical figures, that is—I bet I could drum up some support for a show if we're not too picky about where it is. 'Figures of the Latin American Revolutions.' It's a natural for an upscale Mexican restaurant, if nothing else."

"You think so?" He stood.

Trisha glanced over at him. Just the barest hint of a smile had appeared on his face. "I think so," she said. "Now…what are we going to do about *you*?"

He darkened, appearing more menacing than Trisha had ever seen him, although rationally she knew it was the faded light of the basement. Even knowing him as well as she did, a shimmer of fear flew through her stomach.

"That's what she sent me," Trisha said, seeing no choice but to plow on. "One of your paintings. And it's good, James, really good. I'm not the only one who thinks so."

James scoffed. "You think I don't know that?" he said. "But she had no right." He grabbed his mother's painting by one corner and spun it across the room so aggressively that, to Trisha's horror, the edge of it ripped.

"She did it because she loves you," Trisha said. "She knew what an amazing talent you have. And she didn't want you to end up like her."

"Nothing wrong with that," he said defiantly. "Bed-Stuy is my home."

"You know that's not what I mean," Trisha said softly. "But if you want me to leave, I'll go."

"I think that's a good idea," he said.

Trisha said the briefest of goodbyes, and James disappeared up his stoop. After a moment, Nat joined her, and, silently noting her mood, pulled out her cell phone to call for a car service. (The chances of a cab rolling by in this part of Brooklyn were slim to none.) They stood under the awning without speaking for twenty minutes, waiting where the sleet ripped across the stoop too violently for even Chick or Fat to want to join them.

⊠

Brooklyn left Trisha feeling like a failure, and wondering how on earth she'd convince James to attend the Promettente. Nat counseled her to wait a while for things to blow over—"and if all else fails, offer your bod. Which, I might add, could do *both* of you a favor."

When Trisha got a chance to fill in Tom on the recent doings, she wasn't sure which occurrence shocked him most: that Gresh wanted to include "*that* load of crap" in his show, or that there was a person on earth who might not want to be catapulted to fame and fortune.

"And here's the thing," Trisha said, holding her breath. "I *might* end up having to arrive with him instead of you, depending on what I have to tell him to get him there."

"What kind of asshole doesn't appreciate the fact that you got him into Promettente?" he asked. Trisha recognized Tom's tone as the one he used in closing arguments when he was putting the screws to someone.

"You're not listening," she said. "He doesn't even *know* about the Prom. But somehow, if I value my career, I've got to get him there—in a decent mood." By now, Trisha was beginning to feel like a mythological heroine who had been given a series of unpalatable tasks to do before she could hope to earn her way to the party. She spent her days writing bogus catalog copy for *Junkyard* and her nights juggling all the problems the painting caused.

Tom heaved an annoyed sigh. Given the red tape he battled on a daily basis, the silliest things could set him off at home. Anger welled up in Trisha, at both Tom and James for putting her in this spot.

"So what does this mean, Trisha? I should just stay

home?"

"Oh, no, no, no! I think it will all be straightened out," Trisha said. "And if it isn't, you can always tag along with Carly. If you want."

Trisha had planned to pick Tom's brain for ideas as to how to turn James around, but now she knew better than to ask for help. Luckily for her, good karma finally swung her way. James must have realized that no matter how angry he was at his mother for sending Trisha his painting, it would-n't get him any closer to seeing his mother's works on the wall, or, perhaps more important, girl-magnet furniture in his apartment. He phoned Trisha up and, without apologiz-ing, made the peace. They arranged a few dates for Trisha to come over and photograph Graciella's portraits, so she could scan them into her laptop, from which she would pitch them to a few friends in the business.

"Okay," she said, "but if I'm going to do you these favors, you've got to do one for me."

"Shoot."

She told him her gallery was holding its annual gala, and she didn't have a date. James wasn't happy about the prospect of escorting her, but his doubts were somewhat assuaged after she described in detail the open bar and the quantity and quality of food on the buffet. He answered in the affirmative after finding out about the "hot chicks" that would be attending.

And then, ready or not, the day of the Promettente dawned. It was time for the "up and comers," including James, to arrive.

Careful not to muss her $75 chignon, Trisha donned a sleek navy dress with a plunging V-neckline and "walked the runway" for Tom, who was sitting on her couch, nose buried in a book. "Well?"

He twisted his mouth ever so slightly but gave no indication of what, exactly, his objection was.

"Too daring? Too mature?" She looked down. "Oh god—too tight? Does it make me look fat?"

Tom made a face.

"*What*, then?" Trisha could hardly hide her frustration. Was he honestly unimpressed or was he getting back at her for making him ride with Nat/Carly?

When he didn't answer, she shook her head and made an executive decision to wear the dress. Who needed his approval? "*I* happen to think I look great," she said as she returned to the bathroom/dressing room.

Tom cleared his throat. "It's, maybe, do you think the neckline is flattering?" he called out.

Trisha looked in the mirror from one angle, then another. "I guess not."

"It's just that when you're flat-chested...."

"Thanks." Hiding her hand behind the bathroom wall, she gave him the finger.

"Jeez," Tom said, "if you don't want my opinion, don't ask."

Trisha had already wriggled out of the thing. From her closet, she pulled out the same black Donna Karan sheath she always wore. She threw it over her head and stomped over to the center of the living room to retrieve her shoes, which she'd kicked off in anger.

"Now, *that* I like."

"Yeah, I know. You told me the last four times I wore it." Trisha sighed and began fishing bobby pins out of her hair. The chignon wouldn't work with this look; she'd have to rewash her hair, which meant taking off and reapplying her makeup, too. And James was due any minute. She had no idea why Tom was hanging around.

As if on cue, the downstairs buzzer rang. "Shit!" Trisha yelled as she buzzed up her date. "Could you just—I don't know—keep him busy?" she asked Tom.

"No problem-o," Tom said. "I'm looking forward to meeting the guy."

When she finally emerged, dressed, from the bathroom, Tom was perched on the side of the couch with his coat on, chatting with James about the stock market.

"Better get moving," she told him.

He nodded and continued to talk. Apparently, something about James's job gave him in-depth knowledge of the stock market; Tom's questions were endless.

She tried again. "Shouldn't you really be heading out?"

"Sure thing." He pecked Trisha on the cheek, and, with a "nice to meet you" at James, he was off.

Trisha turned toward James, who was seated on the couch. His bald head shone in the track lights as if polished.

His suit was as bad as Trisha had feared: a black pin-striped number far too stodgy, which hung poorly and was too lightweight for winter. And it was simply too big. Trisha silently cursed the salesmen at all the big and tall stores in the world. The tie only made things worse. James actually looked like the pallbearer he'd once said he was.

"Well!" she said, screwing a diamond earring into place. "Don't you look nice!"

He shrugged. "You too," he said stiffly. Trisha offered him more beer. She'd purchased two six-packs especially for this occasion. On a whim, she took a bottle as well.

"James," she said then. "Before we go, I have to tell you something." She took a breath. The plus side of doing this at the very last minute was that she had to plunge ahead without thinking too much. "Remember how your mom sent me your painting? I'd like to believe it was destiny, that it happened for a reason. A very *good* reason. Anyway, when I got it, I didn't know it was yours. All I had was an address on a package."

James sat up straighter on the couch, perhaps sensing that he wasn't going to like what came next.

"*So*, anyway, in the meantime, one of the heads of my gallery—who is, by the way, a very highly regarded expert—saw it, and, as they say, it *spoke* to him. He got it in his head to put it in this yearly exhibit of his. Which is a really big deal. And which is tonight."

The phone rang, and for perhaps the first time in her life, Trisha let it go. Meanwhile, James looked confused. "Yeah but…they can't do that, right?" he said. "I mean, the paint-ing is *mine*. They can't just do whatever they want with it."

Trisha felt almost sorry for him. "Actually," she said, "they can. We had our lawyers check things out, and we can prove that the painting belongs to me. And…I gave them permission to display it."

"But how did they know it was hers to give away?" he asked bitterly.

Trisha looked down. She picked up her beer and had a drink of it. He had a point. "I don't…I'm sure…I'm sure our lawyers looked into that. Anyway," she said, not without empathy, "I don't think you're getting it. James," she plead-ed, "This is an *amazing* thing. It could mean…I don't want to promise *too* much, but it could mean fame. And fortune." She paused. "And, I might add, it's a *huge* turn-on for the 'hot chicks.'"

"I don't care about that shit." James hopped to his feet and began pacing the floor, a difficult endeavor in such a small space. "I know you don't *get it* or whatever, but this

is *my* work and this is *not* what I want. Look it." He turned
to stare at her, menacingly close. "Don't worry. I won't mess
up your little party. But don't expect me to be happy about
it, okay?"

"Fine." Trisha turned toward the bookcase on the wall,
determined not to cry. Things had actually gone far, far better than she had any right to expect, only now, she realized
that she was bitterly disappointed that when it came down
to it, he didn't thrill at the opportunity. How many times
had she wished she could offer *any* hope, much less *one of
the biggest exhibits of the year*, to a young painter? And now
that she had the chance to uncork the bubbly and celebrate,
she was forced to act blasé or worse about the undertaking.

After several minutes of silence and beer-drinking,
James cleared his throat and spoke up from his perch on the
couch. "So what do you want from me, anyway?"

Trisha looked at him. "Excuse me?"

"What do they want me to do."

"Oh. Um." She hadn't given much thought to what
would happen if he actually cooperated. "We're going—
soon—because they'll want to take some pictures of you
and the other artists. And the curators. And you and your
work. And then all evening, reporters will want to talk to
you about your painting, and what a great honor this is,
blah blah blah, but I told Gresh—that's my boss—that
you're cultivating 'an air of mystery,' so you can get away
without talking to them. Just say 'no comment.'"

"So I can go for thirty minutes and cut out?"

Trisha nodded. "Absolutely," she said. "Although, that
would minimize the amount of free food and drink you'd
be able to consume. And hot chicks."

The car ride was nothing, ten city blocks. On the way,

Trisha realized: She was nervous. Her breath was stuck high up in her chest, and she couldn't get it down again. And she couldn't attribute it to James, because all had turned out well—and she didn't *think* he was the type to act out in public just to spite her.

That thought made her even *more* nervous.

No, this was something else. But God knows she'd been to fundraisers before, and she hadn't had enough to do with Promettente to be concerned about the success of the event itself. So what was it?

She realized, reluctantly, that it had something to do with James.

In a great display of superficiality, she was worried about how James's looks—his suit, his tie, and, of course, his face—would be received, and how that would reflect on her. She didn't want to walk the red carpet with him, didn't want to be there if and when the photogs were cruel or just indifferent, not shooting as he approached to save their film for people who mattered, or from some horrid superstition about breaking their cameras. Even if they did snap them, she didn't want to be immortalized in the art magazines as a girl who couldn't get a handsome date; even though she had Tom, she couldn't claim him. And she hated herself for caring.

"Let's get this over with," she murmured. She left the limo and blew by the few early paparazzi in such a flurry that they couldn't have shot her if they'd tried. And then it started once again; they had to go inside and talk to people.

Although only a handful of people—mostly catering staff and other hired help—were already in attendance, they bustled enough to make the place seem full. The beautifully arranged tables of food reminded Trisha, as always, of props for an exhibition of Wayne Thiebaud still-lifes.

Jaunty pink beheaded shrimp perched precipitously atop a mountain of ice. Cheeses reclined on silver trays. Lavishly decorated cookies sprawled out at the opposite end of the banquet. The smorgasbord was beautifully untouched; a roasted pig was intact, as if it could stand up and dance a jig, or juggle the red apple in its mouth.

James made his way to the feast but Trisha—as well as a black-clad stylist who appeared out of nowhere—jumped forward to stop him. "Excuse me sir," he said, "but we're photographing the banquet."

"Jeez," James said. He raised his arms, like a criminal, and backed away.

Just then, an impossibly skinny woman in a skimpy black dress dangled herself in front of them, like the hoop earrings that peeked beneath her iron-straight Seventies Cher hair. Doreen.

"Patricia," she said, holding out her arms to take Trisha's in a greeting, as if they were bestest friends—and she the hostess of this party. "You made it." As if she could have just stayed home. "Aren't you going to introduce me to your sexy friend?" She draped her hand over James's arm and threw out her breasts, presumably the only soft part in her entire physique.

"Doreen, this is my friend James," Trisha said. "James, this is…Doreen."

"*Hello.*" Doreen held out a hand dripping with red polish—the color of James's living room—and allowed James to paw it. "A pleasure. Has Trisha bored you silly yet with her shtick about the public's lack of appreciation for female abstract impressionists?" She rolled her eyes. She was somewhat softening her usual rapid-fire, drill-sergeant speech, but not by much.

"Something like that." James smirked.

"You found the bartender pouring hundred-year-old scotch?"

"Nope."

"Let me be of assistance."

Trisha allowed her to lead James off without protest, shaking her head. *That* had been easy; maybe the world of people obsessed with looks were actually *kind* to people like James, because...because....Nope. Doreen had something up her nasty little sleeveless dress.

Trisha planted herself on an Eames sofa in the gallery's deserted foyer and loitered, thankful for a moment away from the stress. She tried to massage her own back. The white noise of the crowd picked up, but in the absence of an audible conversation, she almost did the unthinkable; she almost fell asleep. Then a familiar voice broke through, loud and clear, from the room on the other side of the wall.

Doreen, on her high-tech cell phone. ". . . your costume...Okay but what's the code?....Two *four*? Did you say *four*? It's so loud....Thanks, Gresh." A snap as she shut the phone. "Got it. I'll get you fixed up in no time." Trisha craned her neck around to watch Doreen leading James toward Gresh's office.

Trisha was puzzled, until she woke up enough to put two and two together. Doreen was in charge of the publicity. Her job was to make James presentable.

Trisha yawned. Maybe there *was* a method to her madness. And if James got hurt when Doreen turned on her stiletto heel and walked away after the last shutter fell, too bad for him.

Trisha made a quick trip to the ladies' room, where she dabbed cold water on her temples, then took a moment to look around at the exhibit. Instead of the usual big rectangular box, the gallery was as big as a small museum, complete with a foyer and a set pathway along which one weaved in order to see an exhibit. Trisha started at the end, as was her wont; in the same way that she liked to read the end of novels first, she wanted to take in the final work, the one in the position of greatest renown: this year, a Cy Twombly-esque piece—except that the swirls were made of thousands of letters cut from newspapers instead of pencil marks—created by Sharon Dixon, a soft-spoken African-American from Baltimore. This main work could make or break the show, because every lazy or tipsy reviewer who attended—which accounted for most of them—would make a beeline for it, so as to forego using actual brainpower to make their own judgments. In the next few weeks, this piece, and its creator, would be mentioned in three-dozen newspapers; then the magazines would come to call. Trisha was thrilled for Dixon, who'd spent years paying her dues before rising to prominence thanks to a few curators around the country, Gresh included.

She turned the corner and gasped. What was *Junkyard* doing there? Galina and/or Gresh had made a last-minute switcheroo.

Well. It was no wonder Doreen had paid attention to the producer of the moose caca.

Framed and hung properly, and spotlit, the variegation emerged much more dramatically than before, and the layers of unpredictable but hardly insignificant textural changes rose to prominence. Trisha cleared her mind and looked. Here was a prototype for a wacked-out new type of fabric. It was a visual simulation of the genome project, in a way, quite literally a reimagining of a human. (Which made Trisha wonder: Who had done the expanded catalog copy? Did he or she even know that James used parts of other paintings in his work? Without verifying, Trisha knew they hadn't.)

Two entirely unrelated thoughts came to Trisha. First: Gresh is the real deal. One sideways glance at the painting and he'd picked it as a winner. And, two: *I want that painting in my home.* Actually, it was more a feeling, a covetous craving lustful and even jealous *urge,* than a thought, and it was one that Trisha—who as an adult had never even felt tempted to possess *posters* of her favorite works, preferring to own the memory alone—had never come close to experiencing.

And then they took the photographs, and then James was free to go. Only, he didn't.

About said photographs: James emerged, in a police line-up with the other thirty-nine artists whose work was featured in ways big and small. They asked to feature him *more* prominently in the group pictures.

This, Trisha surmised, was due in equal parts to the prestige of James's painting; his screw-you-all attitude, which oozed importance; and Doreen's fifteen-minute makeover. She had ripped off the sleeves of his suit, freed his white shirt from being tucked and wrinkled the rest of it to match the bottom. The tie was turned backwards, to proudly display the JC Penney tag, and only very loosely knotted.

Over his useless eye, he wore a patch, one that Trisha recognized from Gresh's Halloween costume.

He looked like a member of AC/DC, circa the punk schoolboy era. Too cool.

Now he didn't look a bit like a morgue attendant; he looked like a badass.

He looked like the star of the show.

After the photographs, and just as the first members of

the public pushed their way inside, James rushed to the food. At a distance, Trisha watched him overloaded a square white napkin with meats. Then Doreen flew off on gallery business, and Trisha took a breath and approached, hoping against hope that he had come around. She smiled at James's napkin; the delicate paper, too precious to bear its load, bent at one edge, then the other, and it ended up taking both of his hands to stabilize it. Trisha accepted a flute of champagne from a handsome, tuxedoed waiter—another frustrated artist, no doubt. "Good spread, huh?" she asked James.

"Yeah." He attacked a chicken wing.

"Told you so." She took a long draw of much-needed alcohol. "You certainly seem to be enjoying yourself."

"I like getting my butt kissed as much as the next guy," he said, mouth full of food and not kindly.

"I like the, uh—." She pointed at the patch.

He didn't answer, just turned his body to make it clear he was *not* standing with her.

While he gorged, she stared at the patch. Actually, in no time, she'd almost forgotten he wore it; it blended into his face. Her subconscious corrected the part she couldn't see, made the face symmetrical. By contrast, when you could *see* the most damaged part of his face, your mind always wanted to correct it.

"I don't know if they told you," she said, "but it's amazing that your painting is hanging where it is. That's prime position. Congratulations. Like it or not, you should know that it's a great honor."

"Yeah," James said coldly. He turned to glare at her. "Who gave it that dorky-ass name?"

"What is it again?"

"*Junkyard*."

"Wow," she said, playing dumb. "That *is* bad."

"It was you, wasn't it?"

"Yeah." She stood to his side and, feeling no need to make eye contact, surveyed the crowd. "What would you call it?"

"*Shithole. Sewer. Mutant.*" Trisha nodded. James continued, looking at her now. "*Betrayal.*"

At that, an imposing, silver-haired man approached. "Oh, my!" he exclaimed, chuckling. Then he turned to Trisha. "My dear Patricia! I've been looking for you! How do you like our little party?" From his vantage point so far above it all, Gresh looked James over with a curiosity just bordering on rudeness.

"We've only just arrived." She noticed, alarmed, that she was sweating. Normally, she would have diverted attention from herself by introducing her companion, so she could discreetly daub herself, but she needed time to work up to the accolades Gresh was about to lavish. "It certainly looks lovely." The live band stopped warming up and finally kicked into a Sinatra tune. "And from the sound of it, I'm sure the band will be fantastic." They played a group of off-notes in rapid succession. "Or not," she joked.

"Now, correct me if I'm wrong," Gresh said, nudging her elbow with his fingers, "but this is your first Promettente. You weren't with us last year."

"No sir," she replied. "I've only been at the gallery for, uh, three months."

"Gresh Martin." He abruptly held out a hand to James, having had his fill of small talk.

"James. James Morales," Trisha was forced to say when James didn't open his mouth.

"Yes, yes." Gresh raised one finger to his thin lips. "*Yes*, of course. Our mystery man, in the flesh. *You*, my dear boy, are *hot hot hot*. I must tell you that you're one of the most, ah, *intriguing* talents to come down the pike in quite some time. Since the hair on my head was a bit darker, *I can tell you that*. Ha ha." He looked to see how his compliment was being received and to his credit, figured out that something was amiss. He nodded and began to survey the room for his next target. Trisha muttered a goodbye, and Gresh patted her on the shoulder to dismiss her. He pivoted on his perfectly polished heels and then—*turned back*. He wasn't quite done with James yet, apparently. "Now, hmm," Gresh said. "Tell me. Something. Tell me something about art. Or yourself. Or the price of tea in China. Something."

"Knicks won."

"Ah, of course!" Gresh laughed in pure delight. "Of course they did! The Knicks won!" He acted as if this was this were brilliant commentary. "Well, listen, my young Knicks fan. This is what I want to know. What else do you have in that head of yours. In those fingers. What do *you* want to do? I simply don't—tell me, when did you paint that picture there?"

"The one on the wall?"

Gresh squinted at him as if he were an idiot. "Yes."

"Huh. When I's like, eleven? Ten?"

Gresh gasped visibly, like a scene-chewing actor in a Vincent Price movie, only his was an honest response. Trisha wondered if he might have a heart attack right then and there. "*Gracious!*" He shook his head. "Well I'll just put it out there then, although now I see that you"—he pointed his long knobby finger—"*you* are a risky one." He turned to Trisha. "You never know *what* he will say." He put his arm around James, like father to son. Trisha realized that Gresh was pleased to have no idea what to make of James. Was he a comedian? He couldn't have believed the age James had named. Trisha wasn't sure she did herself. He smiled, bemused.

"At any rate, we are prepared to offer you your own show, an exhibit, to your liking. Name your price." Now it was Trisha who gasped. "We can discuss the wheres and whys and hows, unless you already have enough paintings, and perhaps you do. You know how to get in touch with him, yes? You can make this happen?" Gresh asked Trisha. She nodded, weakly.

"Good. You can be his liaison. And, well, there it is! So go and have fun! Enjoy! Much fun and much sex to you! *Opa*!"

Trisha exhaled as he walked away, not sure if she was glad to see him go or worried about facing James alone.

"What was *that* all about?" James asked.

"Pure craziness," said Trisha. "Welcome to my world. Want to date supermodels? Make big bucks? Here's your chance."

Soon enough Carly (as she was known at these gatherings) and Tom showed up, then along came Rhonda, who spent her evening helping the caterers keep the food presentable. At first, Tom held a grudge about their chaotic evening, but even he found it impossible to mope to Sinatra. And so he danced with all the ladies, Trisha and Carly and Rhonda; while from the floor Trisha watched Doreen and James sway, with Doreen draped over him like a scarf. He smiled and whispered something into her ear and she flung her head back, laughed, and ran her hand up his neck. They looked like a couple.

Trisha watched them all night out of the corner of her eye. James looked to be in his element, eating, drinking, laughing, and, of course, creating a ruckus wherever he went—with Doreen at his side. And he gave interviews, actually appearing to relish his moment in the spotlight. Watching from the sidelines, Trisha felt small for underestimating him.

She waited until Doreen had left him momentarily, to go to the restroom, perhaps, and then approached. He had just thrown his cigarette at the floor and was stomping it out beneath his feet.

"I'm so proud of you, James," she said, and on an alcohol-induced whim, threw up her arms to give him a hug.

He turned, denying her.

She quickly ducked back to the bar, hoping no one had seen.

An hour later, she was still there, ordering another amaretto sour and chatting with Rhonda. Tom had disappeared to make a phone call. From the corner of her eye, she saw James and Doreen leave the dance floor halfway through a song after conferring—probably about whether or not it was time for a cigarette, she figured at the time.

It would take her the better part of the evening to accept that what she'd seen was no cigarette break. That James and Doreen had gone somewhere. Alone. Together.

It would take her a lot longer to own up to caring.

1992

College

Philadelphia

The holidays came and went. On the train back to Penn after New Year's, Trisha tried to come up with a resolution that would improve her life, but upon reflection decided she was already doing every single thing she could to be happy. She couldn't figure out why none of it was working. But returning with lowered expectations helped her relationship in one big way: ironically, it allowed Mitch to please her more easily.

In February, for instance, after a surprisingly sweet Valentine's Day dinner at the Palladium, Trisha was actually multi-orgasmic. Unfortunately, this discovery occurred within 6H. Her post-coital euphoria lasted only as long as she remained inside Mitch's actual bedroom. As they prepared to leave the room, they heard a growing ruckus outside. At first, Trisha, paranoid, thought the guys had somehow seen them do the deed. Then she realized the noise centered on the refrigerator.

"Where'd she go?" Phil wailed. *"Where is she?"*

Glenn pulled at what little remained of his hair around the fringes. "Aw, naw, baby, naw, baby, naw," he said. "Why ya wanna leave ol' Glenn?" He stopped and zeroed in on Phil; he stood as tall as his 5'9" frame would allow to look *down* at his friend. "You whackin' off to her, ain't you?" he asked. "I knew it! Pussy thief!"

The object of this anguish was James's dream girl. Cindy's picture got more action than most girls on campus. Every time Glenn walked past it, he greeted her with a "hey baby" and a kiss (delivered from his mouth to hers via stubby fingers). Phil periodically took the photo down and studied her like a scientist examining an especially rare butterfly. For all Trisha knew, Mitch had his own relationship with her; she didn't want to know.

Phil harrumphed. He opened the fridge and withdrew a carton of milk, from which he poured a chunky fluid into a dirty glass from the sink. He took a gulp, recoiled, stuck his nose into the carton, gagged, and replaced the carton into the fridge.

Glenn turned to Trisha, who stood back, enjoying her rapidly diminishing post-coital daze. "It was *you*, wasn't it, Yoko? I bet it was! I always knew you was a lezbo."

Trisha gave him a withering look.

"Well, you best return it, that's all I'll say." Glenn leaned over and ripped a blank piece of paper from a notebook on the table. He grabbed a pen and scratched out a sign: MISSING: BELOVED HO. REWARD! SEE GLENN, ROOM 1203. He posted it in the photo's place on the fridge.

Phil walked over to study the note. "What's the reward?"

"Why? You got information?" He bustled up next to Phil. "Naw, you're just jonesing for some weed. The reward is, I don't kick yer ass, that's what."

For days, the mystery was the subject of much talk around the Rump. Then James confessed to Mitch that he'd removed it himself, de-Cindyfying the place to prepare it for a visit from the goddess in the flesh during her spring break, which fell a week before Penn's. James hoped to keep this news away from the rest of the guys, but it soon became obvious to everyone that things weren't normal around the Rump. James removed two garbage bags' worth of beer bottles; did his laundry—an accomplishment in itself, given the odor emanating from his room; and turned down the heat toward Trisha to a simmer, perhaps to increase the chances of her being kind to *him* while his guest was around.

"Whoa-ho-*ho*," Glenn whooped the next time he visited. He looked around for an explanation.

James had ultimately decided it was better to get things out in the open before Cindy arrived—to explain in detail what he would do to Glenn, for instance, if he screwed things up in any way. Glenn was, at first, too juiced about the prospect of the meeting the babe in person to pay any attention to James's instructions. "So when, exactly," Glenn wanted to know, "is this hot pussy delivery arriving?"

"Let me make this clear: I have a *zero tolerance policy*," James told him. "Do a goddamn thing to embarrass me, on purpose or not—and this goes for all of youse—and I will cut your nuts off and feed them to you. Don't think I won't. Remember: Two separate palm readers have predicted I will kill someone someday. There's no reason to believe it won't be you."

"Jeez, chill out, dude," Glenn said. "I got your back."

James glared at him.

He kept her actual arrival date a secret, but Mitch and Trisha knew as soon as she arrived, late one Thursday, due to the murmuring voices and the croon of The Cranberries coming from his room. Mitch and Trisha sat on the couch watching Letterman, hoping Cindy would duck out for a bathroom break, a glass of water—*something*. Two hours later, when they said good night, giggles still pealed from James's room. Trisha felt a pang of jealousy. She and Mitch never laughed like that.

The next day, when Mitch came over to study, Trisha asked right away: "Did you meet her?"

Mitch nodded.

"And?"

Mitch raised his eyebrows and fanned himself.

"What's that mean?"

"This morning, she was wearing a slinky nightgown."

"*Really*." After the Hooters debacle, Trisha had sworn to herself that she wouldn't be jealous. "What does that mean? Do you think they slept together?"

Mitch shook his head. "No. He slept on the couch. But they seem close."

That evening, Trisha answered a knock at her door and was shocked to find James standing there.

"Oh. Hi," she said. "Are you looking for Mitch? He's on an errand." Actually, Mitch was at WaWa buying Trisha some sanitary pads, but lord help him if James found out. "Can I give him a message?"

"Actually I need a favor from both of you. I need you to go to dinner with me."

"Sorry?"

"I got this friend in town," he said. "She wants to hang out with my friends. And you know Glenn and Phil...." His good eye focused on the door beside Trisha's head. "So can you go? Tonight?"

Trisha whacked her forehead with her palm. "I have a meeting at nine," she said. "Hmm. But we could meet up early. Say, seven."

"Fine. Beijing?"

Trisha nodded. "See you there." She let the door close behind her. "Did you hear that?" she asked Nat.

"Sure did." Nat was painting a heart on the couch to make the best of the red nail polish she'd spilled on it.

"What do you wear when you're having dinner with two guys and a supermodel?"

Nat looked up and examined her roommate. "A bag over your head?"

By five o'clock, every piece of clothing Trisha owned had been called to duty, given a dishonorable discharge, and dumped into a massive, teetering pile on Trisha's bed. Nat came in for an emergency consult. The juxtaposition of her cool demeanor with Trisha's frou-frou clothes and décor made the bedroom feel like a Laura Ashley store.

"You know what you need," Nat said, hands on her hips. "The Fuck-Me Dress."

"*Nat.* I can't wear that."

"Sure you can. You're not *that* much bigger than me."

"That's not what I mean." Trisha ignored the slight. "I mean I can't wear that to a Chinese restaurant. I'd look ridiculous."

"Suit yourself," Nat said. "Wait: scratch that. Do not wear anything remotely resembling a suit."

"Very funny."

"All right," Nat said. "If you won't dress way up, you have to do the Dress Down. *Way* down. As if you aren't trying. We're talking your oldest jeans and a white t-shirt."

"Are you *nuts*?"

"No. Don't you have any jeans? What kind of college student—" Nat was rummaging through the mess on the bed. She finally emerged with a pair of denim trousers and a dusty blue t-shirt Trisha hadn't worn since it shrank in the dryer. Nat put a finger to her mouth, squinted into the distance, and nodded. "She'll come in all dolled up. You'll be the natural beauty. But for this to work—this is crucial—you've got to have 'tude."

"'tude?"

"'tude. You've got to walk in there with your head held high, like you're beautiful and you know it. If you doubt for one minute, it's all over, and you'll look like a forty-year-old housewife from Des Moines."

Given the horrified look on Trisha's face, Nat set about identifying and nurturing her 'tude. She applied Trisha's makeup, caking on far more than Trisha would have used, albeit in subtle colors. She loaned Trisha a thong and forced her to go braless. She toyed with individual strands of Trisha's hair until she achieved the just-fell-out-of-bed quality that made Meg Ryan famous. By the time Trisha walked out the door, she felt sexier than ever—and as comfortable as if she had on pajamas. "Go get 'em, Tiger!" Nat said. "Remember: It's all in the 'tude." Nat was onto something, because when Trisha left the building, Rhett was rendered speechless but for a wolf-whistle and a "You *go*, girl!"

But given the effortlessness of her own beauty, Nat had neglected to take into account two things. One was Trisha's naturally wavy hair. It was only a matter of time—five minutes after it hit the nighttime humidity, to be exact—before it went from chic to shriek. By the time Trisha hit Beijing, her 'tude had sprung a leak. And that was *before* Cindy showed up.

"You okay?" Mitch asked when Trisha sat down across from him. "Hard day?"

"Not particularly."

"You feeling all right? You look...tired."

"Uh...*yeah*," Trisha said, grabbing onto the excuse. "Actually, I'm not feeling so good." How could she, when her 'tude had turned to turd?

And then Cindy walked in, which brought into play the *second* thing that Nat had overlooked: Cindy was such a natural beauty that she could have turned up wearing a gunny sack and rendered every man in the room speechless.

Trisha was so out of her league that if she'd felt a little

more secure, she would have marveled at Cindy for pure aesthetic reasons, like she did when she flipped through the pages of *Vogue* or viewed a Botticelli. Cindy glided in wearing a forest green coat with a big fur collar, which she hung on a hook at the end of their booth. Trisha made a note to tell Nat about Cindy's coup: She had on a Fuck-Me outfit that was also a Dress Down—a black sleeveless t-shirt with red rhinestones proclaiming her a ROCK GODDESS, atop weathered mahogany leather slacks, which in places were worn to a thin black sheen.

The rest of her was just as perfectly pulled off. The auburn streaks in her artfully mussed honey-colored hair were so skillfully placed that any straight male would assume she'd been born with them. And even Trisha, who looked for it, failed to detect one iota of makeup on her. It had to be there; eyelashes didn't grow that long in nature.

In a nutshell, she was a tough girl—make that woman—but all femme.

Trisha's estimation of James went up a notch.

"Wow," Mitch muttered under his breath. Trisha slapped his arm.

"Trisha, Cindy. Cindy, Trish," said a bored-sounding James.

"Ooh, it's so good to meet you," Cindy said, holding out her hand to Trisha as she sat across the table. She had just enough of a Brooklyn accent to be cute. She put Trisha in mind of a fly girl from *In Living Color*.

The waitress came and dropped vinyl menus at their table. As the group perused the offerings, Trisha checked James out. He had spiffed himself up; he had on grey slacks and a black turtleneck, and looked almost civilized.

"Trisha, I have *so* been looking forward to meeting you," Cindy was saying. She used a French manicured finger to hold her place in the noodle dishes. "I hear you're studying art. Do you spend much time at the Philly Museum? I love it there. We used to run up those stairs and pretend we were Rocky Balboa." She used her arms to mimic a runner's movements. "Didn't we, Jimmy?"

Trisha wondered how many hours a day she worked out.

"Of course," she replied. "Although I've always preferred the Barnes Collection. It's this little-known museum about an hour outside the city—"

"Sure!" Cindy said. "It's just so tough to get in there, don't you find? And with the hours so irregular.... "

"You've got to love those *Rocky* steps," James cracked.

Cindy rolled her eyes. "We ran them today," she confided to Trisha. "Funny how when you're a kid, you don't realize how *many* there are."

"You went to the museum?" Mitch chimed in. Trisha glanced over. He was rapt.

Cindy nodded. "I *love* the Degas room. Of course, Jimmy loves it, too, but for his own reasons." She punched him in the arm and smiled, crinkling her nose like a rabbit. "There are several nudes in there," she told Mitch. "But then, you must know that. I'm sure this one has you there all the time." She gestured toward Trisha.

"Yeah, right." Trisha snorted. "He always has something better to do."

"Yeah, we need to go. We're overdue." He looked at Cindy. "I've been so busy this semester, with my thesis and stuff."

Cindy asked what he studied and did a decent job feigning interest, laughing whenever something went over her head. *Maybe she's dumb*, Trisha thought, and took her first unlabored breath of the evening. Then he returned the question.

"I'm in my first year of medical school at Columbia," she said. Trisha choked on her water and coughed for so long that tears streamed down her cheeks, leading her to wonder momentarily if Cindy would have to do the Heimlich to remove…*water.*

So Cindy was beautiful *and* smart. Mitch, obviously annoyed at the interruption, glared at Trisha.

The waitress came at last to take their orders. Trisha went first. She asked for her usual: tofu delight. Cindy ordered General Tso's chicken, quite possibly the fattiest item on the menu.

"Now *that's* what I call a meal," Mitch said.

"I try to eat healthy," Cindy told Trisha. "I just can't always get my palate to go along with it. It takes over when I'm ordering—like I'm Dr. Jekyll and it's Mr. Hyde."

Beautiful, smart, and witty.

"So how do you two know each other?" Trisha asked. If Mitch wasn't going to act as wingman for James, she'd do it.

"Ma baby-sat Jimmy. We used to take baths together." She winked at James, who looked away and turned bright orange.

"You don't have much of a Brooklyn accent," Mitch said.

"See!" James said to her.

"Yo, you knows I'm still your homegirl," she said, elbowing James. "I's still fly."

Their meals came impossibly fast. James resumed an apparently long-standing campaign to teach Cindy to use chopsticks. She was comically inept. Finally, a flaw—and it was inconsequential. Right off the bat, a chopstick flew from her hand and landed across the room, in the lap of a man in a business suit who seemed angry until he saw the perpetrator. "Wow. Such hand-eye coordination," Mitch cracked. "Let's hope you're not planning to become a surgeon."

"I am!" Cindy giggled. "I've been thinking about becoming an eye surgeon. I keep telling Jimmy here that when I'm done, he can pay for my house and my kids' college educations."

"Dude, I'd look out," Mitch said. "Excuse me? Could we get some more chopsticks over here? Two pair!" He waved to the waitress, chopping at the air with imaginary utensils. "I've never gotten the hang of those things myself."

Trisha tried to catch his eye. He had always rebuffed her offers to teach him by coughing up pigheaded arguments about the superiority of the fork. Now he took them up happily and soldiered through an entire dinner, often scooping up mere nibblets of rice without complaint.

The conversation slowed as everyone concentrated on eating, which proved more difficult for some than for others. Trisha reminded herself that red-blooded American males needed to feel attractive, and that flirtation was a natural, healthy behavior.

But obviously, James hadn't gotten the memo on that. In public, at least, he seemed more uncomfortable around Cindy than he was usually. It was cute. *He* was cute. Trisha was rooting for him, and not just because this would knock Cindy off the market.

"So what else have you two got planned tonight?" Trisha asked.

Cindy looked from one guy to the other.

"I thought we'd get some coffee, take a walk," James said.

Mitch pointed his chopsticks at them. "You guys should go out." After an awkward pause, he clarified. "I mean, it's a great night—you should go clubbing." He chewed, mouth open, for a while, and swallowed. Then smiled. "I mean, I *realize* the clubs in Philly can't compare to the ones in New York, but drinking's drinking and dancing's dancing. I vote we go out."

Trisha noted the switch to *we*. Maybe she was being paranoid, but she thought she saw Cindy flash to attention when Mitch came aboard.

"I like it!" Cindy said. "My man!" She offered up her hand for a high-five and then scooched her body up next to James. "You up for it, homie?"

"Okay."

"Trisha? You willing to be seen with these white boys who can't dance?"

"Hey!" Mitch held a chopstick like a sword. "I'll make you eat those words. I'm a great dancer."

"Trisha? Is this true?"

"News to me." Trisha and Mitch had gone dancing once before. He had stood along the sidelines, refusing to set foot on the dance floor. "Anyway, I can't go," she added, in case anyone cared. "Amnesty International called a last-minute meeting, and I'm secretary. I have to take the minutes."

Mitch frowned. "What kind of emergency *possibly* couldn't wait until Monday?" The look on his face suggested that this was the most preposterous thing he had ever heard. He and James laughed.

Trisha cleared her throat. "The Singapore government is set to execute Bryan Albert Dennis if the international community does nothing about it by a midnight Sunday deadline."

Mitch refused to lose face. "Okay, okay," he said. "But what kind of campus group thinks *they're* going to do something about it?"

Cindy slapped his arm. "Loser. How about cultivating a worldview for a change?"

"Sheesh."

"Maybe I could meet you—wherever—later on," Trisha said. "The meeting can't last all night."

"Actually, that'll be tough," James said. "Does anybody know where we're going?"

"Yeah, babe, plus, I thought you weren't feeling well," Mitch chimed in.

The waitress dropped off the check, but no one paid any attention. Trisha pulled out two twenties and watched as her dinner companions tossed in too little cash, without a break in their debate about where to go. As one, the three rose to leave.

Trisha looked down at her cold tofu. She hadn't finished eating. Not that anyone had noticed.

⊠

After a too-detailed briefing on torture practices, Trisha was certainly in no mood to boogie. Plus, she'd had it with Mitch, and she wanted to tell him so.

As she approached her place, she heard the Sex Pistols's "Anarchy in the U.K." blasting out of 6H and rushed to the guys' room, thrilled and, she admitted, relieved that they'd returned so early. Then she realized the sound was coming from her own room. Nat had left the stereo on.

Trisha sighed and tried to imagine what Mitch was doing at that moment, but nothing that came to her was good. She scavenged a pint of chocolate-chip cookie-dough ice cream from the freezer and ate it draped across the couch. With Johnny Rotten still wailing, she turned on the TV and channel-surfed, but found nothing worth watching. As an excuse to walk past 6H again, she wandered to the sixth floor lounge, where she chatted with Ror-Dawg, a hyperactive sophomore just getting over both mono and pink eye. Neither health condition prevented him from downing a bottle of Molson while he purported to study calculus. "And *how* exactly do you pull a 4.0?" Trisha asked him.

"I got my ways."

The Dawg challenged her to a game of ping-pong in the Rat, and she accepted, but downstairs, they discovered that the game room was closed.

Back in her room, Trisha shut off the Pistols and called a high school friend who'd left her repeated messages. When the girl asked about her boyfriend, Trisha felt her stomach jump strangely; she realized that for her, tonight might be the straw that broke the camel's back. Trisha said he was doing just fine and fought to change the subject, despite the girl's attempts to find out if there was a future and what would happen once they graduated.

Afterward, Trisha dozed for what might have been five minutes or five hours, until a familiar old refrain from Metallica returned her to the world. She went over and knocked on 6H, picked the sleep from her eyes, and then let herself in.

James was pacing the room like a hyped-up tiger.

"Hello!" Trisha screamed. "Where is everybody?" She approached the boom box on the floor; James beat her to it and turned it off with a sharp kick.

"What's up?" Now Trisha was shouting; her ears were ringing.

"What do you *think*? They're fucking right now."

"*What*?" Obviously, James had Lost It.

"They hooked up at the bar and then we came back here, and they started making out again in Glenn's room." At Trisha's puzzled look, he added, "We ran into Glenn in the lobby."

This hardly resolved Trisha's confusion, which was mammoth. "Are you sure?"

James squinted at her. "Unless you can think of another excuse for Mitch's tongue to be in Cindy's mouth and his hands on her ass."

After several abortive attempts to speak, Trisha walked to the Kegerator, drew a beer and plopped down on the sofa. She stared straight ahead as her beer sloshed into her lap. "What are we going to do?" she asked.

James, already drinking, sat beside her. The couch crumpled in such a way that she sunk toward him and their knees touched. She quickly sat up and relocated to a lumpy hill on the outside edge of the couch.

"Okay," she said, ready to answer her own question. "This is what I'm going to do." She took a deep breath. "I'm going to fucking wait right here for them to get back from wherever the fuck they are," she yelled, still half-deaf. "And drown my fucking sorrow in the meantime."

"Fucking okay."

She took a long, long draw. "And think about how I'm the most fucked person in the world right now, thanks to you." She was almost proud; she'd never said *fuck* this many times in her entire life. Or drunk beer entirely of her own volition.

"Wait, what do you mean, 'thanks to you?'"

"I mean you bring in a supermodel and dangle her in front of my boyfriend. Thanks a lot."

"First of all, that shouldn't matter if you were keeping him happy at home. Second of all, *I'm* the most fucked person in the world. Don't even kid yourself."

"Bet five bucks on it?"

James looked amused. "Deal."

Trisha took a swig. "Okay," she said with mock cheeriness. "I'll start. I made love to my boyfriend of six months less than twenty-four hours ago, and now he's screwing someone he just met. That's pretty messed up, wouldn't you say?"

"Fucked," James said. "You *fucked* him less than twenty-four hours ago. And in answer to your question, sure. That's pretty fucked." He clicked mugs with her and upended his, and then went for more. "But how long have you known him?"

"Excuse me?"

"Mitch. How long have you known him?"

Trisha did some calculations, which would have taken

far less time if she weren't already feeling the alcohol's effect. "Um. Six months?"

"Well, I've been in love with the person he's sucking and fucking since I was six. And I've never told her how I feel, so you could say I brought this on myself by being a pussy, and I'll have to live with that for the rest of my life if they, like, get married. How's *that*?"

"Ouch," Trisha said. "I'll drink to that." She wiped her mouth with her fingers. "Okay," she said, "But the entire dorm, plus my mother and my friends from home—basically, everyone who knows me—knows that I'm dating Mitch, and now they'll all think I'm a loser who's awful in bed."

"You're screwed."

"I'm *fucked*!"

"That's the spirit!" They clinked mugs and drank.

When James didn't say anything, she said, "Your turn," and nudged him. "Well?"

"I'm thinking."

"In the meantime, I'd like to mention that I live right next door to the guy who cheated on me, and I have to see him every day."

"I have to *live* with the cocksucker who fucked me over." He shook his head.

"Good point."

They drank.

Trisha sighed. "This is sort of fun!" For all of Nat's efforts over the years, she had never been this drunk. Her parents' problems with alcohol had turned her off to drinking. She sighed. "You know, the day I first saw you in the laundry room, I would never have imagined us sitting here drinking together. God, I thought you were such an asshole. You're really not such a dick after all."

"Jeez," James said. "Is that supposed to make me feel

better?"

"Sorry. But—I mean, are you aware that you put a purple rug in a dryer, and it ruined all my clothes? And then you stepped on my foot on your way out."

James breathed in and out, as if trying to work out complex math problem. "Well, you know," he finally said. "Sometimes I don't realize."

"Oh." Trisha reddened. "God." She put her hand to her forehead and sat there for what felt like a year. "I feel like such a jerk. I was so angry." She shook her head.

James made a *pffffffffff* sound, like leaking air, and rolled his eyes. "Jesus. Don't *cry* about it." He shook his head. "Look, even if I'd seen you, I would have made you hate me. I follow the dog-eat-dog philosophy of laundry: You snooze, you lose. Kill the weak."

"But that's wrong!" Trisha folded her feet beneath her and sat up straighter on the couch, to gain the moral high ground.

"Why? Just 'cause someone like you's too chicken to put their stuff in because *somebody might get mad*"—he said this in a mocking nursery-school voice—"I'm supposed to wait? *Fuck* no. That's ridiculous."

"What if somebody got tied up on a phone call? If they're two seconds late, they should be set back an hour?"

"Fuck yeah. Not my problem. They know the rules."

"I believe in rules just as much as you do, if not more, but I also have empathy."

"But empathy only works if every other person in the world is empathetic, or if the world itself is empathetic, which, of course, it's not—"

"No wonder you can't find a girlfriend." Trisha was entirely drunk now and suddenly knew it. "I don't think you have feelings. What are you, a sociopath?"

"Probably," James said. "Yeah. I don't doubt it. But don't change the subject. I don't think it's too smart to, like, empathize. People, or animals even, only do what gives 'em positive feedback. What is the payback for being *nice*?"

"Don't you think karma takes care of that?"

"In a word: *no fucking way*. And I've thought about it. Why do bad things happen to good people? Their *karma*— he used the singsong voice again—says they shouldn't. And besides, if you're doing things just to get the prize in return for being good, what's so noble about that? Not that I'm making a moral judgment. Far be it from me."

"I don't think karma should be the *reason* for doing any- thing," Trisha said. "You should do good things because they're *right*."

"Then you're doing it to think of yourself as good."

Trisha was tiring. "So?"

"I like to think of myself as bad."

"Time out." Suddenly exhausted, Trisha made a "T" with her arms. After a minute, she apologized. "I didn't mean what I said before," she said. "That thing about not getting a girlfriend. It's been a long night. I'm fucked in more ways than one. And I don't know why you get under my skin like you do."

"I hate apologies, so I don't accept," James said, "but that's cool." He turned to her and held out his palm. "So give me my five dollars."

"No way! I won!" Trisha said. Truth be told, she had no idea how the game had ended, but this was the way she always operated with guys. She flirted, and they let her win.

But James gave her a stern look. "Aw, don't even pull that," he said. "You *know* I'm more fucked than you."

"What about everybody knowing about Mitch? Huh?"

Although she hardly cared about the money, now that she'd started, she didn't want to give in so quickly. That seemed like the wrong thing to do.

James wasn't being playful. He took a deep angry breath and, after a minute, began to speak. "Look, I'll keep going if you want. I can't get a friggin' second interview to save my life."

"I know. I can't get a *first*—"

"And in fact, if you look at every single person on campus, I'm the one who's *really* fucked. Everybody else has got daddy's bank account to fall back on. I got shit—except for $20,000 in student loans to start payin' off." He shook his head. "Admit it: I win. I'm more fucked."

"No, *I* am," said Trisha. At this point, she thought it would be downright *rude* to admit that he was, in fact, the bigger loser.

"*I win. Say it. I win.*" James's face was turning red.

"Gosh. Take it easy. It's a game." She pinched his elbow.

"Maybe to you it is," he said. "To me, it's life."

"Fine." Trisha was breathing shallowly. "You're more fucked. Happy?"

"No. I want my five dollars."

She reached into her back pocket and pulled out a five. Out of habit she added, "I'm sorry."

"Jesus. Don't be." James looked disgusted. "I hate when people say they're sorry about things that have nothing to do with them." He stood. "Anyway, I'm going to bed."

Just then, Mitch walked through the door.

✠

"Oh, hi," Mitch uttered, in a tone that meant, *Oh, shit*.

"Hey man." James glanced up.

Trisha jumped to her feet, almost lost her balance, and went to pour herself a glass of water.

She waited for Mitch to say something. Instead, he opened the fridge and removed a slice of American cheese, which he unwrapped and popped into his mouth. He glanced over at James.

"Well," he said, "I'm off to bed." He started for his room. James said, "Me too," and followed.

"Mitch," Trisha called out. She walked to the far end of the hallway, so she could see him.

He sighed but didn't turn around. "Yeah," he said, back still turned.

"I'm sure James would like to know where his house-guest is."

Mitch cocked his head around just far enough to scowl. "Well *I'm* sure James would like to ask his own questions." He turned to face James head on and folded his hands across his chest. "By the way, James," he said. "Cindy fell asleep on Glenn's couch, and I didn't want to wake her." He started for his room again.

"*Mitch*."

He looked at the ceiling. Trisha stared at the back of her alleged boyfriend for a good ten seconds, and then said, simply, "Fine."

Mitch went into his room and shut the door behind him.

Trisha felt the sudden need to drink five gallons of water and sleep for three days straight. Confused, dizzy, and a little nauseated, she stumbled home.

Trisha's horror was so immense that it awakened her at five-twenty, five-fifty and six-fifteen in the morning. At eight-oh-eight, she woke up so tense that she sat up to feel her pulse to make sure she hadn't suffered a heart attack in her sleep. She looked around for the remote and turned on the television, on which a slick Southern evangelist was insisting that *Jaysuhs* was the answer. She fell back on the couch.

Warily, she replayed the night in her mind. First things first: Had she said anything to James that she might regret? Had she told him anything about her father? As far as Mitch or Nat or anyone else here knew, he was dead. In fact, he was a drunk and a compulsive gambler who'd been in and out of jail for fraud and now lived somewhere in Tennessee. No, she was sure she hadn't said anything about him. She might have told James how her mom couldn't deal without having a husband and drank too much and walked around talking about how she needed a man, any man, even a *gay* man for that matter because what she really wanted was *someone to talk to, just someone to talk to, anyone to talk to…*

God.

And then there was Mitch and Cindy. Cindy and Mitch.

To go there at all, she would need fortification. She tried to stand but her legs shook; she fell back. She was shaking and too confused to figure out what form of sustenance might stop the tremors. Water? Hair of the dog (whatever *that* was)? The Ho-Hos snack cakes that Nat kept in the freezer for her own mornings after?

She wasn't sure she could make it across the room to the kitchenette in the first place. She thought with a start: This must be how Nat, and her mother, often felt in the morning. If only she'd known. She could have shown more compassion.

After fifteen minutes of concentration and five of moti-. vational speaking—i.e., chanting, "C'mon, you can do it"— she was able to weave to the kitchenette and procure water and a handful of saltines. She held onto the counter for a while, contemplating sitting but too daunted by the prospect of having to stand again. She ultimately stumbled back to the couch. There she lay back, holding her glass like a baby bottle; she raised it to drink, and half of the water splashed all over her. She threw out her arm horizontally to put the empty glass back on the coffee table, and somehow it landed safely.

Able at last to relax, she closed her eyes and saw yellow-tinged movement. The sun streaming through the window hit her like a sledgehammer. She wanted to cry, but that would require additional hydration.

Why had Mitch left her in this state? Put another way: Why was he giving up daily sex for a one-night stand? A cretin like James would say it was obvious: Cindy was hot. But their relationship was about more than sex. Wasn't it?

She replayed it, looking for clues. Sure, he'd said he wasn't ready for marriage. But wasn't that just something guys said right up until the day they proposed? And all those wisecracks about the infeasibility of monogamy. Could he have been *serious*? God, she was stupid. She whacked her palm against her forehead repeatedly. Stupid stupid *stupid*.

James had asked, at one point during the evening, if Trisha loved Mitch, and Trisha had surprised herself by saying no. That was the truth. Now, in a calm, quiet moment, breaking up seemed…okay. If only she could make that state of mind last.

She sighed. She needed words of wisdom from Nat. She wondered how late she might sleep. Three or four in the afternoon if she'd gone to a frat party. And even then she'd be in no mood to offer advice. Of course by now, Trisha knew what Nat would say. "Dude, it's for the best. If you'd listened to me—and your list—you might've met Mr. Right by now. It all boils down to one thing, T-bone: You're afraid to be happy."

Of course, Nat might have said something entirely different, but Trisha knew enough psychology to understand that this monologue was what she, Trisha, believed, or it wouldn't have popped into her hung-over head.

Hours later, Nat walked in from her bedroom, hair a mess, wearing nothing but silk panties and mascara. Trisha stopped, eyes filled with tears, and looked happily toward her roommate. Meanwhile, Nat paused and draped one hand across her bare breast to scratch gently. She looked like a heroin junkie about to recite the Pledge of Allegiance.

"Look what the cat dragged in," she drawled, with an accent straight out of *Cat on a Hot Tin Roof*. "You feeling all right, Trishie?"

"Let's just say I had a very eventful night." Trisha began to cry wholeheartedly. "And morning," she added, tasting saline. And feeling better already.

"Mornin', Trishie," came a Texan drawl from around the bend in the hallway. And then Glenn walked into the living room, clad only in Ren and Stimpy boxer shorts.

1997

Life

New York

⊠

Every day since Trisha had arrived at the Galina Woodworth Gallery, Doreen showed up wearing the very same ensemble: black slacks, black Helmut Lang t-shirt, stilettos and a doubled-over strand of pearls as a choker. Trisha would have given anything for a peek inside her closet: How many black t-shirts and pairs of slacks did she actually own? Did she have several sets of pearls? Were they disposable?

The morning after the opening night of Promettente, Doreen walked in wearing a thin white scarf instead of the pearls.

This shook Trisha. Although there were surely less troublesome reasons, Trisha had one thought only: hickey camouflage. Doreen was hiding a hickey, or she wanted Trisha to *think* she was doing so.

Otherwise, she was cold toward Trisha—no change there. Did Doreen secretly feel smug about walking off with Trisha's date? Or was Doreen too self-involved to know that James had come with her in the first place? She was almost certainly too self-involved to know that Trisha had a boyfriend, even though the two women had shared an office for several months now. And even if she'd known, she hardly seemed the type to think that any woman could be monogamous.

Trisha tried to go about business as usual, but it was difficult with Doreen leaning back in her Herman Miller chair, feet on her desk, whispering sweet nothings into the phone. Granted, Trisha had no idea if she was speaking to James, some unknown lover, or, for that matter, her hairdresser, but Trisha assumed the worst—and at the same time, thought, *it simply can't be.*

But of course it could. She and Nat had even discussed it after she spilled the fantastic gossip that Doreen and James left the party together. Was it *conceivable* that Doreen had taken a shine to James? She expected Nat/Carly (she was making a renewed effort on the name thing) to roll her eyes.

Instead, Nat just shrugged. "There's a history of that kind of thing," she said. "Remember when we were kids, all the fuss about how that model, Paulina something, married the guy from the Cars? The one with the Plasticman face and Dumbo ears? And, god knows, models marry hideous and smelly rock stars all the time."

"But *why*?"

"That's easy: They want someone who reminds them of the way they feel."

"Excuse me?"

"All those models, they think they're hideous. They were gargantuan as teenagers; nobody wanted to take them to the prom. They think they're ogres. So they feel right at home dating social outcasts. Plus," Nat said, raising her eyebrows. "I'm sure you've noticed: He's got a body on him. And…dating someone deformed is….kinda *kinky*. This Doreen chick, I didn't really see that much of her; is it possible she's into S & M?"

"She wears stilettos," Trisha answered. "And she's got this black-black hair she pulls waaaaay back…."

"Enough said."

Trisha nodded.

Later that night, Trisha wished that Nat had never pointed this out. She developed an awful case of insomnia and spent the wee hours of the night trying to banish from her mind images of James and Doreen rolling around in bed in various configurations: with and without eye patch, with and without stilettos, with and without whips and chains, and in all sorts of positions. And always, *always* with the two of them cackling and moaning in cruel, filthy, sexual *joy*....

But *Doreen*?

Trisha chalked up her obsession to her hatred of Doreen, and her disgust that anyone she knew would have carnal knowledge of James. Had she plumbed deeper into her psyche, she might have realized that she saw James as fundamentally broken, and her purpose in life to make him happy—much as she'd rescued her family dog, Gus, when she was a child. This is not to say that Trisha wanted James to fall in love with her, although she wouldn't have minded; but she wanted to be the conduit to his happiness, by giving advice or matchmaking—whatever it took.

And if not her, certainly not Doreen.

At work the next day, the bags under her eyes were prominent enough to draw a crack from Gresh during the morning meeting, "Somebody had a little too much drinkie-drinkie last night...."

But it was all fun and games: Gresh was in the mood to laugh with, not at, the world. Thanks in large part to *Junkyard*, and, apparently, all of the frank and scintillating things James had to say before he bolted at such a fashionably early hour, the Promettente was a raging success.

There was a knock at the door. "Excuse me, Mr. Martin?" Rhonda was the only person who called Gresh that. "We just got another one. I know you said you wanted to know the second they came in." Meaning *rave review*.

"Let's read this one aloud, shall we?" Gresh said.

'DETRITUS' NOT ALWAYS SYNONYM FOR 'TRASH'

NEW YORK—It would be easy to designate "Urban Detritus" just another of those ubiquitous gimmicky theme shows that have lately gummed up the art world. Whoever named this year's Promettente (at Galina Woodworth; see events, below) made that conclusion only too easy to draw. But this is no mound of excrement, but a diamond in the rough—as is the show's centerpiece: *Junkyard*, a masterpiece by Gresh Martin's latest *and perhaps greatest* discovery, James Morales....

When he was done, everyone broke into applause, including Galina. Gresh gratefully nodded his head in acceptance, like an Oscar winner.

Marcus, the supercilious events planner, raised his hand. "Yes?"

"Does this mean we'll be doing a Morales show?" he asked. "I heard *several* clients asking last night about buying his work."

"*Mrs. Lipshitz*," the room sang out in unison. Mrs. Lipshitz was an elderly collector who lived by the credo that she who dies with the most talked-about paintings wins.

"You've perfectly anticipated what I have to say, Marcus," Gresh said, clasping his hands together. "I have several announcements in light of the success of our show. First of all, after a *remarkable* job handling the publicity throughout the opening, I'd like to announce that our own Doreen Philbrick has accepted the new post of senior communications director." Doreen stood briefly to acknowledge the polite applause.

Never mind that had *Junkyard* been less than a success, Gresh would have had Doreen's ass on a platter. Trisha had only seen the interviews with James in the *Post*, but if that were indicative of his frame of mind…. ("What kind of idiot would you have to be to spend thousands of dollars on this shit?" he'd asked one reviewer. "It took me ten minutes to paint it.")

From now on, Doreen had official sanction to party her butt off, smoke out the window of her new private office, and submit Dolce & Gabbana outfits on her expense accounts. Trisha was happy for her—ecstatic, actually, that they wouldn't have to share an office any longer.

"And while I haven't had time to pull her aside yet, I'd just like to commend Ms. Trisha Portman for wrangling *Junkyard* and bringing it to our attention." The room exploded. "As a result, I plan to ask Ms. Portman to broaden her job, to include scouting for more outsider artists. We'll call her our Assistant Director of Acquisitions." Galina pulled him aside and whispered in his ear. "*And*, if she handles putting together our Morales solo show as well as I know she will, we plan to make her our Associate Director of Acquisitions!"

By now, the conference room was full of hoots and hollers. Not even Reginald Crowley, who'd been working on a summertime exhibit of Rwandan photography, could help but show his excitement for the show that would bump his—as it would certainly be the hottest ticket in New York. It would be a sensation.

"It's going to be a disaster."

Trisha truly believed this, but said so only when she was safely at home with Tom. "I'm clearly being set up to fail." At the Promettente, when she'd agreed to be his liaison, she'd been comforted by the thought that she had months and months to work on him, or at least figure out some way out of this mess. Now she had a matter of weeks to pull the whole thing off.

"I find that hard to believe: They just gave you a super promotion! Besides, who would want you to fail?"

"Well...no one, I guess, besides Doreen. But, what I mean is, this show—it's never going to happen. James will never allow it."

"He sure seemed to have a good time last night. Why don't you give him a call?"

Trisha served herself more mashed potatoes, letting the spoon loudly hit the plate. "Why do you have to make everything sound so easy?"

"Because it is," Tom said, swallowing his last bite of chicken.

Unfortunately for Trisha, he was wrong. Trisha didn't get through to James on the phone that night. Nor did she on her next two attempts.

Without James's cooperation, she was spinning her wheels at work. For several days, she did her best to cobble together the makings of an exhibit, not knowing anything about the art—or whether the artist would even allow her to see it. It wasn't difficult; she really was quite the bullshit artist. And so much of the copy she needed to generate for various calendars and "coming soon" sections in quarterly magazines was painfully formulaic anyway. It was as if she'd been given a box of magnetic poetry in which the words included "façades" and "grittiness" and "powerful" and she had to string them together. "Hidden selves," "the honesty of flaws"...it wrote itself.

Since she had no way on earth to reach James short of stalking him at home—a resort that was looking better all the time—she hit upon another, perhaps more forthcoming, way to get to the bottom of his reluctance. She just had to dial the operator to get a number for a Dr. Cynthia Dorado. She looked at it off and on for several hours, and finally picked up the phone and made the call. She left a message saying that Trisha, James's friend from Penn, wanted to stop by and say hello. The receptionist rang back an hour later, saying that Dr. Dorado could see her a week later, before clinic hours.

Even now, years later and in the absence of any significant others, Trisha cared about how she looked compared to Cindy. No Dress Down this time: Trisha cranked her workday look up several notches.

There wasn't much she could do to her hair; Trisha had recently chopped off her college locks in favor of a flattering chin-length bob that looked pretty much the same no matter what she did or where she was going: to the gym, to work, you name it. She did, however, break out the big guns in her cosmetics bag: foundation, eyelash curler, eyeliner, shadow, blush, matte lipstick and a touch of gloss. Once done, she looked no more made up than any other woman on the street, but she felt like Tammy Faye Bakker. Then she paired a silk blouse with a long slim skirt that showed off her tiny waist, and zipped on her tallest pointed boots.

Cindy's office façade resembled a Park Avenue apartment building but for the brass nameplates bolted to the right of the doorway. (Cindy, obviously the least senior of the doctors, was listed last, Trisha noticed with pleasure.) The waiting room was a grand living room. Cindy had come a long way from her humble Bedford Sty beginnings.

"Dr. Dorado just got in," the receptionist said. "She usually does her paperwork now." She waved Trisha into an examining room painted subtle yellow, lit with track lighting. She handed Trisha a peach seersucker gown and then laughed. "I'm sorry," she said. "Force of habit." Trisha, who was used to waiting upwards of an hour in crowded waiting rooms, gave serious thought to switching her records to one of Cindy's partners.

In a moment, a woman in a white coat walked in. If Trisha hadn't known whom she'd come to see, she would never have recognized her as the girl who'd stolen her college boyfriend. She still had her looks, but she had her hair pulled up and wore black-rimmed glasses. Her emphasis now was seriousness, not sexiness.

"Why, Trisha! How *are* you?" She sat in a chair and waved Trisha down from the exam table to a similar one. "What a *long* time it's been."

"I'm great!" Trisha said. "But you—*you're* doing *really* great." She waved around her arm to encompass the surroundings. "Congratulations. How long have you been here?"

"Just a year or so. A year now, I guess. Wow. Time flies." She crossed her arms across her chest and frowned slightly. "But, please tell me—this isn't why you're here...."

Now it was Trisha's turn to frown. "I—I think I'm as healthy as they come. Actually, I'm not even clear on what exactly you do."

"Oh! Whew!" Cindy smiled. "I'm an oncological surgeon."

"Meaning?"

"Meaning, unfortunately, that I do a lot of biopsies and mastectomies."

"*Oh.* I see. No, I'm fine—although they always tell me I have, what are they called? Fibrocystic breasts? And that I should watch them. They get sore sometimes." She couldn't believe she was talking about *breasts* with Cindy.

"Right. That's nothing as long as you keep up with it."
Cindy hesitated. "I could check them out if you like."

If only Mitch were here, Trisha thought, he'd be, well, tit-illated. "That's okay. I just had a physical." Realizing that this sounded like idle lunchtime chat, rather than something that should take up valuable office time, Trisha rapidly continued, although truth be told, with all this talk about breasts, she had lost her poise entirely. "I wanted to talk to you about James—specifically, James and his art.

"I'll try to be brief," she continued. "Remember how I was an art history major? I work at a gallery now—Woodworth." Cindy murmured, suggesting that she recognized the name. "Long story short, I have an opportunity to give James his own show. I don't know if you know any of this already? If he's told you?"

"*No*," Cindy replied. She leaned forward in her chair. "I have to say, I haven't seen Jimmy lately. Gosh, it must be"— she thumped her fingers on a desktop—"I don't know, several years now. Since I moved out of the 'hood. How is he?"

"He's good! Great, actually. I mean, for the most part, same old same old, but—it's a long story. But one of his paintings got shown recently, and it caused a huge stir."

"Well, do tell him I said hello," Cindy said. She stood and repositioned herself on the edge of the desk, hinting that her time was running short.

"Anyway, the reason I came to you is that—he's so...*ambivalent* about his art, that I'm afraid he's not going to let us exhibit it."

Cindy gave a hollow laugh. "That always *was* the issue."

"I don't want to keep you, but—I was just wondering if you had any ideas about how I could convince him. Or if you thought you might be able to help in any way."

Cindy sighed. "For obvious reasons, I don't want to get

involved. It would probably do more harm than good."

Trisha had no idea what the "obvious reasons" were, but for the time being, she let this pass. "Why do you think he holds back his art?"

Cindy shook her head. "He tries to put on a good show, but it's all...so *raw* to him, even to this day. I guess that's what happens when you don't deal with your grief."

So it had something to do with his family, Trisha thought.

"But don't you think it would be good for him to pursue his talent? He's so gifted, and this is a huge opportunity."

"*Sure*—if he *could*. But I'm not so sure he can. If he actually confronts what he's been hiding all this time, it might be too much for him. He might just, I don't know, explode."

Trisha nodded, wide eyed. She opened her mouth to press Cindy for details—about what James was hiding from himself, how Cindy was involved, what was so "obvious"—but just then, a nurse knocked on the door and opened it simultaneously. "Dr. Dorado," she said, "I hate to interrupt, but they're waiting for you with the conference call."

Cindy stood and held out a hand to Trisha, smiling warmly. "It's good to see you," she said. "At any rate, I'm glad James is with you. Be good to him."

It took Trisha a moment to figure out what Cindy meant. She turned to correct the misperception but had once again missed her chance to speak.

"Oh, and Trisha," Cindy said, turning back from the door, "you really *should* do monthly self-exams. Breasts like yours can be tricky." And with a nod, she was gone.

⊠

Trisha was nothing if not persistent when it came to reaching James. Her job depended on it. But knowing the state of the New York phone system, she finally decided his phone must be out. She decided to head out to Bed-Stuy the following Saturday.

On Thursday night, with Tom working late, she decided to pamper herself as a reward for facing up to her college rival. She slathered her face with a bright green avocado mask, combed a hot-oil treatment through her hair, donned her Cookie Monster-blue robe, and put in a CD of Neil Diamond's greatest hits. Then she poured herself a cup of chamomile tea and prepared to begin her yearly reading of Jane Austen's *Emma*.

She had just sat down on the couch when the phone rang. Trisha looked at the white plastic handset in dismay, knowing that answering it would cover it in avocado. But she couldn't not answer. She gingerly picked up the receiver and held it an inch away from her head.

Right away, she heard a man breathing, and knew it was Tom, making his nightly call. "Thomas," she said. (He had recently requested that everyone call him by his entire first name, thinking it would be of use at work. What's next, Trisha wondered. Should I decide to go by Trixie?)

"Uh, might I please speak to Trisha," said a stilted, low-pitched voice.

Damn. A telemarketer. They'd been calling all night.

"I'm sorry," she said curtly, "but would you mind taking me off your list?" And then waited. She was a telemarketer's dream, a consumer who couldn't hang up without having been given permission.

"Um...okay."

Trisha waited to be released, or, at least, resolicited. But instead, she was met with silence. She wondered what new mental torture *this* was. "Hello?" she snapped.

"H-Hello?"

"Can I help you?"

A gulp. "Yeah...I'm trying to reach Trisha."

"*James?*"

"Trisha?"

"Since when are you a *tele*—oh. Hi!" She was so taken aback that he'd actually called of his own volition that she forgot about the mask and cradled the phone, smearing avocado everywhere and causing the receiver to slip to the floor. "Hold on!" she yelled. The green was all over her gold- and cream-colored Oriental rug, and, once she picked up the receiver, her fingers.

But he had called her.

"Sorry," she said, panting slightly. "I'm back."

The call waiting clicked. Under extreme stress, Trisha now reasoned, mistakenly, that the other party was a telemarketer. "Hold on," she said to James, and clicked over, furious that some numskull would interrupt the call she'd awaited for *weeks*. "*Take me off your list!*" she said.

"*Patricia.* I'm sitting here with Harvey."

"Oh jeez." Hearing feedback, she warily realized that he had her on speakerphone—in front of his humorless boss. "Tom. *Thomas.*" The phone began to slide again, but she was able to catch it—although not without a measure of noise. "God. I'm so sorry. I thought you were a telemarketer."

"Patricia, Harvey and Eileen wanted to know if we could come to dinner next Thursday night. Do you know if you're free?"

"Absolutely! That will be lovely," she said. "Please tell him we'll look forward to it and ask if there's anything we can bring."

"Will do. I'll let you go now. Have a nice evening." *Click.*

Trisha hung up, shaken. In a daze, she went to fetch a paper towel to begin taking care of the avocado. Only then did she remember: James.

She picked up the phone, praying she'd find him on the line. But he was gone, and, when she tried back, busy. She tried to get through for two hours, to no avail. She wasn't sure if he was on the phone, or if the phone had chosen this inopportune moment to go out of service, or if James had taken the thing off the hook to teach her a lesson.

Finally, *finally*, she got through.

"Were you on the phone?" she asked James.

"No," he said, through a mouthful of something. "Just took it off the hook while I's eating."

"What's for dinner?"

"Huh? Oh. A slice of American cheese, a Twinkie, and some steamed pork dumplings."

Trisha made a face. "So listen," she said. "I've been dying to talk to you."

"Yeah?"

"Yeah." *Yeah*, Trisha wanted to say. *That's why I called you twelve times.*

"Phone wasn't working," he said. She wasn't sure whether or not she believed him. "Whassup?"

"Originally, I wanted to talk to you about doing a show of your work," she said. "You know, like Gresh, my boss, mentioned to you? It, um, would probably mean a lot of money for you. Like, thousands and thousands of dollars. There's been a lot of interest in your work."

"Yeah?" Trisha couldn't read a thing from his tone of voice.

"Yeah. So, um, maybe we can get together and talk about that sometime? You can come here, or we can meet at my office, or I could come to you—whatever."

"Whatever."

"And I wanted to finish cataloguing your mom's paintings," she said, hating herself for using this to her advantage. "Do you think I might be able to stop by sometime this weekend?"

"Sure," he said. "We're painting the bedroom. So listen," he said. "I was thinking. Where's your office again?"

She told him.

"Oh, right. I forgot you were in SoHo," he said. "I was thinking if you were in Midtown, we could have lunch sometime. Nevermind."

Trisha held out the receiver and stared at it. That's when she realized: *he* had called *me*. What was this all about?

Oh, right, she thought, as she hung up. Doreen.

Trisha had two days to suffer through at work until Saturday, the day she and James agreed upon. Ironically, she was thankful that her new promotion hadn't taken away much of her busywork; at least it gave her something to do. It had taken her no time to decorate her new office, and she had to admit, she missed the chatter of another person in the room. Although she *did not* miss Doreen.

Try as she might, of course, Trisha could not avoid the person entirely. On Thursday afternoon, she was in a stall in the women's room when Doreen, having noticed to her horror a few white hairs mingling with her crop of jet black, came in to have a bit of color applied by Marcos Carlos Denis, her ultra-fabulous Brazilian hairstylist (who, given what she paid him, always came running when Doreen needed a quick lunchtime fix). They carried on their dirt-filled chatter as if they were alone in the universe. And that's how Trisha found out how the Doreen and James episode had ended.

After telling Doreen for the umpteenth time that she was *not* going gray, that she was *not* old, that this was *one* stray fluke of nature, Marcos finally gave in and dished up what she obviously wanted: lies from 180 degrees in the *opposite* direction. Now he told her she was hideous, looked like trailer trash, and was too ugly to live—"like that Elephant Man freak of yours." He tut-tutted. "So you never did tell me the story of how you got rid of him."

"*God*," Doreen snarled. "You'd think standing somebody up five times would be enough, but I think in his twisted little head he thought that was part of the game. "

"Oooo-kay, I don't *even want* to go there."

Inside the bathroom stall, Trisha barely breathed, afraid to remind them that they weren't alone.

"So finally I just had to be blunt. I had him meet me at Starbucks, and when he got there I pulled out my compact, and I went, here: Look. Did you *really* think somebody like me was going to go out with someone like you?"

"*Damn*. You're cold!"

"Not really," Doreen said. They were done with the color application now. "It's common sense, really. I mean, if you'd *seen* this guy. Although, I have to say, the dude knew how to move."

"So how'd he take it?"

"Called me a cunt. So, get this, you'll like this: I couldn't stand for *that*, right? So I accidentally on purpose knocked my cappuccino over him—which was really hot—and then started quivering my lip and acting like I was going to cry.

And when these cute guys came up, I acted like I was afraid this pervert was going to *molest* me."

Marcos chuckled under his breath. "I don't know *why* I love you," he said, catching his breath, "but God help me, I do. So what did the guys do?"

"He's a pretty big guy, but there were *two* of them, and they looked like they just got back from the gym. One of 'em threatened him but, dammit, this undercover cop was there and asked if anything was wrong, and I had to say no."

"Or *did* you?"

"*Ooh*," Doreen said as she left the restroom. "I like the way you think."

Trisha took half a sick day and went home early. For hours, she lay propped up in her bed, mindlessly reading *People* and *In Style*, eating chocolates and shaking her head every so often when she thought about what she'd gotten James into. She didn't know how he dealt with rejection, but whether he would admit it or not, it had to hurt like hell. And this particular instance was *brutal*.

She envisioned James turning thirty, forty, fifty, alone, ever more trapped in his own thoughts and routines with each passing year, without the slightest thought of asking a woman out because the one time he'd taken a chance, he'd been bitten by a she-wolf.

James needed a girlfriend, someone who would kiss his sore spots, soothe the savage beast, turn him into the teddy bear he was capable of being.

She needed to *find* James a girlfriend.

She started going through the mental Rolodex of single women she knew.

Maureen. Superficial (as evinced by her insistence on

lime-colored Post-Its, her $60 weekly salon hair blow-outs, and her overly manicured toy poodle). Would veto James for his ill-fitting shirts and scuffed shoes—*if* she managed to get past his scarred face and lack of a six-figure salary.

Cathy. Ditto.

Cynthia. Ditto.

Doreen. Ha!

Melinda. Forty-nine years old.

Liza. Wouldn't get the video game thing.

Kristy. Listened to Celine Dion.

Rhonda.

Trisha sat up. Rhonda, Gresh's assistant, was lonely, and James was lonely; Trisha was brilliant. Rhonda wasn't superficial; would not just understand, but also *indulge* his video game habit; was not above bringing brewskis to him and the boys.

She decided to broach the topic with James that weekend. All in all, they had much to discuss that Saturday. Trisha would have to hope her karma was in good shape.

At work on Friday, Trisha was scraping the bottom of the barrel, surfing the websites of graduate programs in studio art for photos of their star pupils' work. Suddenly, an instant message popped up on her screen.

Yo we need to talk, said someone named DaSandmann.

Trisha considered just logging off IM, since this was obviously a wrong number, or wrong—whatever—but that would be rude. WHO *ARE* YOU? she typed.

Yr fave metallica fan of course.

She started to type another angry query but then got it. The heavy metal. She smiled, as she did whenever she thought of college. Funny, the power of nostalgia to make the worst experiences of your life seem like the best.

HOW DID YOU FIND ME? she asked, aware of the irony, given that he had only tracked down her IM name, while *she* had shown up on his front doorstep.

Net white pages, James replied.

WHAT'S UP?

Change o plans need to tell ya something over dinner pick nice place im payin

I DON'T KNOW. WHAT DO YOU LIKE? MCDONALD'S? KIDDING, LOL.

Its gotta be nice, im serious, how about bouley?

Trisha knew there was no way they were getting into Bouley on such short notice.

She made a quick phone call to an acquaintance who owed her a favor and then turned back to the screen with an odd twinge in her stomach. THE RAINBOW ROOM CAN SEAT US FOR SATURDAY IF WE DON'T MIND EATING AT 9:45, she typed. HAVE YOU EVER BEEN? She usually didn't like rubbing elbows with tourists, but the view made it worthwhile. Plus, it wouldn't be too expensive for James; Trisha could cash in a favor.

Now the question was, why was James spending anything in the first place?

1992

College

Philadelphia

[*]

There was no way, given the circumstances, that Trisha and Mitch would honor their plans to go to Daytona Beach for spring break, and Mitch kindly offered to deal with the ticket refunds. (Which only angered Trisha all the more: one less thing to be angry with him about.) Once again, Trisha found herself stranded on campus entirely alone.

Alone—except for James, who had seemingly become her rival for Biggest Loser on Campus. Or, to put it another way, Most Fucked.

"I was supposed to go on a road trip with Glenn," he explained when Trisha found him loitering in the sixth-floor lounge, playing with his Nintendo GameBoy, "but then he hooked up with some piece of tail—"

"Hey," Trisha said. "That 'piece of tail' happens to be my roommate."

"Anyway, here I am."

"Why don't you go home?" she asked him. "The city's just two hours from here on the train."

"I'd love to go see my ma," he said. "But I got lots of stuff to do. I got to find a *job*."

"Me too," Trisha said.

James frowned at her.

"What?"

"It's not the same thing," he told her. "If I don't find something, I'll be flippin' burgers at Wendy's."

He was right to be concerned: Already, the two of them were wallflowers in the great employment dance. Mitch had his consulting job set up in Boston. Nat planned to spend a month sipping lattes in Paris, spending her trust fund, and then move to New York to pursue acting. Glenn would sell cars on his dad's lot in Texas. Even Phil the pothead knew where he'd be come July: answering phones at his uncle's ad agency in New York while studying for the LSATs.

On paper, James was a dream applicant: a dual economics/statistics major with a 3.9 GPA and actual paid consulting experience. When he submitted his resume to Penn's Office of On-Campus Recruiting, *forty companies* signed up to interview him during the two-week period when corporations and other businesses sent delegates to scope out potential future employees. James should have had offers for several plum jobs by now.

But something had gone very wrong. Only ten companies requested a follow-up. And James received just one bona fide offer: a glorified admin job at a third-tier consulting firm in New Jersey. It paid only $20,000, which was all that liberal arts majors like Trisha could expect—but a slap in the face for someone with a *real* major. And James needed the money. He was on the hook for a cool $20,000 in student loans. It was starting to look as if James would be putting his $100,000 education to work delivering pizzas in Bed-Stuy.

"So what's your problem?" Trisha said, terrified that she *knew*. She chose, however, to disregard his appearance. "What are you doing, picking your nose at these interviews? Leaving the boogers on your thank-you notes?" For a moment, James looked like a deer caught in headlights. "Oh, c'mon," she groaned. "Don't tell me you aren't sending thank-you notes."

"What a waste of time! It's all bullshit," James sneered. "Like they should be looking at how much I *smile* during my interview? Or what *suit* I wear? Or, if they actually condescend to eat lunch with me, whether I use the right fuck-ing *fork*? *Bullshit.*"

"I'm going to tell you why it's important in a way you can understand and respect," Trisha said. "The whole point of the thank-you note is to make them feel guilty about, A, how pathetic you are—here you are spending all this ener-gy to get a job they're waaaay beyond; and B, the fact that they *haven't given you one second's thought* since the minute they walked away and you've obviously been thinking of them non-stop, because here you are sending them a note after all this time. The gushier you make it, the worse they feel. And what do people do when they feel guilty?"

"They act." James looked stunned. "That's, like, the whole key to telemarketing. People would rather spend their money than be rude. You're brilliant."

"And they'd rather give you a job than feel guilty," Trisha said.

"I never thought of it that way. Is there more?"

"Are you kidding?" Trisha said. "Stick with me, kid. Bullshit is my specialty. Now," she continued, "what can you do for *me*?" Dirty thoughts ran lightning-fast through her head.

James grinned. "Why are *you* here, anyway? Why didn't you run home to mama or off to 'the Continent' or whatev-er you trust-fund babies do when you're heartbroken?"

"I'm doing some work at the Institute of Contemporary Art," she replied. "They need someone to look up refer-ences for the copy for an upcoming exhibit. And since I wasn't exactly going to Daytona...."

"I thought it was illegal to work-study during a vaca-tion."

"Um...it's not work-study, exactly. It's an internship. Because, gosh, when it comes to getting a job, I need all the help and experience I can get."

"Well, isn't *that* special?" James shook his head. "While students who need real jobs have to slop your shit at the dining hall for less than minimum wage, you get to go get these juicy recommendations from the director of some big museum. Real nice."

"Tell me where the protest is and I'll go."

"Oh, I get it," James said, nodding, "a bleeding-heart liberal. A rare breed on this campus." He looked at her out of the corner of his eye. "I got some big problems with that but the way I figure it, you're too naïve to know any better. That's cool."

"You're one to talk," Trisha said. "Why aren't you 'slopping shit' at the dining hall?'"

"I bargained with 'em." At Trisha's puzzled look, he explained, "I didn't want to work-study. Why spend so much on school if you're too goddamn exhausted from your job to learn anything? And they had to give me what I wanted. They needed me. You know, diversity and all that shit. They needed a poor blind kid." He patted a catalog full of on-campus recruiting participants. "Now if I could just find some nice corporation with the same desperation." He smiled.

"So—what's the deal, then. Don't *you* feel guilty?"

"No," James said. "If those dining hall kids are too stupid to negotiate, then let 'em slop."

Trisha guffawed. "So what was all *that*, then? All that crap you said about *me*?"

James shrugged. "I don't know," he said. "It's just fun to see what-all you got stuck in your ass." He smiled.

Trisha's situation was, in all honesty, much trickier than James's. She had known this without really knowing it for three years, and now it was time for her schoolgirl idealism to come back to haunt her. Everyone she knew, and even complete strangers who had asked her major in the last three years, had questioned the wisdom of studying perhaps the least practical of all majors at the most expensive university in the country. More than once, Wharton undergraduates—preppy boys in oxfords—had broken into spontaneous laughter upon hearing her plans, or lack thereof. She had always energetically defended her choice.

Trisha had composed her first few cover letters in a daze of optimism, sure that her passionate, earnest prose and resumé bursting with internships would levitate its way out of the stack of mundane applicants. She poured out her heart to these human resources lackeys, creating convincing cases that she wanted to work for their companies more than just about anyone they could hope to find and would therefore give them 150 percent of herself, including her very blood if so required. (She didn't include that last part, but it came through nonetheless.) So if there were no positions to be had—they would *create* one for her.

She found herself getting annoyed at Nat when she lingered on the phone at first, wanting to keep the line clear in case someone wanted to call to set up an interview. She checked the mail several times a day before it was even due to arrive.

By spring break, however, her expectations had fallen in line with reality. She wanted one of two things: a non-paying internship at a middling (or piddling) museum that within a year she might parlay into a paying job, or a paying job in a related field—and the term "related" was broadening with every passing day. Her cover letter prose had changed, too, from overheated to lukewarm.

Only now was she beginning to feel the full impact of

what she'd signed up for: namely, undignified begging for the chance to prostrate herself in front of snooty heirs and heiresses and grovel for the opportunity to do their bidding for sixty to eighty hours a week—and make $18,000 a year for it. She'd written to dozens upon dozens of museums and other art-related institutions and come up with...nada.

"What I don't understand," Trisha said, "is how you can talk people into giving you more than their starting salary when they're doing you a favor hiring you."

"First of all, never think that way. You're doing *them* a favor. Do you know how hard it is to acquire a competent work force?" James began gesturing with his whole body. "Second, when you're talking money, never, *ever*, mention a number first. Make *them* do it. Even if they ask you straight out how much you'd like to make, do *not* answer the question—even if you have to be rude. The one who talks first *always* loses. Not just with salary, with any negotiation. You got to control the flow of information or you get fucked."

"Hmm, interesting," she said. "I'll definitely put that to use if I ever get a job offer. Or an interview." Then she had a brainstorm. "James," she said, "Do you stick to a similar philosophy when you're still trying to *get* the job? Because that could be another one of your problems right there."

"I don't follow."

"Well, I bet you never ask a question about the company because you don't want them to think there's anything you don't know."

"Sure," James said. "I hate it when people go in and don't know shit about the company interviewing them. What a dick move."

"Big mistake. You *have* to ask questions. Otherwise, they assume you aren't interested. Wouldn't you be upset if they didn't ask a single thing about *you*?"

"So you're saying I should act stupid?"

"Either that or come up with some smart questions."

James shook his head in amazement. "You know," he said, "if you put the two of us together, we'd make one *hell* of a candidate." Trisha saw that he was smiling.

"In the meantime," she said, "I bet that between us, we've got more rejection letters than anybody." In the last several weeks, Trisha's had begun to arrive in full force. A postcard. A letter comprised of one sentence: "We regret to inform you that we have no suitable positions available at this time, but we will contact you should a position for which you are appropriate become available."

This was the week, then, that Trisha felt that she and James became *friends*. At first, they just ran into each other accidentally, ordering hoagies at WaWa (since dining service was closed), or sunning on the Green, or buying snacks at the downstairs Rathskeller, the one campus establishment, it seemed, that stayed open during the bleak break. Soon Trisha found herself running out into the hallway when she heard James leaving, and tagging along to the movies or wherever he was going. They never did get to the point where they were intentionally seeking each other out—or at least, not to the point where they admitted it— but they probably logged four or five hours together a day.

Of course, Trisha had to bite her tongue to stop from asking about Mitch. Her first item of business was to find out whether he was spending the week in New York with Cindy. She later found out that he *was*—but James refused to verify this.

"God." Trisha shook her head. "I don't understand you guys. Look what he did to you, and you're still loyal to him."

"It's not like I *owned* Cindy." James shrugged. "She was fair game. I don't believe in possessiveness. People can't own people."

"So I take it you don't think I should even be upset then."

"Nah, you're humiliated. I get that," James replied (as Trisha harrumphed). "But"—he shook his head. "The whole monogamy thing is a crock."

"God! Do you—do you guys really think that? Honestly?" Trisha was even angrier that James would feel that way than Mitch. If a woman ever *could* find it in her heart to be true to him, how could he not be faithful?

"Yep." After a minute, he added, "It's not like he was out to hurt you. This is my point. Men aren't made to be faithful to one woman. Things just…happen sometimes."

"So you're Neanderthals? Big brutes with no control over your dicks?"

James shook her off, apparently convinced that the conversation wasn't worth continuing with someone so emotional.

That only made Trisha angrier. Somehow, she had expected more of James. She thought if he ever did find a woman, he'd treat her like a queen. Sure, he didn't exactly have NICE GUY tattooed on his forehead. Quite the opposite. But she had secretly imagined, she now realized, that he was a beast that would one day be tamed.

"So let me get this straight," Trisha said. They were entering a sushi bar. (James couldn't afford it, and in fact had never even tried it, but Trisha had a craving and insisted on paying.) "You're fine with what Mitch and Cindy did. You wish she wanted you, but she doesn't, and she wants to snog your best friend instead, and he wants to snog her, so no biggie."

"'Snog?'" He cocked an eyebrow. "Basically, yeah."

Trisha shook her head. "I don't believe you for a minute. You're repressing your feelings, big time," she declared. "You're in love with her and you're heartsick about it and this is too mortifying for you to process."

James guffawed. "Bullshit."

"You certainly thought you were in love with her the other night."

"I was drunk." They both folded their arms and stomped to the table.

"Can I just ask one question?" Trisha asked as they neared the high rises, after James had put down more sushi than Trisha had ever witnessed in one sitting.

"That's the third time you've said that," James said, "but okay."

"What should I do about Mitch?"

"What do you mean, *do*? It's over." He laughed.

"That's not what I meant," Trisha said. (Actually, it was.) "But, well, out of curiosity: What if I *did* want him back? Hypothetically speaking."

James gave the universal symbol for a blow-job. "It ain't rocket science," he said. "Seduce him. No guy will turn down free sex unless the girl is hideous. Maybe not even then."

"So I'm not hideous?"

James made a *pfff* sound. "C'mon, Trisha," he said. "Of course not." He said this clinically, as if describing her hair as blond.

"Really?" A pit appeared in her stomach as she waited for his reply, because she knew he'd tell the truth. He wasn't one for massaging egos.

James considered. "I don't know if I'd say you were *hot*, exactly," he said, "but then again, I like my women slutty. You're slim. You have a pretty face. A lot of guys go for that sexy librarian thing." He shrugged.

"Well, thanks," Trisha said curtly. "I'll take the compliment." She felt the hotness on her cheeks.

"Aw, come on," said James, as they got off the elevator and walked past the lounge. "Let's play a little ping pong." As they picked up their paddles, he added: "Oh—but one thing. You might want to wait a while to try that seduction thing. I mean, let's face it: He just had the kind of sex guys *dream* of."

The ping-pong ball shot past Trisha's elbow at something like twenty miles an hour.

"In the immortal words of James Hetfield, lead singer of Metallica: 'Kill 'em all!'" James raised his fist.

"I don't want them *dead*," Trisha said, jogging back with the ball. "Just miserable. Besides, I thought you were fine with what they did."

"I am—but *you're* not, and I aim to please. Besides, any excuse for violence...." Half of his mouth curled into a smile. "C'mon, don't be a pussy. I got boys in Crooklyn can do the job," James cupped his hand around his mouth to keep the conversation between them, even though there was a grand total of only *two* more people downstairs in the Rat. "Chick, Fat, Puppy—m' boys."

"Are these your friends or your pets?" Trisha served, but the return again blew right past her. She went to pick up the ball and then tossed it to James. "Five love."

"Just, we'll have to be careful around Puppy on this one." He paused, juggling the ball in his meaty right hand. "He's had this thing for Cindy since we were, like, twelve."

In the spirit of Who's More Fucked, while opening their mail one day, Trisha and James got into a debate about who had collected more 'dings' (as Trisha referred to rejection letters). Trisha was in the throes of obsession with these letters; she used much mental energy to analyze them down to the minutest detail. She always wondered who wrote them and searched for the smallest signs of personality in the corporate-speak. After determining that both she and James had far too many of these letters, they settled into the lounge and spent a long afternoon in the fascinating, if masochistic, endeavor of parsing the letters for the smallest variations from the standard form letter, as well as mocking the companies whose bullshitting skills left something to be desired.

"It keeps getting worse," James said as he sipped a beer he'd brought in from the Kegerator. "Today I got dinged by *someone I didn't even apply to.*" He pulled a piece of paper from his backpack and held it up. "Someone passed my resume to another branch of a consulting company, and then guys from *both* branches sent dings."

"Get this: I got a ding today that said I was unqualified for a proofreading job—and it contained three typos," Trisha said wearily. "I thought about writing back, to see if that was a test, but if that's the way the company operates, I don't want to work there anyway. I mean, how *embarrassing* for them."

"I don't know," James said. "It's obvious they got no one on the job now. They got a great excuse for mistakes." He flipped through a ream of letters in his backpack. "Oh, here's a good one." James handed it over.

"'Dear *Jack Morals,*'" Trisha read aloud. "Oh, that's classic."

"Keep in mind: That's from someone who spent *two*

hours with me."

"Here's something *I've* been trying to figure out," Trisha said. "Which is kinder: when they straight-out reject you in one measly sentence—'thanks but no thanks'—or send a really flowery note about how they're so impressed with you and promise to keep your information on file in case something opens up, when you and they know nothing will. It's like trying to figure out whether you'd rather die a slow, horrible death of cancer, or sooner but more quickly—like, by guillotine."

"Give me cancer any day," James said. "*Pain! I loooooove pain!*"

Trisha thought of his mother and shuddered, but decided not to ask after her.

"Anyway," he said, "someone ought to collect this shit and print it so everybody can see it."

"No kidding! Or it could be an exhibition. I can see the catalog copy now: 'A tribute to the death of the American dream, one loser at a time.'"

"Shit—let's do it," James said. "Why hide the fact that we're total losers? We should *celebrate* it."

"*What*?!"

They spent the rest of the afternoon on their project. For the remaining three months of the school year, their personalized wallpaper would cover the hallway from their dorm rooms to the elevator bank. At the top they tacked the explanatory title: WALL OF DINGS. Beneath this, they stapled dozens of no-thank-you letters. Eventually, the wall became a Mecca for desperate job seekers, who made pilgrimages from all over campus, bringing their own contributions and often spending a good half hour or more perusing other people's dings. Trisha smiled whenever she walked past. More than once, she heard strangers say the wall made *them* feel less pathetic. "Losers unite!" she always had the urge to shout. "Losers rock!"

On Saturday, the last night before the students returned with their tans and tales of debauchery, Trisha saw James lope past the lounge at an unusually fast pace. She yelled after him, and upon getting no answer, jumped up and followed him into 6H, which, unfortunately for him, he had failed to lock.

James was at the kitchen table, huddled over a paper bag in a vain attempt to keep her from spying what he was doing.

"What's up?" Trisha asked. She pointed at the half-wilted white roses sprouting from a stuffed brown paper bag. "For me?" She smiled, but James looked distraught. "Seriously, what are you up to *this* time?"

James appeared ready to pounce if she came any closer. But he was stuck, and he knew it. He stared at the floor and bounced from foot to foot, considering. "If I tell you," he said, "you got to swear not to tell nobody. Never."

"Sure," Trisha said. "Triple pinkie swear."

He overturned the bag on the already dirty table. Trisha cringed but had little time to be bothered by the mess because of the fascinating cornucopia of items James had just revealed: roots, plants, cacti, ginger, weeds, dandelion, and various unidentified roots and plants. Her mouth dropped open. "What…what is it?"

"My grams," he said, "she…she sent me some stuff to make, um, like a traditional soup from where she comes from in Nicaragua," he said, "on my pa's side. I'm supposed to make it tomorrow afternoon.…We all are, because of, you know, Ma. But, um, since she was sending me that stuff anyways, I asked her to get me what I needed for like a success soup too." He winced. "Sounds stupid. That's not what it's called but it's the best translation I got."

"Wow," Trisha said. "It must be nice to have a tradition like that."

"You want some?"

"Um, sure," Trisha said. "Goodness knows, I need it. Would you like help, by the way, with the cooking?"

"No. I got to do it. It's sort of a…religious thing. But I can't really say it's gonna work." He shrugged.

"What do you know about this…religion?" Trisha asked, trying not to be concerned.

"You know those kids who died down in South Texas a couple months ago? They were doing it too, just more…hard core."

Trisha *did* remember. They died after consuming a fatal amount of peyote and other hallucinogens. Among other things in their cauldron was a human heart. "Oh."

"I'll bring some over, when it's done," James said. "You might wanna dress up a little. For, like, the religious part."

That evening, she put on a black shirt and skirt and even stockings and heels, and flittered around the apartment. A brothy smell, with a strange minty kicker, had wafted in all day; but it was after eleven when James came over, bearing a pot full of his soup atop a frayed old notebook. "Hey," he grunted, and set everything down on the table; then he slid out the journal from underneath. "You ready?" Trisha saw then that he was wearing a backpack, which he sat on one of her chairs and half opened. He pulled out two pens, a pad of paper, a tiny bowl, a lighter, and two blood-red candles.

"Ooh! Hold on," Trisha said, and went to fetch saucers to spare the table. "Here you go," she said. "What's the notebook for?"

James shrugged. "There's some chants and shit. I haven't checked this one out entirely."

"Oh." Trisha's mouth twisted into a troubled pout. "Then you should probably count me out."

"Why?" He frowned. "You scared of my cookin'?"

"It's not that. It's… against my religion."

"*What*?"

"I just think it's blasphemous, is all…. "

"You telling me you still believe in *Jeeeesus*?"

She winced, exaggerating the gesture to apologize for what she was about to say. "Maybe."

"Has *Jesus* answered your prayers and given you a job?"

"No."

"So he'll understand if you consult other deities." James lit the thick red candle. "Look at it this way. You're an art history major, and these are the *black* arts—the best arts of all!" He handed her a piece of paper. "Here," he said. "Write down what you want." He pulled the cap off a red marker with his mouth and scribbled something, then folded the paper and placed it in a silver bowl. Then he waited. "C'mon," he said. "It ain't rocket science."

Reluctantly, she wrote JOB AT MUSEUM, but on second thought, changed it to JOB AT MoMA. If she were going to blaspheme, might as well be for good cause.

"Fine," she said. "Now what? Do we prick our fingers? Sell our souls?"

"*No*." He looked offended. "We just hold onto these pieces of paper so we remember when they come to be. That's all. I'll read this chant, and then we eat." He opened the journal, which looked ancient and was filled with long, scrawled script, and scanned the pages until he found the right place.

"What's it say?" Trisha leaned forward.

James laughed. "Yeah, just *try* to read it. It's in Spanish, but, like, really *old* Spanish. It's my grams's. I think it's some shit about giving up control, saying, yeah, I get it, I can't control shit and I'll stop trying and therefore stop fucking it up…. Something like that."

He proceeded to stumble through a Spanish poem that went on for several minutes and several pages. Trisha tried her best to tune him out—imagining that this might lessen her sin. And then it was time to eat.

Trisha peered into the bowl at what looked like an upscale broth, like something she might order at a Thai restaurant but without recognizable slices of egg or chicken. Her first sip took her off-guard; it tasted sweeter, and spicier, than she had imagined. "Interesting," she said. She was just about to say it was something she might actually eat voluntarily, but her second spoonful held a root so bitter she had to spit it out.

"Yeah," James said, watching her, "it's got all the tastes of whatever—sweet, sour, salty, bitter. Like life or whatever."

"How much am I supposed to eat?"

James rolled his eyes. "Whatever you want," he said. "That's enough."

"So James," she said as she sipped another spoonful, telling herself it was just soup. "You believe in this stuff?"

"Naw," he said, guzzling it. "But, we ate this shit every night when I got wait-listed at Penn, and I got in." He laughed. "The way I figure it, some poor schmo got run over and killed so's I could take his spot. It's potent shit."

Trisha chose to ignore this. "Why didn't you get accepted in the first place?" she asked. "I thought you were supposed to be Mr. Brilliant."

"I am," he said, still smiling. "I suck at standardized tests."

Trisha continued to take small mouthfuls, and before she knew it, she had finished the bowl. "That wasn't bad," she said. "But how are we going to make this happen?"

"Did you totally miss the point? You're not supposed to worry about it. The soup takes over."

She sighed, exasperated. "Okay then, let me ask you this: What are you going to do next in your job search?"

"Interview with anybody who'll have me, I guess."

"Me too," Trisha said. "Although I have to say, there aren't many people coming for on-campus recruiting that will interview liberal arts majors. By the way, can I borrow your catalog tonight? To write them all down?"

"Sure. I left my stuff in the lounge."

She walked down the hall with him, and they admired their newly installed art exhibit.

"If I had a buck for every ding I got," James said, "I wouldn't need a job."

Trisha stopped short. Without a word, she turned and made a beeline for her room.

James laughed. "What?" he called after her. "You want the catalog or what?"

"Nope!" she called back. "Thanks!"

She didn't need it. Whether or not she wanted to admit it, she had the power of the soup.

Inside her room, Trisha hastily booted her computer and opened the Word file of her latest cover letter. She made several significant changes, rendering it appropriate to be sent to her top ten choices—all at modern art museums and venues; she introduced herself briefly and directed the powers that be to the enclosed sample of her work.

Then she created a new document: a sample proposal for a fictional, albeit entirely feasible, exhibition.

EGG ON THEIR FACES: THE REJECTION OF BRILLIANCE IN THE ARTS, she titled it. EVERYBODY LIKES TO BELIEVE THAT THEIR DAY WILL COME, she wrote, AND THAT THE PEOPLE WHO REJECT THEM WILL ONE DAY BE SORRY. HOW BETTER TO INTRODUCE AN EXHIBITION OF WORKS BY THOSE WE NOW RECOGNIZE AS MASTERS—FROM JAMES JOYCE TO HENRY MILLER, FROM VINCENT VAN GOGH TO JEAN-MICHEL BASQUIAT—THAN BY EXPLOITING THOSE WHO, IF THEY'D HAD THEIR WAY, WOULD HAVE KEPT THEM FROM US FOREVER? LET'S TAKE A LOOK AT THOSE SAD SACKS WHO REJECTED THE GIANTS.

It was a brilliant idea, one that would appeal to anyone who'd ever been sent a ding or otherwise rejected. People would come to read the rejection letters and stay to see the manuscripts, pieces of art, other creative works.

Now if only her prospective employers would get the hint: Heaven help whoever *dared* to reject Patricia Portman.

⊠

Nat arrived on Monday night with bronzed skin and a tattoo of Minnie Mouse inked on her right shoulder. She and Glenn had driven all the way to Key West—"clar to Florda," she said, having taken up Glennese—and spent the week eating surf and turf and screwing their brains out on the beach. "Oooh, it'uz beautiful," Nat swooned. "I even loved the cheesy motel room. I had half a mind to stay thar."

"Good thing you didn't," Trisha said, feeling like a parent. "You've only got, like, seventy more days of class until graduation."

"Aw, I know."

Nat was so full of stories about crazy drifters and tropical drinks that she never managed to ask about Trisha's week, other than to ask about the new wallpaper in the hallway (which Trisha answered with a raised eyebrow). Trisha didn't bother to enlighten her. Then, on Tuesday, as Nat spread glitter on her shoulders at the hallway mirror, she blocked Trisha from passing. "So I hear you and James were the only people on this floor all last week," she said. "What's the deal? I'm glad you're both still alive, given all those threats you've issued where he's concerned."

"It was fine." Trisha hesitated. "No biggie."

"I see." Nat threw her hands to her mouth, accidentally getting glitter on her chin. "You hooked up, didn't you!"

"*God* no. We were bored. We played some ping-pong, that's all."

"And wallpapered the hallway. So…what else?"

"*Please*." Trisha folded her arms over her chest. "Look,

you never told me: What's the deal with Glenn, anyway?"

Her attempt to change the topic didn't fly. "Okay, listen," Nat said, brushing off her hands. She walked to the mirror and began picking off stray glitter, piece by piece. "I know you're not in love with James. You don't even *like* him, although I bet you're telling yourself you *do* so you won't feel guilty about using him. Just be careful in the meantime, that the boy doesn't fall in love with *you*."

Trisha looked at Nat incredulously. "I have no idea what you're talking about."

"Look at him and look at you! You don't think it's crossed his mind? When he's ever gotten all this attention from a *girl*?"

Trisha folded her arms. "And what exactly am I supposed to be using him for?"

"Access to Mitch, of course."

"That's ridiculous. I'm so over that."

"Well, it's one thing to feel that way when you're hundreds of miles apart," Nat said wryly. "Let's see how you do now that he's right next door again." She turned on the water and stuck her hands under it, then placed the cap on the bottle and smacked it shut with a *whack*.

Trisha's middle name might as well have been GUILT. She was the kind of person who left twenty percent tips for waiters who were blatantly incompetent, clumsy, and rude. She said "I'm sorry" when people bumped into *her*. So Nat's offhand comments had hit her where it didn't hurt, which hurt even worse.

She examined the charges one by one. She maintained that she genuinely liked James and, once she got to know him a bit, had sought him out because she enjoyed his company. She might have bought him that sushi lunch to get the goods on Mitch, and yes, it had crossed her mind how Mitch might feel when he discovered she'd spent so much time with his own roommate. But...Jesus, maybe she *was* using him.

And there was another area that Trisha found herself repeatedly avoiding, her mind circling around it and retreating, shying away quickly when it approached, like a bumper car or a finger to a hot stove. Did Trisha enjoy spending time with a guy so soon after the guy in her life walked out (*just like her father*, the psychologist in her intoned)? Sure. But...if Trisha liked James so much, and enjoyed his attentions, why wasn't she interested in him?

How would she feel about James if he looked like Mitch, or even a bad Mitch clone (which would make him a David twice-removed)? At the very least, she would have been interested in using him—there was that phrase again—as a rebound.

So...was she denying the attraction because of the way he looked? Probably. And she hated herself for it. She was doing what she despised Cindy for doing, rejecting him because of his scars. She tried to rationalize; it wasn't his scars that would make them a bad couple, but what the trauma had done to him—made him bitter, and cynical, and sometimes mean.

But even so: Was *that* fair? Would she want someone to reject *her* for things *she* couldn't control, if she were him?

He *could* control how he *handled* his trauma, she told herself. But...who's to say she wouldn't do the exact same thing, if she suddenly looked deformed, different from everyone else on the streets? Jeez, she couldn't even handle a lousy fever blister!

Trisha let her head fall into her hands. It was exhausting, arguing with herself in this manner, and she did it constantly ever since that conversation with Nat.

The only saving grace was that James hardly seemed interested in her, no matter what Nat had to say. But out of curiosity, what if he *were*? He *had* mentioned her pretty face.

For now, Trisha decided, it was a non-issue. If James wanted to make a move, she would entertain the idea of dating him. In the meantime, with the rest of the campus back to normal, they'd no doubt go right back to hating each other, if not avoiding each other entirely. Just as soon, that is, as they were done…*using* each other…to help coach each other through on-campus interviews.

As planned, Trisha met James in line at a food cart near the nondescript McNeill Building on the fateful day. They sat on a concrete overhang and exchanged last-minute pep talks over egg-and-cheese-on-a-roll sandwiches. To wit: "Your mission for today is to go in there and manipulate those suckers into thinking you're the biggest suck-up they know," Trisha said. "You can't BS them enough, I guarantee it; just keep laying it on. Just think how screwed they'll be later on, when you join their company and turn out to be a total jerk."

"I like it. I like it," James replied. "And your assignment is to do the exact opposite. Be tough." At the last minute, Trisha had decided to hedge her bets by interviewing with the few companies that had *anything* to do with art. If nothing else, she could practice her interviewing skills. "Let's review," James said. He straightened up into a middle-management pose. "Trisha," he said in his best interviewer's voice, "what did you have in mind as far as money is concerned?'"

Trisha paled and cleared her throat. "Gee, you know, this position seems to fit me to a T. I'd hate to have money come between me and the job. What did *you* have in mind?'"

James raised his brows. "All right," he said. "A little much—remember, the less you say, the better—but we're making progress." He raised a fist of solidarity in the air, and she enthusiastically joined him. "Here's the deal. I go in there and be you, and you be me."

"Deal." They banged fists together.

They were far less upbeat two hours later, at the lunch break. Trisha's first meeting had been cancelled; the company cited lack of student interest (perhaps explaining the ad agency's willingness to meet with *her*). During the second round, she was supposed to meet a recruiter regarding a graphic arts position for which she was only peripherally qualified. A snarky fellow reeking of aftershave asked what she had wanted to be when she was a kid; what she saw when she looked at a scarlet inkblot that clearly depicted female ovaries; and which character on *The Simpsons* was her favorite.

"Surely that can't be relevant to my graphic art skills," she said. Maybe, she thought, this was a psychological test of self-respect—to see if the candidate was desperate enough to do *anything* to get a job.

"Actually, we absolutely want someone with a finger on the zeitgeist," the guy said, "seeing as how we're a comic book company."

"Oh," Trisha said. "I guess…Lisa?"

She was merely disappointed. James, on the other hand, was seething. All day, he'd had to weather the rapid-fire grilling techniques that consulting companies sprang mercilessly to see how well candidates handled the unexpected; he faced scenario after scenario and was forced to come up with a game plan for each potential client. "They don't give a shit if two other companies just did the same thing to you," James said, "because they like to think *they're* the only company you'd ever work for."

He continued. "In fact, they even ask which companies you're interviewing with, and they expect you to say only them, which is ridiculous. You'd think they'd want a smart candidate who hedges his bets. But they don't want someone who's smart. They want a cookie-cutter who gives the same old stupid bullshit answers." He yanked off his necktie. "I'm blowing off Teloitte & Douche," he said, screwing up the company name on purpose.

"There are still nine days," Trisha said. "You've got what, eighteen more companies?"

"Oh great! Fifty-four more scenarios!"

Back at home, as exhausted as she was, Trisha did a bit of housecleaning; if she didn't do it, nobody would, and it took just a couple of days for the place to look as bad as the Rump. She grabbed the trashcan and brought it over to the kitchen table, where she started to sweep the mass of junk mail, printouts and old *Daily Pennsylvanian*s into it wholesale. Then something scribbled on an old envelope caught her eye. After wiping off a coat of tomato sauce, she could just make it out. Dated yesterday. FRAUNCES (?) CALLED, it said, and there was a (212) phone number.

"Nat?" Trisha asked, her voice growing louder by the nanosecond. "*Nat?! What did this Francis person say?*" She didn't wait for a reply. She was already on the phone with the secretary of Mr. Francis McManning, head of human resources at New York's Museum of Modern Art.

Twenty-four hours later, she was sitting in his midtown Manhattan office.

Francis, as he wanted Trisha to call him—Francis!— explained that one of the museum's new hires had just had a family emergency that prevented him from taking the job after all. Trisha's letter had landed on Francis's desk the very moment after he received the bad news. Which was fortuitous: The few candidates who had been in the running had since accepted jobs elsewhere. "It was almost—and I hesitate to say this, given the unpleasant circumstances for our initial hire—as if *fate* had acted on your behalf." Francis smiled. "I don't know if you have a guardian angel, but if so, by all means give him, or her, a raise."

Fate, or God, or some Jamesian deity. Trisha thought back to James's idea that someone had been struck down to get him his place at Penn, and suddenly, she wasn't sure she wanted to know.

More likely, of course, it was fate, but she was willing to give the credit to the soup if it would give James a little hope. The next day, after Trisha accepted her assistant curatorial position and went on a Manhattan shopping spree that her generous starting salary didn't begin to cover, she knocked on 6H to share the good news.

But Mitch opened the door instead. "James here?" she chirped.

"No," Mitch said. He cocked his head and, for a second, looked puzzled. "Haven't seen him in a few days, actually." He put down a bag of potato chips on the table and wiped his hands on his Levi's. "How are *you*?"

Trisha paused just a minute. "I'm fine. Actually, great: I just got a job curating at MoMA. Well, *assisting* with curating. But—at *MoMA*!"

"Momer?"

"MoMA. The *Museum* of *Modern Art*?"

Mitch shrugged.

"Only one of the most prestigious museums in the country."

"I would hope so, given the name."

"Huh?"

"Whatever. Congratulations." Mitch leaned against the corner of the table to return to his chips. "That's great." After a minute, he continued. "By the way, I liked the hall decoration," he said. "The 'Wall of Dings.' Clever. Is that what you did over spring break?"

Trisha sniffed. "Among other things."

"Aren't you going to ask what *I* did?"

Trisha's eyes shrunk into little beads. What gall he had. "Okay," she said. "What *did* you do, by chance?"

"Went to Daytona. Sure was lonely." Mitch tilted his head sideways and fluttered his eyelashes. He tapped her shoulder lightly with his hand. "How you been, Trishie?" he asked softly.

"Fine."

"I've missed you."

"Like you're missing your girlfriend right now?"

"Wha? I don't have a girlfriend."

"Ah. That's right," Trisha said. "You don't believe in commitment. What do you call your women now? Concubines?"

He put his chips on the table and folded his arms. "Who told you that? James? You should know better than to listen to him. He's jealous. He doesn't want anyone to be happy because he's miserable."

"God, you're such an amazing best friend," Trisha said. "Anyway, nobody had to tell me anything. I saw enough for myself."

"Oh, did you really?" Mitch asked. "Ask yourself how much you really saw. You should have seen *James* the night we went out. I wish you'd been there. James didn't want to dance, but he didn't want Cindy dancing with anybody else either. She was talking to some grad student from Penn Law and he freaked. He just took off, just like that. Left his guest totally deserted. We came back right away, of course, and went to try to find him at Glenn's."

"I—I don't know," Trisha said. Her head was spinning, but truth be told, she didn't really care *what* had happened: She didn't want to be with Mitch, regardless.

"Oh, so now you believe James instead of the guy you've been dating for six months?"

Trisha was confused. She liked to think she wasn't totally naive, but it seemed inconceivable that even Mitch would tell lies this blatant. "So why'd you act like such a jerk when you got home that night?"

Mitch smiled gently. "I wish you'd seen the look on your face, Trishie," he said. "You scared me."

She let out a confused whimper. She actually felt *guilty* now for being mean to *Mitch*. And she hated herself for it. "Look," she said. "Did you or did you not have sex with Cindy?"

"What gave you that idea?" Mitch looked hurt.

Trisha noted the non-denial denial. She also observed that Mitch wasn't particularly attractive; he had all the raw equipment, but his face gave away his deceptiveness. But, wow, it felt good to let go of the feeling of rejection she had lugged around for weeks now. It felt so nice to be wanted. And—what if she turned him away and didn't get a chance to have sex again for *years*? She'd never forgive herself if she closed the door on Mitch and later determined that she wanted him. She was 95 percent sure this would never happen, but what if it did?

And besides, couldn't a woman have meaningless sex if she wanted? Men did it all the time. And so, believing full well that Mitch was a scum who had lied before and was lying again, finding him unattractive to wit, and altogether convinced she could do so much better, she allowed Mitch to take her hand and lead her to the bedroom.

After they removed their clothes but before any intimate contact, James walked into the Rump, sounding strangely hoarse, asking Mitch an unusual question: if he knew where Trisha was. He quickly stomped down the hall and opened the door to Mitch's room—another strange move— without asking him. Given his poor eyesight, it took him a second to realize what he was interrupting. But his eyesight wasn't *that* bad. "Ooooo-*kay*," he said. "I'll be going now."

Trisha left as soon as she could get dressed; she had nothing to say to Mitch, really—and although she wondered why James was looking for her, there was really no way she could ask now. Little did she know it would be years before she found out.

1997

Life

New York

⊠

Trisha might have wondered why James wanted to take her to dinner, but Carly, the drama queen, had her own ideas. "*Oh my god* he is *totally* in love with you!" she screamed. "This is it!"

Trisha fumbled her end of the phone. "I don't know," she replied. "I don't think so"—although at that very moment she was eating Ben & Jerry's Chunky Monkey ice cream directly from a pint container, which she never did except in cases of extreme distress. If Nat was right, she was heading for disaster. She would have to pretend she liked him— be a whore for art—or else screw up the friendship *and* her career.

"Why not?"

"Excuse me?"

"What evidence do you have to the contrary?" Nat asked.

"Well." Trisha thought for a moment. "He once told me he was hot for slutty girls. That they were his type. Not exactly what you'd say to a girl you liked."

Nat had an answer even for this. "*Unless* you: A, wanted to hide your true feelings; B, wanted to make sure she knows you *are* straight; C, didn't think it mattered what you said because you thought you'd never have a chance in hell. Then there's D—"

"Wait a minute," Trisha said. "Let's go back to C. Why *would* he think he had a chance?"

"Do you ever talk about Tom with him?"

"No." It seemed cruel to gloat about her good fortune.

"There you go."

"But he knows Tom and I are serious—that we're practically engaged."

"*See*?" Carly shrieked, theatrically. "He has to speak now or forever hold his peace before he loses you forever!"

Trisha sighed. "What exactly are you thinking is going to happen here?" she finally asked. "And why are you so happy about it?"

"I don't know," Carly said quietly. "I just think it's sweet. That's all. I'm proud of him. Even if an evil bitch like you *does* feel the need to blow him off."

"I liked you better as Nat!" Trisha cried. Then she added, "Think whatever you want, *Carly*, but as far as I'm concerned, it's not even a *date*."

It was date-like in one vital way: Trisha worried about what to wear.

Had she been meeting anyone else, she would have put on a skirt and blouse and been done with it. But she felt uncomfortable dressing up for James. It felt like leading him on. On the other hand, it seemed disrespectful to dress *down* for him.

The top half was the more problematic, given a conversation James and Trisha had had in college about breasts. He'd admitted to Trisha that he—and, he assured her, *all* men—stared at women's breasts constantly. Worse, he'd explained that if a blouse showed off a woman's breasts—if it were tight or showed any cleavage—then this meant that the woman *meant* for them to be seen and enjoyed.

Trisha had branded him a Neanderthal and told him she found this philosophy disgusting. But she had to bear it in mind or send the wrong signal, and possibly put up with James staring at her breasts the entire night.

Finally dressed (in a skirt and blouse, with a cardigan

tied around her shoulders as protection, she frittered around her apartment straightening paintings on the wall and thinking about a nagging issue: She hadn't told Thomas the identity of the "friend" she was meeting for dinner. He would have asked *why*, and cross-examined her. Given that she had no idea why this dinner was taking place, she wouldn't have made a very good witness.

Really, it all came down to this. Dinner was a non-event. One that, if she were lucky, would help make her a curator and James a star.

James was already at work on a bottle of red wine when Trisha arrived. "Hey," he mumbled when she sat down. He picked up the bottle and poured her a glass, one-handed. "You were right. This place is the *shit*." Trisha's friend had hooked them up with a table overlooking the city, giving them a perfect view, from the sixty-fifth floor, of the Empire State Building.

Trisha looked out at the fog, or maybe they were clouds, as, in the background, the live orchestra played big band classics. Then she gave James the once-over. She praised his eye patch, wondering if it was a permanent accessory. Dressed in his sports jacket and slacks, he looked otherwise very much as he had on that fateful night they'd eaten with Mitch and Cindy at Beijing. She hesitated for a second and then told him so.

James poured another round, and Trisha drank her wine, hoping it would offer her a script for the evening. She felt as if she were playing a part, one that wasn't hers—like when a soap opera actress went out on maternity leave and they had to find a sub. ('Tonight, Trisha Portman will be acting out the role of…TRISHA PORTMAN.')

"That was a fun night, though," Trisha said.

"Huh?"

"When we got drunk and played that game—what was it? 'Who's More Fucked?'"

The tuxedoed waiter appeared out of nowhere. Sensing that he might not be able to read the small print of the menu, Trisha ordered the escargot, and then suggested a few items to James.

"If youse got the snails," James replied in his best Brooklynese, "youse gotta get *me* something raw." Trisha ordered carpaccio and tuna tartare for the table.

"Anyway," Trisha said, picking up the conversation again, "that was one of, if not *the* first time, I ever got brunk. I mean drunk. I'm not drunk by the way," she said at James's bemused smile. "I bit my tongue accidentally."

"Huh," James said. "Yeah. Watch out. I'll drink you under the table, sweetheart."

"Oh, I'm watching you, mister. I'm watching you." Flirting. She was definitely flirting. For the love of god, why was she flirting? She had to change the tone of this dinner, pronto. "So you've never been here?"

James shook his head.

"I'm surprised. It's an institution, and you're such a die-hard New Yorker."

James scoffed. "My version of New York is, like, Gray's Papaya, and Katz's Deli, and Washington Square Park. Aw—and Coney Island. *Definitely* 'Da Isle.'" He smiled genuinely; he looked happy. "Three things everybody should do before they die," James added. "Get trashed, have sex with a supermodel, and visit Da Isle."

Trisha's eyes had glazed over as she stared at a cream-colored votive on the table. Chin in her cupped palm, she grinned sheepishly. "Damn! I'm 0 for three!"

"Yeah. I can croak—but *you* better watch out for buses."

James said. The appetizers arrived. "Lucky for you, by the way, I know the Heimlich. So you really gonna eat snails?"

She smiled slyly. "I have to outdo you." She smiled and paused with her fork at her mouth. "I won't even make you try it, if you'll tell me why we're here." Despite herself, she was glowing like a kid on Christmas morning, complete with visions of sugarplums dancing in her head. She loved surprises.

And deep, deep, deep down inside, she wanted James to declare himself. She recognized this. She dreaded rejecting him, wanted to crawl under the table to avoid it, turned purple at the very thought. But looked forward to afterwards, when, alone, she could relish the delicious thought that he liked her. That was her reward: that somebody liked her. That somebody so brusque would open up himself to someone like her. It was so romantic.

But of course it came at too high a price. Because once the evening ended, he wouldn't be in her life anymore. He was too full of pride, like a man in a Jane Austen novel. Unless she could stall him, tell him she had to think about it. Say she had Tom to consider.

All of this, Trisha considered, drunk, in the blink of an eye.

"So will you tell me?" She held her breath.

"Nope." James tucked his white cloth napkin into the top of his shirt.

"Pleeeeeease!" Trisha batted her eyes, thinking, *I am shameless.*

"After dinner. Here," he said. "Give me that, dammit. I love raw meat. I like my steak to moo."

"Why can't you tell me now?"

"I don't know," he said, chewing. "Mmm." He grabbed another precious slice of carpaccio off her plate. She wanted to explain that the dish was all about quality, not quantity, in case he couldn't see that he'd just eaten two-thirds of it, but stopped herself.

"Are you…scared of how I might react?"

He shrugged. "Sure."

Aha. A hint. "Scared of what?"

"Don't know," he said. "I mean, I'm not *scared*. But I don't know how you'll react, I guess."

"How do you *think* I'll respond?"

He was quiet for a long time, and Trisha wasn't sure he would answer. "I don't know," he finally said. "I hope you'll be happy. I'm scared you'll be upset."

Trisha exhaled unhappily. Even half-drunk, or drunk—whatever—she realized what this meant: He wasn't here to say he'd agree to do the exhibit. If so, he would *know* she'd be ecstatic.

And it might well be the other thing. The declaration of love.

She was breathing heavily, and James watched, apparently interested in her reply for once.

"So what if I am?" she said, recovering. "Unhappy, that is. I'm not sure, but I don't think I can beat you up."

"Nah, I'm not scared of no ass-whomping," James said. "But check out those claws. They'll do some damage."

Trisha considered her fingernails, recent recipients of a rare manicure. She rolled her eyes. Then she took a cracker smeared with some sort of mousse off James's plate and took a stab at neutralizing the strange tone of this dinner.

"Did you know that carpaccio was named after a Renaissance painter named Vittore Carpaccio?" she asked. "What am I saying, of course, you wouldn't, but anyway, he used a lot of red in his paintings. So." There was a long pause. Realizing how condescending she sounded, Trisha added, "I like red. In paintings. It might be my favorite color." She tittered. "So, the Torture Room—I'm a fan." She gave an overenthusiastic thumbs-up across the table.

James stared at her. Trisha noticed for the first time that given the dearth of eyelashes on his working eye, he could deliver a disconcertingly long cold stare at a person.

She redirected. "So, how's your work going?" she asked. She wasn't terribly interested in the answer; she still wasn't sure exactly what he did. But she wanted to get him talking. Or, rather, she wanted to stop talking.

"It blows." His face darkened. "My boss is a dickhead. He keeps dangling this raise in front of me, and I know for a fact I'm never going to get it." The waiter brought their entrees, and James slurped down the last oyster.

"How do you know?"

"I saw a goddamn report on his desk about our review. I'm getting a 3 percent increase—and I'm supposed to be *happy* about that piece-of-shit raise? Like it makes it okay for them to shortchange me because some other people are getting squat?" He sighed.

"Screw the stupid of the world!"

"Fuck the stupid!" he said. "But I can see his point," James continued warily. "He has no incentive to give me shit until I find something else."

"Are you looking?"

He shook his head.

"Why not?"

He'd been reaching for a cracker but froze midair. Then he ate the last appetizer. "It, uh, just ain't worth it," he said quietly.

It's good news, she thought. *He wants to leave his job and pursue his art. That's what he's going to tell me.* Her head swam.

"How's *your* job?" James asked.

"I have to say, thanks to you, it's going well." She took a long drink of wine and was about to continue when James interrupted her.

"How's *Doreen*?" he asked with a jeer.

"Same old same old. She's in the Hamptons a lot. Looking for a cottage for the holidays."

"What holidays?"

"*The* holidays."

"It's *May*."

Trisha shrugged, and then decided to go for broke, whether James wanted to hear it or not. "Listen," she began, "I know you had no choice in the matter, but bringing in your painting was such a big coup that it inspired my boss to give me a chance. They love your work, what little they've seen of it, and they really, really want to present it to the public at large. If, um, if that could happen, it would probably allow me to have what I've always wanted, which is the credibility to get artists that I want into the gallery— and I hope eventually that would get me my own gallery. It's so hard to impress anybody in this business. So now everybody's, um, just sort of waiting, to be honest, to see if we're going to have a James Morales show."

She was breathless with anticipation when she finished. Awful as it was, she knew she looked beautiful, and wondered how that might translate into her getting what she wanted. Inspiration would be dancing in her eyes, and the apple-cherry color of her cheeks would glow in the candlelight. Meanwhile, James's eyes remained on the now-empty plate in front of him as he chewed his last bite of what looked like very rare baby lamb. Trisha's fish sat quietly on her plate.

"They know how I feel about it, right?" James asked.

"Um. Well. I think…I mean, Gresh heard you at Promettente, I'm sure."

And suddenly she knew. It was all over.

She scrambled to say the right thing. "I, I didn't want to say anything until we had another chance to talk. It's *such* a big opportunity, I knew a business guy like you would want to consider it."

"Yeah."

"Seeing as how it could mean tens of thousands of dollars." She paused, but got no response. "I mean, possibly even *hundreds* of thousands…."

"Yeah," James said. "Too bad."

The waiter took their plates away and slid two dessert menus in front of them. Without considering them, they both ordered coffee.

James leaned forward and rubbed his face with his hands; the stubble sandpapered his palm. "I can't do it," he said. "I don't mean to screw you, but I don't want to make a dime from that shit. I just don't," he said, raising his voice in case Trisha had even thought of protesting.

"Why?"

James shook his head. The waiter came with the coffee.

"I'm sure you want to kick my ass right now," James said, "so I guess this is no time for a proposition. But I'll just make it and get out of your face."

Even in her despair, Trisha noted the word: "proposition." Incapable of facing him, she put her head in her hands. Her hands were shaking.

"I've been thinking a lot about what you said, and I want you to know that you're right: I've been a pussy. But I'm ready to go for what I want. That's why I brought you here. I wanted to do this the right way."

James continued. "I had a long talk with my boss's boss. I asked to talk to him, I hated my review so bad. He said he could tell I wasn't happy. I was like, no shit. So he goes, 'You should apply to b-school. You'd make a great upper-level executive or entrepreneur.'"

After experiencing a brief hideous chill, like one second in the electric chair, Trisha realized she'd gotten a reprieve and dropped her hands from her face. She put on the faux-Trisha face, the one she wore on Christmas mornings as a child as she faked it through the mediocre presents.

Business school? He was turning down the Galina Woodworth Gallery for *business school?*

James was still talking, oblivious to Trisha's sheer amazement. "I was like, 'Yeah, I thought about doing the night school thing,' because if you do that, they'll like pay for it. But I always thought that would suck because b-school is all about the connections, and you can't make good connections if you're there with a bunch of other part-timers, or whatever." James continued to ramble, looking down at the tablecloth instead of at Trisha. "I don't know. It just seemed lame-ass to me. Like, you can't go to a good school, you've got to go in New York, and everybody else in the city's trying to do the same thing, so it's really hard to get into Stern at NYU, which is the only place worth going. Whatever. Then he says as long as I come back and work at the company at this whole different position that I always wanted anyway, they'd pay for me to go full-time. During the day. I'm like, blown away."

Another success for the soup, Trisha mused. The wind had

slowly seeped out of her. She had no idea she had so much air inside her.

"I know, I know, it's not art," James continued, "but for the first time since, like, junior year of college, I think I might make it—like, be happy. I hope this doesn't screw you at work but...it's what I want." He finally looked up.

"That's good news." Trisha nodded four times rapidly. "Good for you. I'm glad you decided to do something for *you*." *Even if it's the dumbest thing I ever heard*, Trisha wanted to say.

"Thanks." He nodded.

"But...do you really think, at the end of it all, this will make you happy? Does it fulfill you like painting?"

James laughed humorlessly. "Painting makes me miserable."

Trisha nodded. "Just do me a favor. Call up Gresh, go to lunch with him, kiss his ass. Don't make me tell him."

"Agreed."

"Tell him some story—that you broke you arm and can't paint for a year. Can we get you a cast? At least a sling? I'm not kidding. Although he'd probably want you to paint with your feet. James Morales: The Extremity Years." It would have been funny if she weren't practically crying. Good for James that *he* had his career figured out. What about hers? A question came to her: Would MoMA take her back if Gresh fired her?

"But...why all this?" She pointed at the room around her. Her voice didn't sound like her own. She sounded like Kermit the Frog.

James shrugged. "I knew you'd be mad. And, I wanted a good place to make you an offer. Which I still ain't made. See? Listen to me. I ain't no good at writing." He laughed and slugged some wine. He seemed immensely relieved to have gotten his news across. "Anyway, I got to do all these admissions essays and I got to do them quick, and you know I'm bad at bullshitting. I want to hire you to help me."

Trisha sighed. "There's no need to pay me. I'd be more than happy to look over them. Even if I do think you're making a colossal mistake." She paused. "Did I say that out loud? But it's true. You're too gifted not to paint."

"Naw. You got to let me pay you."

Trisha chuckled cynically. "Will you pay enough to make it okay when my boss fires me for not bagging the James Morales show?"

James tipped his head. "I'm sorry," he said.

"I thought you didn't believe in apologies."

"Only when somebody's done something to really screw the other person." He cocked his head. "Which...I guess you could argue I did." He shook his head woefully. "Listen, I want to pay you whatever's fair. I'm not being nice, I'm being selfish. I want you to treat it as a job. I need to feel like you'll give me one hundred percent, like they're your own essays. Although obviously I will do the writing.

"These have got to be good—*really* good," he continued. "With b-school, it's all about getting in. The classes are totally easy. And it matters where you go, since that determines the caliber of people you know for the rest of your business life."

"I won't take money," Trisha said. "But...paint me a picture."

James frowned.

"It'll be worth more than you could possibly pay me," Trisha said, "especially now that the James Morales market is drying up. As it is, I'm going to have to volunteer to sell *Junkyard* to the gallery's top client just to make amends, since she won't be able to buy any more of your work. So it's only fair, right?"

James considered for a long time. "Would you pick one, or what?"

"No—I want a *new* painting. Doesn't have to be done right now."

He sighed. "Fair enough."

1992

College

Philadelphia

⬚

As the school year rushed to a close, Trisha had her work cut out for her. She hadn't managed to finish her senior thesis on martyrs—or even get it underway. And she'd lost all of her favorite study spots: Thanks to Glenn and Nat, she never knew *what* she'd hear in her own room. She certainly couldn't go back to Mitch's room, or to the sixth-floor lounge or the campus-wide study halls at the Steinberg-Dietrich building, which Mitch also frequented. So she made her way to the last place anyone would think to look for her: a flavorless carrel in the back of Van Pelt Library.

It felt good to rough it, far from the highly sociable snack lounge at "Steinrich" as well as the temptations of home. She had access to just one poorly-stocked vending machine and a broken coffeemaker that dispensed only hot water. Day after day, she consumed instant oatmeal, ramen noodle soup, and hot chocolate out of one frequently washed-out mug. She developed mouth sores from sucking on Sour Patch Kids and Swedish Fish.

She lost all sense of the season, and the time of day; she entered the library each morning around 7 a.m., reported to her windowless underground retreat, and didn't depart until well after dark. Every day—and each hour *within* each day—resembled all others. A nuclear bomb could have hit the United States, and Trisha would have kept on working.

Space as well as time became disjointed. Trisha was like an astronaut floating on a slow, two-week journey, hovering in one spot and concentrating on one thing only: *Martyrs*. She forgot who she was and what she did other than one thing: *Thesis*.

But as her world slowed to a halt, outside, without her knowledge, the school year sped up and reeled toward its ultimate demise. The campus was a hyper-charged atom; buzzing particles careened from exam to party to job interview. So when Trisha emerged from her odyssey, having been gone for just days, she had missed the equivalent of years on Earth. When her feet had first left the ground, students were still concerned with classes, or pretending to be. When she returned to terra firma, students had their eyes on the summer—and seniors were saying their goodbyes.

It wasn't until her way back to High Rise North, after she'd dropped her thesis underneath her professor's door, that she realized she'd never given James her news, *or* found out why he'd been so eager to see her on the day when he, ahem, *saw* her. She hoped it wasn't too important. She'd been impossible to reach, she suddenly realized, for more than a week.

She expected to return to her room for the first time before midnight, to discover that Nat was back to normal, but she walked in to find Glenn on all fours, playing "Three Blind Mice" on Nat's exposed stomach with his mouth. So. The bizarre love match continued.

"Hi," Trisha said.

Glenn flipped Nat over, murmuring in some strange language only they could understand.

"You folks going to graduation? Anybody have that piece of paper about where to get our gowns? I think someone stole mine from my mailbox."

"I'm hungry for something salty!" Glenn roared, licking Nat's stomach like a dog.

"Nat?"

"T-bone?" Nat batted at Glenn tepidly with her hands in a lame attempt to get him off her. "I think we're going to

Atlantic City instead." She glanced up. "You and Mitch want to go?"

"*Huh*?" Trisha shook her head to clear it. Hadn't she and Mitch broken up a couple of months before?

"Oh." Nat flopped over. "I thought you were back together. He's been looking for you."

Trisha stepped over them and exited back into the hallway.

"Hey, T!" Nat yelled into the hallway, "James came by once, too! Woo-hoo!"

Maybe, Trisha thought, Graciella was here for graduation and wanted to invite her to tea. She knocked on the guys' door, but got no answer.

Down in the lobby, Rhett was hosting a game of Twister for a handful of GLAAD buddies whose gender Trisha had a hard time determining. Simultaneously, he sucked on a red lollypop lasciviously. Trisha asked if he'd seen either of the 6H inhabitants.

"Now that I think about it? I just saw your epidermically challenged friend leave the building. But I wasn't exactly paying attention?" Rhett fell. "Oh, fudge!"

"Thanks!" Trisha yelled as she walked away.

"Hey, did you ever find that flyer? About the cap and gowns?" Rhett called after her.

"Nah," she yelled back. Trisha couldn't believe how little she cared about marching. Once upon a time, such rituals had meant a lot to her.

Trisha didn't think she had a chance of catching up with James, but the moonlight reflected off his bald dome, and with a hard jog she stayed within range of his moderate stroll. She called out. At one point he turned and she lost him, but seeing movement to her right, she spotted him kneeling at the door to McNeill, one of the science buildings on campus. She watched as he stood, sighed, and lifted his face to the night sky, concentrating—on manipulating the lock, she realized as she got near.

"James," she said as she came up behind him, panting.

He whipped around like a ninja. Upon seeing it was only her, he sighed. Now he'd have to start all over again.

"James," she repeated. "Were you looking for me?"

"Nope." He bent down to continue what he was doing.

"I heard you were. I thought maybe your mom might be here."

"Uh-uh," he said flatly.

She waited. "Are you mad at me?" she finally asked.

"Uh-uh."

"What happened with your interviews?"

He just grunted. "What're you doing here?"

"Following you," Trisha said. "Isn't that clear?" She laughed and leaned against the door; it fell open, startling them both. "What are *you* doing? Stealing dynamite? Or next year's science exams? Not that we need them."

"You better go back to the dorm." Given that she had been unreachable for a week or more, following the most awkward moment in their short-lived history, she had obviously lost ground. Now she was sorry.

"I'd rather stick around."

"Suit yourself. As long as you don't mind breaking the law." Trisha followed him inside, creeping, as if walking very slowly made what she was doing less illegal. The door clanged shut, sealing out every single molecule of light. Trisha began to breathe in short, nervous bursts. On the far side of the room she heard a refrigerator open and close, then the sound of a Coke being opened. James loved his Cokes.

Complete and utter darkness, James's angry demeanor,

breaking the law—any of these things would make Trisha jumpy under the best of circumstances, and all together, they made her shiver. The thought crossed her mind that just like an imminent murder victim in some stupid horror flick, she'd walked right into a bad situation. And…if she disappeared, wouldn't everyone say how *distant* she'd been in the last several weeks?

That was ridiculous, of course, but it didn't escape her when, just like some horror-flick victim, she made things worse by following James up the stairwell.

"They turn the elevators off at night," James explained in answer to Trisha's question. "And the lights." He was less forthcoming about where they were going.

It was difficult to walk without seeing the steps. Trisha clutched the rail for dear life. They walked what seemed a hundred stairs to the top floor. There, light from the full moon beamed in from a skylight. It faded periodically, as clouds passed, but for the most part, Trisha could see again. She wondered about James. "It's dark," she whispered, to hear the sound of her own voice.

James spoke at normal volume. "By the way, you might as well scream and shout," he said. "No one can hear you."

Comforting.

He opened a door at the end of the hallway.

"What's this?" Trisha asked.

"Utility closet."

She contemplated making a run for it. This wasn't fun. Using every ounce of moxie she had, she kept her voice even. "A *utility closet*? We came all this way to steal a *broom*?"

"Not a *broom* closet. A *utility* closet."

James walked across the room, and then steel hit steel in the darkness. "Where are you?" Trisha asked. Her voice, louder now, shook. She could hear the terror in it.

"Here," came James's dead voice—from the ceiling.

"Where are you?" she repeated. She shifted from one foot to the other, ready to bolt at the slightest signal.

"Calm down." Something creaked, and then a square patch of midnight blue, a clear contrast to the inky black, appeared on the roof. "You coming or not?"

Aha. To the roof.

Trisha had never overcome the fear of heights she'd developed when she broke her collarbone falling off the monkey bars in third grade. But at least now she had a destination in mind. This was almost comforting. Following James was slightly less frightening than staying behind in the dark. And damned if she was going to be a ninny.

She used this internal dialogue to psych herself up to stride to the ladder and grasp the rails, almost too tightly.

Somehow, despite her slippery flats, she made it up and hoisted herself onto the gritty roof. Immediately she scurried away from the hole in the roof that was the stairwell. And then, as she caught her breath, Trisha experienced a wave of nirvana familiar to any mountaineer on summit day. "*Wow!*" She was unaware of everything but the sensation rocketing through her.

The lights of Philadelphia surrounded her, belonged to her alone—unlike the garish New York City skyline, owned by the world at large. She felt an onslaught of nostalgia for West Philly, which in three short days she would leave forever. She would miss the city, with its small but fierce attempt at self-esteem, and its grand old buildings all dressed up with no place to go. There would be no more walking over the bridge to Center City at dusk, window-shopping in Rittenhouse Square, stopping in for homemade apple pie and ice cream; no more watching as a proud fryman sizzled her up one of Philly's best cheesesteaks on a day that was already too hot; no more watching the skaters and patchouli-scented palmreaders of grimy South Street. No more jaunts to Penn's Landing to catch a breeze, or to the Ritz for an art house movie and some much-needed air conditioning.

No more first days of class, new notebooks, or watching *Sesame Street* instead of going to calc. No more having a roommate to talk to anytime you felt like it. No more knowing you *could* shirk responsibility for anything because you were just a student (not that you ever did, not if you were Trisha Portman).

If she'd liked Philadelphia more, she would have mourned it less; at least she could tell herself she'd be back one day. But this chapter was ending. All that was left were goodbyes.

She lay back, ignoring the layer of gravel on the roof, in a daze, seeing stars.

"James," she said, enjoying speaking into the dark. She could have lain there all night. "I didn't tell you why I was looking for you before. I wanted to thank you," she said. "I got my wish."

"I knew you'd get Mitch back." He didn't sound surprised. "I told you if you waited a few weeks...."

"What?" It took her a minute to understand. "No! I got a job—my dream job, at MoMA. In New York. That's what I asked for." She listened and heard his silence loud and clear. "Well if you can't congratulate me, at least tell your mom." She felt as if there were something to say, something to apologize for or explain about Mitch, but couldn't figure out what it was. Finally, she just asked, "What about you? What are you going to do?"

"I skipped out on the rest of the fucking interviews."

She sat up. That was no good. And then she saw that he was close, far too close, to the roof's edge—and the wind was picking up. As James took another step—his right foot teetering over the side—a gust blew at him. She knew he was messing around, but the wind was nothing to mess with.

She wanted to scream but couldn't, and it would have done no good anyway. All she could do was step as far back from the edge as she could, under the irrational presumption that this would influence how far from the edge *he* stood. God. She'd been playing with the idea that James might hurt her tonight, which she'd never really believed, when all the while she should have realized that *he* was the one in danger. It was her fault, her fault, she muttered to herself. Would he be acting out if he were here alone?

Or maybe it was lucky she was here; she wasn't sure. What was she supposed to do? She could go get him but she had a feeling he just might jump to perturb her.

She could try to talk him back, not that she had ever gotten through.

"James." She tried to hold her voice calm, like they did in movies where guys were on ledges—didn't they? "I'm scared. It would really help me if you stepped back now. I'm afraid of heights."

He guffawed. "Then you wouldn't like it if I did this!" He flung his arms open and pinwheeled them, changing the momentum of his body so it could fall in any direction if it so desired.

Her hands flew to her face, covering her eyes. Spittle caught in her throat. "Please come over here to the middle." The words flew out of her mouth, with stress naturally occurring on every syllable. She sounded like a mom. *Her* mom. "I'm not kidding...James, *please*. If you only do one thing for me in your whole life, do this. I *beg* you. I will do *anything. Anything you want.*" God, that sounded presumptuous. But she would have offered more

Thump.

A long moment passed before she could peek between her fingers. More a period of time than a moment.

He'd stomped his boot, hard, maybe to put out a cigarette or maybe to scare her. He finished twisting it and then perched on a stack of concrete blocks, a good five feet from the edge.

"That wasn't funny." She walked over and punched him in the chest as she collapsed beside him. She kept punching. In other circumstances, such a gesture might have been flirtatious; not here. Finally he punched her back, rough enough to get across the message that she should stop. Then he reached into his pants pocket and lit another smoke.

"Seriously, James. What if you'd been up here all alone?"

"Do it all the time."

"Why?" she said. "Do you have a death wish?"

He hocked a glob of spit across the gravel and followed it up with a long drag. "Don't worry about me, okay?"

"I'm not worried," Trisha said. There was a pause. "You might as well tell me what's wrong because you're never going to see me again anyway." Another pause, long enough for him to smoke still another cigarette. "Is it your job?....Your mom?"

He laughed humorlessly. "Thanks for giving me a rundown of my whole miserable life. Oh, by the way, you forgot my love life."

They sat for a long time. Trisha was afraid to say anything until the stars and the skyline once again took over.

"I can see why you come up here. It does make things

better," Trisha said when she finally broke the silence. "Thanks for bringing me."

"You didn't give me much of a choice. You followed me."

"Fine, then. Thanks for not throwing me off."

Trisha shook her head and headed for the ladder, dreading the long walk home.

She left 6J with her last box late on Friday night. It was as anticlimactic an end to her college life as could be imagined, but she liked it that way. She hated tearful send-offs.

There was no sign of Nat and Glenn, but she had already exchanged contact information with them anyway, making plans to meet up with Nat when she passed through New York, after Paris. Unless she fell in love and decided to stay, a thoroughly plausible thought. It was sad; all day, as she'd passed through the lobby, students spontaneously ripped into a cappella versions of "The Red and the Blue." Ever a joiner, she always sang along.

As she was passing 6H for the very last time, she paused. At that moment Mitch emerged, freshly scrubbed and well dressed. It was the first time they'd faced each other since their evening that wasn't.

"Where you guys been?" Trisha asked.

"Chilling with the folks at their hotel—what a minibar!" he said. "Haven't seen James."

"Is he staying for graduation?"

"I assume," Mitch said. "His stuff's around."

"Well...." She considered telling Mitch to pass along her new contact info to his soon-to-be-former roommate, but ultimately decided against it.

"On your way out of here?" he asked.

"Yep. You?"

"Tomorrow." He gestured toward his clothes. "I'm on my way to meet my parents for a drink at the Palladium. The good old Palladium."

"Well. I'm sure you're in a hurry," Trisha said. "Nice knowing you, as they say." She raised her hand for a high-five.

"Aw, now. I've always got a few minutes for my best girl."

Trisha paused, trying to figure out what that meant.

"Want to come inside for a sec?"

That's what it meant.

"I know you gave me your new info," Mitch said, "but you know me. I bet I lost it."

Trisha knew it was a line—and that he was telling the truth. She felt she had no choice but to join him, both because the request was so innocuous and because, well, wasn't fate once again pushing her into his arms at the strangest moment? Maybe it meant something.

Besides, nothing that could happen here could possibly be of any importance, now that she was leaving this part of her life behind her. In a few minutes, she'd be an entirely different person. An alum. A MoMA employee.

Twenty minutes later, she emerged from Mitch's bedroom, feeling like she had used *him* for a change. She knew she was not the same stupid girl she'd been when she arrived at Penn four years ago. She was ready to move on.

She tried to turn on the hall light, to maneuver her way through the boxes, but the guys had apparently seen no need to replace these last light bulbs when they'd gone out.

Click. Click. She jumped at the odd sound behind her. Like a lighter trying to fire. Or…a bomb. She turned and just barely made out James's silhouette. He was standing between her and the couch, doing…what?

Click. Click. Pause. The pattern repeated itself.

"James," she said evenly. "What are you doing?"

He didn't answer. Her eyes adjusted and she saw: He was compulsively opening and shutting his butterfly knife.

"Okay then," Trisha said. "Have a nice life." She bolted from the room.

She realized, with an uneasy relief, that this was the last time she'd ever see him. Except, of course, in her nightmares.

1998

Life

New York

⊠

The invitations arrived, thick as credit cards. Constructed of cream taffeta and warm white vellum, lettered by hand in solid gold. Selected by the bride's mother, a socialite who cared about such things.

The slip of paper that fell out when one opened the invitation could not have been more different. The groom's family had copied directions to a rehearsal dinner at Bo's Barbecue onto red construction paper using a defective Xerox machine, which left the top half of the paper too light and the bottom too dark. And someone had spelled "barbecue" with three b's.

Lucky for the bride and groom, by the time the bride's mom got wind of the add-on, the invites were in the mail.

Carly hand-delivered Trisha's to her doorstep, on the very day she returned from touring the South as Eponine in *Les Misérables*. Wisely, she warned Trisha to sit, in anticipation of the coming shriek. It took a minute for it to dawn on her that GARY GLENN BOSHANKS was, well, *Glenn* and that NATALIE was her Nat. "Natalie," she said, fanning herself with the thick paper as she leaned her torso forward onto her dinner table, "*what happened*? And is Glenn marrying *Carly too*?"

"Of course!" she said. "All very hush-hush. He came to see the show in Houston—with a date, no less—and he recognized me," she said, chuckling. She looked fantastic, like the star she was becoming. "Afterwards, he came backstage to get my number and never really left."

Trisha noticed that Carly had taken on some of Glenn's Texas twang. It suited her.

"You know, it's funny: I wasn't even supposed to be in such a big role. I was just the understudy. But the other Eponine had just broken her leg."

That was enough for Trisha: Obviously, fate approved.

"We spent a week or two together," Carly said, "and then Glenn left his job—actually, he called in sick to the car lot for two weeks and then quit—and then followed us around for the whole rest of the tour."

Two weeks into their lovefest, he whisked her away to a Sizzler in Oklahoma City and proposed. In her excitement, she jumped up on a table, covering the surrounding patrons with juice from her 12 oz. rib eye. "The manager was mad until he found out what was up," Carly said, chuckling, "then he comped us a dessert."

Trisha shook her head. "But what about all those sexy actors you're always meeting? Do you really want to break their hearts?"

Carly waved them away with a whisk of her hand. "They're nothing. Glenn…he makes me laugh, Trishie. And it gets lonely on the road. He's going to be my manager just as soon as we get done with this wedding. Speaking of which: Will you be my maid of honor?"

"You know it," Trisha said, "as long as you don't make me wear a Fuck-Me Dress."

Carly actually looked like she might be contemplating this. "You're lucky," she finally said. "Can you *imagine* Katrina in something like that?" Katrina was Carly's not-so-beloved sister, who always claimed she'd gotten the smarts and Nat, the looks.

Given her touring schedule, Carly arranged for the big event to happen just one month later, in a Baptist church in Glenn's one-horse hometown of Brazoria, Texas. (Which was only fair, given the exorbitant expense of shipping

Glenn's six brothers, their wives and *twenty-three* children to Carly's hometown of Cherry Hill, New Jersey.)

"How'd your mom take it?" Trisha asked.

Nat rolled her eyes. "She cried for, like, two hours, but I told her: I'm not knocked up or nothin'. It's just that I got a spring break off the tour and I wanna have as much married sex with my hubby as possible. Besides, any longer and one of us'll chicken out."

Trisha raised her eyebrows but knew Carly was only joking.

Well. She was *pretty* sure.

Trisha arrived in Brazoria a month later, on the Friday the 13th that fell a day before Nat's Valentine's Day extravaganza. As she schlepped her bags up to the motel, she saw that Nat's mother, Gertrude, had decorated My Cousin's Motel—the only lodging in Glenn's hometown—within an inch of its life. (Carly had, for the sake of the relatives, resigned to marrying as NAT. Plus, it helped for deniability in the press.) Huge bouquets of white roses sat on every coffee table top, mantle, and countertop in the musty, brochure-laden lobby. ("She couldn't get orchids or peonies," Nat told Trisha later, shaking her head. "She went around repeating, 'We're in a third-world country!'")

Due to a particularly tall splash of white flowers, Trisha didn't even spot Mitch sitting on a lobby couch until he shouted "Heeeyyyyyyyyyy" at her as she checked in. Mitch tried to get up but fell back into the couch from which he'd staked out all comings and goings for the past twenty-four hours, with the help of muchos Dos Equis ("should that be *Muchos Equis*?" he kept repeating, as if he'd just come up with it). "Come over Trisheeeeeeee," he called at her.

"Be right there," she said, smiling, wishing he were

sober enough to volunteer to help with her bags. My Cousin's had no valet.

Mitch finally managed to stand. He stretched his back, popping it so loudly Trisha heard it at the check-in desk, and tried to win points by taking Trisha's luggage off of her hands. "Need help?" he asked after grabbing it.

Trisha nodded as she negotiated with a sunbleached young clerk named COLBY for a non-smoking room. As the boy lazily stared at a board of keys to decide where to put Trisha, Mitch tried again for a more enthusiastic hello. He kissed Trisha quickly on the cheek and asked, "So, when's the *man* coming?"

Trisha neglected to acknowledge the kiss. The harder he tried, the colder she got; that was the rule. "He couldn't get away," she said. "Short notice and all." She forced herself to relax her jaw; no use letting on what a bone of contention this had been.

"Jeez, what an idiot. To let a looker like you go away on her own in close proximity to her college sweetheart for the weekend? You look *great*, Trishie."

She couldn't say the same for him, given the bloodshot eyes, as well as the tire around his middle. "What about you?" she asked. "Didn't you bring that girl you were seeing?"

"Naw! Looks like we're *all* flying solo," Mitch said happily. He pointed at James, who was tucking in his shirt as he left the men's room along the side wall. "Yo, Rump, look who's here? It's Trishie!"

Mitch was *very* drunk.

"Yo yo buddy," he said, throwing his arm around Trisha as James approached. "You remember our old next door neighbor? Trisha?"

She gave the tiniest of smiles, a little irked that her name

hadn't come up in the day they'd spent drinking together—
although of course, if it had, Mitch was certainly in no
shape to remember it. At any rate, James and Trisha each
answered with some version of "yeah," and nodded.

They had not seen each other or even spoken for at least
six months, when James went away to Stanford. But in the
weeks before he'd gone, they had spent more time together
than ever. There were the admissions essays for her to edit,
for one; although he refused Trisha's repeated urgings that
he write about how his early tragedy had affected his life,
they came up with bullshit about playing something he
dubbed "blind chess" in Washington Square Park to build
his young confidence. This not only ultimately got him into
school but earned him kudos in the dean's admissions invitation.

And just as time-consuming was Graciella's exhibit,
which Trisha was determined would occur before James left
for Stanford. They put it on at a large restaurant, New
York's most upscale Latin American hot-spot; and even at
such an unusual location, James sold four of his mother's
paintings for several thousand dollars apiece—giving him
a nice bit for living expenses.

Although Trisha had been wondering how on earth she
was going to keep from being fired or at least chastised by
Gresh for her failure on the Morales exhibit (and the lack of
work she'd done in general recently), Gresh was impressed
enough with Graciella's portraits to purchase two of them
himself, in order to capitalize on the Morales movement for
the additional month or so that it might last. Who knew if
some collector might pay big bucks for Morales's *mom's*
work in lieu of the real deal? As it turned out, Gresh's
instincts were on the money; he bought one work at $4,000
and sold it for $10,000. And, thanks also in part to James's

frank meeting with Gresh—during which he promised not to paint for *anyone*, and to give Gresh first dibs if he did— Trisha's job was safe.

Yet, after all that, here it was six months later and Trisha and James had nothing to say to each other. She told him he looked great; California obviously agreed with him. She didn't add that his new tan took the emphasis off his skin problems.

He nodded, but didn't engage. To get away from the chill in the air, Trisha yawned and asked Mitch to escort her to her fourth-floor room.

"Well, this is me," Trisha said at the threshold. She yawned again on purpose. "I'm due for a nap."

"Oh, don't *sleep*," Mitch said, as alarmed as if she'd announced plans to undergo a lobotomy. "My room's just down the hall, and dude, we got all kinds of drinks. Let me get you some wine." A second later, when she didn't jump on the offer: "It's good stuff, totally, I swear. Nat's parents sent a ton of it over. Do you drink red or white? Wait wait wait: I remember. Red."

"White."

He left before she could disagree. When he returned, he sat on the edge of the king-sized bed; Trisha had propped herself against the headboard. She had no desire for physical contact with Mitch, but it was nice to be pursued, and she liked the feeling of danger it inspired. Mitch began to ramble about Boston and the consulting world, and as he did, Trisha wondered: If she *had* been attracted to someone, would she be the type to cheat?

"How are the ladies of Boston treating you?" she interrupted to ask.

"Not great. I was seeing this one girl, or woman, whatever, but she was in the financial industry and both of us worked all the time."

"Yeah, Gloria, right? You e-mailed me about her." Trisha hesitated, and then gave in and poured herself more wine. "What about Cindy? You still see her?"

Mitch looked perplexed. "Cindy?" he squirmed and took a better seat on the bed, against the headboard but on the opposite corner. "Oh! *Cindy*. We never…. We lost touch *years* ago."

"Why didn't you try to make it work with the busy Boston woman? Isn't it worth the effort? If you like the person."

"I liked her all right." Mitch scooted a little closer until he was now in the center of the bed. He thought he was being sly, but Trisha was just amused. "It just seemed like a chore to get together. The way I figured it, if she was the right woman, it wouldn't feel like a chore."

Trisha shrugged. She thought about Tom, and how overly inconvenient he had found the prospect of this trip.

Mitch tilted the beer bottle and considered it. "On the other hand, we're almost thirty. I guess that's when you start giving up ideals and start *settling*, huh?"

"I don't know," Trisha said, wistfully. "Beats me."

"Well, here's to *not* settling," Mitch said, and clicked his bottle to Trisha's glass.

"To not settling," Trisha repeated.

"So how come a beautiful lady like you is still on the market? When am I getting an invitation to *your* wedding? If you'd invite me," he hurriedly added.

"Working on it," Trisha said.

"So what's he like, this Tom?"

"Thomas is a…good guy. A really good guy."

"Unlike me."

"Unlike you." Trisha smiled.

Trisha paid no attention to how many drinks she downed, and even if she'd tried, this would have proved impossible: Mitch refilled her glass every time it was half-empty. When his words began to slur, Trisha decided a change of venue was in order. "Let's go," she said, mustering more energy than she felt. "I've got to go find Natty Bumpo."

She allowed Mitch to lead her outside the hotel and next door, to a neighborhood bar where the wedding party occupied three booths in the back. Scattered locals took the rest of the seats; men in JC Penney suits spoke earnestly to long-haired blondes with red lipstick and headbands.

"Hey hey hey hey!" Glenn shouted, standing as they approached. "Mitchie and Trishie! Pull up a chair!" He bounced up bloatedly to hook an arm around Trisha and pull her into a bear hug that lasted much longer than it should have. This he followed with a kiss square on the lips—complete with tongue. "Woo-hoo!" he shouted. "Last one 'til the divorce."

"That's what you say ever' single time, l'il brother," an almost-bald redhead called from the table.

"What's up?" Trisha asked.

Glenn shrugged and began to chatter, but the redheaded guy talked over him. "I's a-tryin' to figure the chances my baby bro will give up his freedom," he said. He stuck out his hand. "I'm the older brother, Mac."

"The *baby* older brother," said another Boshank, one of a handful of Glenn clones at the table.

"Who's he?" Trisha asked.

"That's Cletus," Glenn said. When Trisha said, "Hi, Cletus," the crowd hooted, and he said his real name was Clyde. Trisha replied, "Cletus, Clyde, what's the difference?" The crowd hollared.

"I can't believe I'm asking this, Mac," Trisha said, "but how do you figure the odds?"

"Two to one he'll go through with it."

A decidedly female roar arose from the surrounding tables.

"But we had to call the whole thang off," Mac continued, signaling with his hands for the ladies to simmer down.

"Yeah, Baby Bro wanted in on the action, himself, he-hee," broke in another Glenn clone. "And Glennie wanted to bet it wouldn't happen, which is when the beautiful Natalie put a stop to it."

"For now," Mac said with a wink.

"Lovely," Trisha said. "Where is Nat, anyway?"

"Oh *shit*," Glenn said, pretending to look panicked. "I lost me a bride!"

"You wish!" Nat said, running full force to tackle her man. She'd been in the bathroom. Then she saw her friend. "Trisheeeee!"

"So Nat's been tellin' me yore married," Glenn said, not letting go of Nat, despite her attempts to extricate herself.

"I did not." Nat hit him in the chest; he coughed it off.

"Well al*most*," Glenn said haughtily. "I'm jest trying to offer my congratulations is all." He shook his head. "Don't worry, Trishie. You'll be next. I'll make the woman here throw you the boo-*kay*."

Nat rolled her eyes and finally disconnected herself from her flabby hubby-to-be.

"How are you?" Trisha asked her.

"*Exhausted*." Lower, she added, "Gawd, he can wear a girl out."

"That's right honey," Glenn said, pushing chest toward the sky. "You tell 'em." He sat and grabbed a biscuit, sopped with cream gravy.

Nat and Trisha ducked right back into the ladies' room. Nat blissed out at having someone with whom she could trash her sister (codename: Ogre), who continued to voice complaints about Nat's choice of red as a bridesmaid's color, as well as her pairing with Glenn's brother—with *any* of Glenn's brothers—for the big day, as well as Nat's barring her sister Katrina's infant daughter from the ceremony. "She actually threatened to boycott," Nat said. "She says no one in this state is qualified to take care of her precious baby. I should *be* so lucky."

Trisha rolled her eyes. She'd planned to tell Nat how awful the Ogre had been to *her*: She refused to let Trisha contribute to any of the shower planning, then had the gall to complain that Trisha had done nothing to help. Now she decided Nat had plenty on her mind.

Too soon, the girlfriend of one of Glenn's brothers entered, and the girls headed back into the main bar area. Trisha met three long-haired strangers who introduced themselves as Nat's high school friends and fellow bridesmaids, Terri, Jeri, and Mary. They looked like triplets, but as she talked to them, Trisha realized it was just the similar bleach-blond hair, dark tans, and colorful makeup.

Someone poked at Trisha's back. She turned to see a girl with an outrageous poof of blazing red curls, eyes buried in black mascara, staring intensely at her. "Got a smoke? We need smokes. Desperately seeking smokes." She sounded like Minnie Mouse. She glanced at the person beside her—which was James, it turned out—and giggled. Both of them already held lit cigarettes.

"Sorry, no," Trisha said. "Hi James."

Almost immediately, it was time for the boys to go wherever they were going (reportedly, a strip joint in Houston) and the girls to a Chippendale's knock-off chosen by the Ogre. The bridal stretch-chariot could not have been more crowded. Trisha enjoyed the naked, bow-tied boys more than she expected, probably due to the wine, but after four hours total of high-pitched screeching in the car and three more in the bar, all she wanted was to bunk down at My Cousin's place.

Standing at last at the motel lobby door, she heard Nat call her name. "You know where we're meetin' up, right, girlfriend?" Nat asked. "For the party?"

"Another party? *Tonight*?"

Hearing Trisha's reply, Nat gave her a pained look. "I'm the bride," she said. "You *have* to come. Just for a while?"

Trisha sighed and nodded. "Just let me get out of these smoky clothes."

"All right," Nat said, wagging her finger, "but if I don't see you there…. " She never finished the threat, having been dragged off by Terri (or maybe it was Jeri).

Trisha wanted more than anything to run a Jacuzzi and order *Good Will Hunting* on Pay-Per-View. But she could hear at least two sets of revelers from her room, and besides, how many times did your best friend marry? (She chose not to think about that *too* carefully.)

Before she set out, she sat on her bed and thought about alcohol. She liked to keep a tight reign on this aspect of evenings out. Typically, her M.O. was to consume two alcoholic beverages per evening, getting them out of the way quickly, so she wouldn't lose track of how much she consumed and would have some time for the effects to wear off. If she nursed a glass here, a glass there, she might accidentally do things she'd regret. She'd seen it happen often enough to her mother and Mitch.

She'd already doubled her usual limit, but it had been, what, at least three hours since her last sip. Did that start the clock again? She knew from experience it was no fun to hang out with people far drunker than herself. She made the executive decision to nurse one final drink throughout the course of the long night. Two, tops.

One of the younger Boshanks—"Scooter" or "Cooter," Trisha thought it was—worked in the dining room at My Cousin's, and, given his "in" with the owners, the boys had had no trouble setting up a full bar in a ground-floor room without fear of discovery. They temporarily cleared the adjoining rooms of all furniture, save the chairs. The lone decorative item was a shiny blue CONGRATULATIONS banner strung, crooked, above the bar.

"Rit-tis-way," Chuck Boshanks said as he steered Trisha into the "bar" room teeming with people. (Trisha suspected that many had no relation to the wedding party at all.) "We got acid, we got 'shrooms, we got happy gas, we got all kinds o' pharmaceuticals. Hell, we got E, X, *and* ecstasy."

"Aren't those all the same thing?"

Chuck looked disappointed, as if Trisha were determined to cast a pall over the festivities. "Only if you want 'um to be. Anyhoo, we got herb, we got ganja, we got chronic, blunt, everthin' in between. You name it; Crazy Charlie's got ya covered. It ain't ever day a Boshank boy gets married."

"Just *most* days," a well-wisher in a gimme cap leaned over to interject.

"Thanks," Trisha said, "but I think I'll stick with wine."

Chuck whistled. "Ain't got no *wine*, I'm a-ferred."

"Beer, then."

"Suit yourself, li'l lady," he said, shaking his head. "But feel free to try one of our many other liquid specials, including my own personal favorite, the Septic Tank." He pointed her toward a line of kegs with little to distinguish them. Before she filled her cup, she stopped to admire the mammoth bar, complete with dozens of bottles and a serious-looking bartender in a maroon, black, and white get-up. She paused to watch him work.

"What's a Septic Tank?" asked one of the youngest Boshanks, wide-eyed and probably no older than fourteen, awaiting his chance at the bar.

"An extreme kamikaze, little man." Chuck put a hand on the boy's shoulder.

"What's that?"

Chuck looked around and lowered his voice. "See that wet rag in the bartender's hand? He makes a Septic Tank by wiping down the bar with it and the floor, too, and squeezin' it into a shot glass. And you add some Yager if there still ain't enough liquid."

"Oh." The boy turned white.

"Yeah," Trisha said quietly, "I think I'll stick with beer."

Chuck heard her. "Your progtive," he said.

Ever the conservationist, Trisha took one of the full plastic beer cups from a line-up on a nearby table rather than pouring her own. It was a bit warm, but, after all, it would mainly serve her as a prop. She struck up a conversation with Glenn's mother's cousin's daughters, twins named Stacy and Tracy, nurses in Baton Rouge who said they were exhausted from the drive to get there—and cranky, since, given their proximity to the kegs, people kept asking them what kind of beer there was. They suddenly stopped minding when Nat's sister's husband's (handsome) brother stopped to ask. (Actually, he asked Trisha, but Stacy and Tracy quickly enlightened him that *they* were the experts.)

Trisha took the hint and made the rounds looking for Nat, the reason she was here in the first place, but to no avail. Before she knew it, she'd consumed her beer, refilled with cold stuff, and had some of that to make the bad taste go away. She may have had a third cup, given that Chuck "borrowed" her almost empty glass as he tapped a keg. She felt very strange. Maybe she needed food.

After a while—she couldn't read the numbers on her watch—she spotted James laughing with some of Glenn's friends across the room. Fresh from the strip joint, she realized what a prude she'd been in college over that whole Hooters episode. It seemed so stupid now. She should tell him so.

"James!" she stumbled over and lurched into him; he went to great lengths to keep hold of his beverage. "Sorry!"

she wailed. "How are you?" She reached to grab his bicep, bulging as he held onto his beer for dear life. "Wow!" She raised her eyebrows, squeezed again and laughed. Then she patted his arm. "Listen, do you have a second?" She beckoned outside. "C'mere." She swung the door open wide.

The first thing Trisha saw upon leaving the motel room was the large, shiny, silver fender of a red-and-white pickup truck, the perfect seat for two. But its vantage point, just ten feet from the party, didn't offer the privacy she had in mind for her apology. It made what she knew to be her ridiculousness too obvious. She called for him to follow, saying this was important, and they circled the parking lot, their shoes increasingly filthy in the sandy Texas dust. Finally, out of dizziness and frustration, Trisha settled on a patch of dried-out grass and sat.

"So, how are you," she said.

"I'm fine. I'm not so sure about *you*."

"I'm great! Great. So sweet of you to ask, though." And really, it was. She reached to give his wrist a squeeze. "Listen, I just wanted to say…. Well, first of all, I *miss* you, Morales! Can you believe *that*?" Which wasn't what she was going to say at all. "You liking California? Because you always struck me as a New York guy. But the tan's working for you. Really, I mean, it totally is. She paused for a reply, but upon getting none, plowed ahead. Anyway, um, I just wanted to say … oh. Right. Remember that whole Hooters thing?"

"Hooters?"

"Yeah, you know, Hooters. I wanted to say, I mean, look at us. We all went to our little strip clubs tonight, and it was fine. I mean, totally fine. If that's the worst thing you've got to worry about, I mean, really!" She scoffed.

"Trisha." James cut her off. "Is this about Mitch? Because I don't think you have anything to worry about. My advice is: Go for it."

"*Mitch? No way!* This is not about *that*." She put her hand on his wrist.

It was just then, under a million stars, in the thick Gulf Coast air, with the Charlie Daniels Band and at least four-dozen partygoers and, in the distance, someone barfing as accompaniment, that Trisha realized what it *was* about.

She wanted to be with James, but had been too scared to admit it, even to herself. And he obviously had feelings for her, just like Nat always hinted. Wasn't it perfect that these thoughts and feelings should break through to the surface at Nat's wedding?

Could there be any doubt it was meant to be? Their paths had crossed too many times for it not to be true. How else to explain the visceral reaction she'd had when she'd first laid eyes on him? Didn't they say that love and hate were two sides of the same coin? Look at how they'd become friends against all odds—not once, but *twice*.

She had known they were bound together in a special way; even James's mother had picked up on this. But Trisha, and for that matter Graciella, had believed that Trisha was merely meant to discover James as an artist. Maybe so. But perhaps she was meant to discover him as a person, as a lover. In which case he was truly a starving artist. God, this was amazing!

"James." She looked into his eyes—his *eye*—and then chickened out and redirected herself toward the full moon. "This is sort of, um, embarrassing," she said, hand to her brow, "but do you remember when you said that I was— that I wasn't hideous?"

"Huh?"

"Remember? When Mitch and I broke up? I was upset, crying, and you said I shouldn't have trouble getting dates because I had a pretty face? You said some guys go for the 'sexy librarian' thing? I mean, basically, you said I was not hideous?"

"I, uh, prob'ly said something of that nature."

"Do you still think that?"

James hesitated. "You still look the same, if that's what you mean." He hesitantly stood and brushed off his jeans. "We oughtta get you inside."

He was scared. So cute! She was scared, too. "Because—" Trisha stood, too, and put her hand on his arm. "I'm thinking you're not hideous either. And, um, I think we should do something about it."

James did not react. He blinked, and breathed, and held onto a plastic cup, and presumably did some thinking. Trisha, meanwhile, tuned into the universe. Although she had removed her hand from his arm, she knew his pulse had quickened and the blood inside him thickened and pounded, sending out an electrical charge that her body received and logged in.

"We can go to my room," she whispered hoarsely, in case he had misunderstood. She tried to send the psychic message that whatever worried him, it was all right, they were friends, she cared about him.

But he wouldn't look at her.

At last came his reply. "Listen, Trisha, I'm sorry. I...can't."

Her throat tightened. She squeaked out speech before it could close completely. "*Can't*, or don't want to?"

He sighed again. "Both. Look, I'm, I'm, like, flattered, but you can do a whole lot better than me."

"Uh-huh." Trisha stood. "I sure can."

"Look. I'm not a dick. I don't *like* saying this shit, y'know, but—"

"Uh-huh." She stalked off. She listened for him to call after her, to make her stop and turn around, but he didn't.

"I was drunk, I was drunk, I was drunk, I was drunk, I was drunk, I was drunk, I was drunk." Again. *"I was drunk, I was drunk, I was drunk, I was drunk, I was drunk, I was drunk, I was drunk."* Trisha repeated her new mantra as she brushed her teeth for bed, spewing froth all over the motel room sink.

And then: *"Stupid stupid stupid,"* although she wasn't sure if this was directed at James or herself.

And: "Omigod," at the idea that he would share what had happened with anyone, with *Glenn*, although she knew he would not. At least, that's what she prayed. And: "God god god god," at the idea of facing him again.

Somehow she realized that confronting him again would be much easier now, drunk, at night and surrounded by unknowing friends, rather than later. Besides, she could not allow herself to be shamed out of attending her best friend's wedding bash (even if her best friend didn't seem to be in attendance). She made the decision—the remarkably *brave* decision, she thought—to rejoin the festivities.

She switched into a trailer-trash ensemble perfect for inviting the catcalls of the Bubbas, pairing a black corduroy miniskirt and a ribbed maroon tank top with spaghetti straps, which she'd originally meant to wear to bed.

Well, that could still be arranged, a naughty voice in her head said.

And then the *good* voice, the one that had masqueraded as the *real* Trisha Portman for the past twenty-seven years, had something to say: Weren't you supposed to call your boyfriend hours ago?

"Shit."

She ducked back inside, dialed, and got Tom's answering machine. *Yes,* she thought, and raised a victorious fist. Maybe she could even get away without his knowing that she was drunk. But then she blew *that* by leaving quite a long message: "Hi, Tom Thomas"—her new nickname for him, since she could never get it right the first time—"I'm calling again from the motel, still not catching you, I hope I gave you the right number which is...uh, which I left for you, and...I just wanted to tell you...uh, I love you, and I really miss you, and I really really wish you were here, and I'm sorry about our fight, and I think the reason I got so upset is that I really love you and miss you, and, uh, I hope you're having a good weekend, and I'm going to try to have a good one, but I really miss you. So—" Then the machine cut her off.

After reapplying her lipstick, she returned to the party, re-entering the main room with her head held high, reminding herself that James couldn't see very well anyway. She spotted Mitch on the makeshift dance floor in the center of the room, bouncing in his approximation of dancing to "Ice Ice Baby" amongst the big-haired Jersey girls. She waved and caught his eye; he pointed at her and gestured to let her know he'd be right with her. The song ended, and, using the bottom of his navy polo shirt, he wiped the sweat from his brow. Then he walked over to plant a sweaty kiss on Trisha's cheek.

"Hey there, Foxy," he said. "Isn't it past yer bedtime?"

"Didn't yer Maw teach you it ain't nice to mock the locals?" she said, laughing. Then she sobered a bit. "'Foxy?' You really think so?" She lapped up the flattery.

"Why I shorely do. Yew shore is purdy." He grasped her hand. "Will yew be mah Valentine?"

He coaxed her out on the dance floor.

The amateur deejay segued into Al Green's "Let's Stay Together." Mitch pulled her close, arms on her lower hips. Trisha wished that James, wherever he was, *could* see her. She closed her eyes and swayed. Who needed James, anyway? Mitch pulled her tighter; she felt his hardness. She peeked and saw that his eyes were closed; he was doing the white man's overbite, his front teeth grabbing hold of his bottom lip.

She began laughing, so hard she had to pull away and double over.

She recovered quickly and steadied herself. Gently, she bit the scruffy skin on his chin and worked her way up the side of his cheek. She wrapped her left leg around his body and rubbed the back of her calf up and down the back of his.

"Whatrya *doin'* to me," he murmured. "You're *killin'* me."

"I'll stop if you want."

"Don't you dare," he said.

"Oooooohhhhhhhwwg."

Trisha Portman was hung over. She could tell by the strength of the light coming through the motel curtains that it was well past 7 a.m., her usual wakeup time.

She looked at her watch. Well *well* past 7 a.m.

And then the full horror of the night before came back to her. She simultaneously heard and felt a rumbling behind her and realized—*someone was in her bed*. And she hadn't the slightest recollection how—he?—had ended up there. She remembered, vaguely, saying goodbye to Mitch, and she had never run into James when she'd gone back to the party. At least, she didn't *think* she had.

She took a deep breath and held it. With a pained look on her face, she turned around—and found Thomas, eyes flittering open, with a huge smile on his face.

"Hi!" he said. "I came in on the red-eye. Didn't want to wake you when I got in." He smiled. "Surprise."

Her breath exploded out of her like a popped balloon. "Hi," she said, and fell back onto her pillow, with a thankful grin on her face.

They lay there, smiling at each other, for quite some time. Then Thomas rolled over to the side table to get something. Instead of rolling back over, he fell to his knees. "Trisha, I realized something," he said. "I love you, and I want to be with you. Will you be my wife?"

Trisha looked at him, with her eyes wide open, and was just going to respond—when suddenly, a wave of nausea like none she'd ever encountered hit her stomach and head at the same time. She ran to the bathroom, decisively ruining what should have been the most romantic moment in their entire relationship.

The rest of Trisha's afternoon was a near-comatose blur. Later, she would vaguely remember sex and room service, with Thomas questioning her in depth about the college friends he'd meet at this event, making a special point of inquiring about her college boyfriend, Mitch. This worried her, although she was fairly certain she'd been a good girl the previous night—or at least not a bad girl. Not where Mitch was concerned, anyway. Given all the time she'd spent wondering why Thomas never got jealous, she couldn't believe he was doing so right now. But no wonder; he was a great lawyer. Two grunt-like syllables from her and he'd deduced that the power structure of the relationship had somehow shifted. He could sense *something,* probably her guilt over the James matter.

To avoid having him figure out anything *else* about her psyche, and avoid any awkward situations, Trisha insisted that she and Thomas bypass the afternoon's festivities and spend their first afternoon as an engaged couple together, perhaps by seeing what Brazoria County, Texas, had to offer. The best they could find in the motel's brochures was the Varner-Hogg Plantation, an Antebellum/Colonial Revival mansion in nearby West Columbia that was the former home of Ima Hogg. Trisha made a great show of wanting to see if her home was as ridiculous as her name.

Her two worlds finally collided at the rehearsal dinner. Even given the somewhat muted energy level of the crowd, it was a raucous good time. (One muted Boshank proved as entertaining as a roomful of people in high gear. What can you say about a mother who begins her son's toast with the immortal words, "For those of you who've been wondering, yes, Glenn *was* a master flatulator, even as an infant"?) Trisha realized how dumb she had been to worry; although James was at their table, he was entirely wrapped up in Polly, the redheaded smoker. And for all of Mitch's touchy-feeliness, he came off as a bombastic white management consultant-slash-wannabe player. Every time he came over and put an arm around her to say hi, she grabbed hold of Thomas's arm, putting both men in their proper place. And there were plenty of congratulations flying around, now that Trisha had her *own* fiancé. She sighed with relief. She'd had cold feet about Thomas, that was all—albeit *before* she got engaged. Thank God the waiting was over.

And then it was time for the big show. Nat and Glenn had the perfect ceremony, surrounded by the rest of Texas's white flowers as well as a capacity crowd, with Nat radiant and Glenn in a blue tuxedo (complete with a frilly shirt). It was the right mixture of class and home-style tradition; Glenn's brother's steel guitar band suited up in their tuxedos and banged out beautiful processional music. It took a good twenty minutes for all of the bridesmaids and groomsmen to make it down the aisle, because there were just so many brothers, and of course, several of them had to ham up their parts. (Nat would always appreciate the perfect timing she and Glenn had shown by getting married right away. Just another year, and Carly would have been too famous to throw such a shindig, particularly without the paparazzi catching on.)

The ceremony was fairly raucous until Nat walked down the aisle. The look on Glenn's face as he awaited his bride clearly showed the teddy bear desperately in love with the vision before him. Nat was beaming back, and it was all just perfect enough to make believers out of anyone who couldn't imagine how the Texas cut-up and the New Jersey princess could make this work.

From her perch up front, Trisha looked out into the crowd and found herself, as in a dream, looking at Thomas, who was beaming at her. But although she was entirely full of joy for her friend on the biggest day of her life, and although it looked as if Trisha herself were due to finally get exactly the same thing, something in her said that she could never count on a wedding as beautiful as Nat's—or a marriage as successful as this one, in all its improbability, promised to be.

2004

Love

New York

⊠

She stood on the sidewalk, hardly sheltered by an almost-leafless tree that seemed to think, months prematurely, it was fall. Every so often, she shifted an inch to the right, an inch to the left, seeking the paltry shade. She did this in part to keep her pale skin out of the sun, although she was far more concerned with staying hidden from the house across the street. She would have made a terrible spy.

The tiniest breeze stirred, just enough to kick up the odor of dog urine on the pavement. It was really too hot outside for a stakeout, particularly for someone—well, someone like her. She should have marched up and rung the doorbell twenty minutes ago; when the cab dropped her off; she'd had plenty of time to figure out what to say.

She told herself she was just being careful. In the past week—had it been just a week?—she'd learned that for now, at least, she wasn't all there. She'd left water boiling on the stove, the iron sizzling on the ironing board, her purse under a table at Starbucks—twice. She'd been honked at repeatedly by well-meaning drivers who didn't want to run her down. What if this, too, was a calamity waiting to happen?

The way her luck was running, the visit was bound to be detrimental to her wellbeing, or at the very least, her ego. But she felt drawn here by some invisible but very powerful homing device. There was an urgency about it. The first moment that she could, after her week of chaos and constant attention, she had sneaked away. Maybe this would help. Lord knew, nothing else had.

Besides, he probably didn't live here anymore, and if he

did, he surely wouldn't be home on a beautiful Saturday afternoon. Bolstered by the thought that this was just a dress rehearsal, she stepped out from behind the tree, crossed the street, squeezed between a dinged-up Datsun and an Accord with a sign that read NO STEREO AQUI and climbed the fractured stoop. She wiped her feet on the Astroturf welcome mat and pressed the rusted doorbell.

After a minute, she pushed again. And one more time.

She sighed and lowered herself into a squat on the top step. She had no plan B, hadn't even thought about how she might get home. Panic rose inside her; maybe this time it would take over entirely. She hoped it would, although she knew that hard-core Brooklyn was not the place for it. But, who would ever have guessed how hard it was, what an accomplishment, to go crazy? She hyperventilated, causing her heartbeat to speed up. Splotches appeared, blocking out her world. Her hands rose to her face and her body rocked back and forth. It felt good, safe, to leave her senses this way. She had done this so many times in the past week, but was obviously missing some crucial step. She had new respect for the insane.

A vision came to her, of a thug driving by with a gun and a grudge, of his bullet racing through her brain, ending her with a bang.

This was not an unwelcome vision.

Heavy footsteps sounded behind her; a door opened. "Yeah?" the man said. She turned and looked up.

He squinted, shielding his eyes with a palm; his eyes met hers but didn't see them. She had watched him wince in the sunlight before, knew it felt like the needles that once punctured his eyes in reality. She also knew he was waiting for her to speak, to identify herself, but she did not. Instead, she examined his face.

Even knowing what to expect, and although it had hardly changed, she couldn't help but recoil, not out of disgust but a fresh horror that so much pain in the world could settle upon one person. No longer a student or a young professional in Manhattan's looksist culture, however, she recovered quickly.

"Yeah?" he repeated.

She saw not a monster or an outcast but a man of profound pain, bad luck, and sadness. His scars spoke, saying: Look. This is what my life has been about. This is part of who I am, all that I am if I allow that. She wondered what her own face said, and shuddered. She was afraid to find out. Whatever it was, it was changing, dying, growing extinct.

"James," she said at last, more steadily than she'd said anything for a week. Had it been a week already? Having re-acclimated to his face, she could look past it to the changes in his physique. Where once had been sheer bulk sat clearly defined muscles, the kind built during many dedicated and lonely hours at the gym.

He wore no shirt, only the khaki work pants men wore now instead of jeans.

"Can I help you?" He hadn't placed her. She was hurt. But she could still walk away. Pretend to be a Jehovah's Witness.

She had decided to say what she had to say matter-of-factly. She had neglected to take into account that she had never before said it aloud, made it real in that manner. Halfway through, her voice cracked and blurred, as if a glass of milk had broken and coated the inside of her throat.

"I hope you can. I'm dying." She gasped and by sheer willpower wheezed in enough air to continue. "I guess in the end, I was right. I *am* the Most Fucked."

James sighed and rubbed his temples, and then he opened the door and waved her in.

She thought she could read what he was thinking quite clearly.

Damn. So much for my *Saturday.*

As Trisha brushed past him, she squeezed shut her eyes and tightened her hands into fists, unsure if they were meant for him or herself—or, maybe, for the cancer. She rolled her eyes to the ceiling and tightened her jaw, cursing herself for being so cheesy. And hating him, because she would not have felt so squirrelly and ashamed if he had not allowed or even encouraged it.

Jerk.

She hated herself for coming here. For having thought she needed anyone, having thought anyone could help her. Especially him.

Dick.

She brushed away the slobber with her shirtsleeve, preferring to ruin the linen of her blouse than to request a tissue. Shame churned in her lower stomach. She'd give anything to take back what she'd just said.

She wished she were here under other circumstances—to help *him*, maybe. She'd give anything to pretend, even for five minutes, that everything was normal.

As he went to his bedroom for a shirt, she sank into his black leather couch. It was amazing how fast the years had flown past, and how little had changed in that time. The Torture Room remained, the theme buried now under takeout menus, junk mail, paperbacks, coat racks, bookshelves. The Oriental rug had faded from black and maroon to gray and pink from exposure to the sun, the outlines muted with the accumulation of dirt. But now all one saw upon entering was a tasteful armoire housing a large flat-screen TV;

currently, the bottom half of an action star froze, mid-kick, sparing the jaw of his opponent.

James re-entered the living room from the bedroom, pulling a tight v-neck over his head. The influence of a woman?

"How have you been?" Trisha asked. "Did you like Stanford?"

James nodded.

"What are you doing now?"

"I went back to the bank for awhile, but it didn't work out. Then, some classmates and I started a business," he said. "A consulting firm." He shrugged. "It's probably about to go under."

"What do you do?" Trisha asked. "Will your skills translate into the open market?"

"CFO," he said. "Chief negotiator. Dick for hire."

"A job you were born to do." A wry smile hid in the corner of her mouth.

Normally, she would have nurtured her smile into a laugh, or brightened her eyes—added MSG to her personality, you might say. Age, and now tragedy, had erased her need to please.

"Are you dating?" She kicked the coffee table absently. "Or, I guess I should say, are you married?"

"No," he said. "Almost was."

He didn't ask, but she volunteered a few of her vitals. That she had left the gallery. That, after a failed bid to fund her own space, she had settled in at the Met, the largest of the large museums she had foresworn during her sojourn through the gallery world. "It has its plusses. I'm a full curator," she said. "American contemporary. Nothing you'd recognize." *Was* at the Met, she should say. *Was* among the youngest female full curators in the museum's history. Not that that mattered now, other than to plump up her *Times* obituary.

The course of her life had changed. Once, it was love, then marriage, then Trisha pushing a baby carriage.

Now it was different. First came disability, then death. Then nothing.

The minute she knew she would soon be dying was the minute she realized definitively that she no longer believed in the afterlife. She felt the nothingness as it approached, cold and dark and hard.

"Do you ever paint anymore?"

James shook his head.

"Would you tell me if you did?"

He smiled at last, shook his head again.

"—*ZZAWIP! ZAZZZIZAWIP!*" Having waited long enough, the action movie had kicked abruptly into high gear. The floor shook under their feet. James fumbled for remote that lay in plain view on his coffee table.

"Feel that subwoofer?" he yelled. "That's the DTS."

"The what?"

"It's like Dolby five-dot-one. Six-channel surround."

"Oh."

"You should hear *Saving Private Ryan* on this baby."

"I imagine."

"Wanna hear?"

"Maybe later."

She sighed, folded her arms, bounced her foot up and down, stared at the rug—all of these actions designed to make him realize what even an imbecile would see: that he should have asked about *her* by now. She kicked the ground, releasing clouds of dust, and lapsed into a coughing fit. "Could you"—she fanned her face and coughed.

"Something to drink?" she got out.

He nodded, returned with a glass of water. Miniscule bubbles danced inside, forming clouds. Trisha brought the glass to her face; it smelled sour, no doubt due to germs left over from an old sponge—a pet peeve. She set it down without drinking.

"Can I ask you something?" she asked.

"Shoot."

"Why haven't you ask me about . . .what I said?"

He sighed, pained. "You came here for a reason," he said. "Sooner or later, I figured you'd let me know what it was."

"Don't you give the tiniest fucking shit? About what I said?" She had read somewhere that swearing was the release of emotions by those who weren't smart enough to do it in a more charming manner.

Fuck whoever said it.

She watched the wheels turn in his head. "Not really," the answer finally came.

Trisha set her jaw and bit down, so hard that she wondered if she'd cracked her molar. "*God*. What's *wrong* with you?"

He shook his head briskly. "What am I supposed to say, exactly? You come in here after, what, how many years, and for whatever reason, and I'm supposed to be your—your—your I don't know what?"

Trisha shook her head. As usual, she tried to see the other side. James had experienced more pain than anyone she'd ever met. Who was she to expect him to feel for others?

"Like I'm supposed to sympathize? I don't do that easy. Especially when somebody's trying to drag it out of me."

Still. She was dying. She didn't want him to feel sorry for

her, but she did want him to be upset at the prospect of her being gone. Even as she thought about it, she realized how stupid that sounded. They hadn't seen each other for several years. Until an hour ago, for all he'd known, she could have been run over by a bus. He had never bothered to call when he came back from Stanford.

"Look," James said. "I don't know what state you're in. I just thought it was better for you to tell me what you want to tell me. Like a privacy thing. If it was me"—he shrugged—"I'd want to just be alone and tell nobody."

"Well, we're different. I guess I knew that."

James nodded.

"But if I died, you wouldn't cry?"

"I can't," he said.

She looked at him quizzically.

"My tear ducts got fucked up. In the fire."

"Oh. But... you wouldn't feel sorry?"

Another shrug. "I'd be—kind of sorry, I guess." He glanced at her. "Do you want to know the truth?"

She nodded.

"I wouldn't want anybody to go through the pain I went through, or my mom. At the same time, it's kind of nice to know that we aren't the only ones that go through it." He sighed. "And by the way, I think you'll probably find out that most people are like me, they're just too self-righteous to own up to it."

Trisha scoffed. "You wouldn't know that from the looks on people's faces the past week. You would have thought their world was ending."

"Who? Your family?"

Trisha nodded. "Sure. Everybody."

"That's not empathy, though. That's selfishness. They want things from you and don't want you to not be here to give it to them."

Despite herself, Trisha laughed. She had missed him. "You're nuts," she said.

"Probably."

She took a huge breath and slowly let it go, like the yoga teacher she sometimes watched on television at five in the morning.

Come to think of it, the way people reacted *had* been bothersome: the puppy dog eyes, tears, hugs, pity. As if they were looking at her for the last time. Like she was dead already. They looked through her, not at her.

She gave him the short version of what had happened. That a couple of weeks ago, she had felt a lump. That one week ago, the lump was just one of those things. How the doctor said it grew too quickly to be a tumor, how it was too big and painful to be a tumor, how the technicians were so sure it *wasn't* a tumor that they joked about it.

Then they came back into the room with ashen faces and reinforcements. They drew comfort from sheer numbers while she sat, the freak among them, the which-one-of-these-things-is-not-like-the-other. Some guy stuck her with a needle, and another looked at the cells under a microscope, and delivered even worse news, that of all breast cancers, she'd gotten the queen bitch.

How she knew it was bad when her primary doctor cried.

And how in the past week of hell, she had frozen her ass off, naked, having tests run on machines that had to be kept *very, very* cold (and they of course were more important than people who weren't long for this world anyway), and how she was scared as all hell, thinking that she'd been so unlucky that one of the tests *had* to go her own way, and how not one of them had. And how it was already in her lungs.

And how each doctor contradicted the previous one about the best course of action, surgery or no surgery, talking down to her while explaining the obvious, rushing through the incomprehensible.

Trisha told James all of this, not because she wanted him to know, not exactly, but because she wanted to make it clear How Fucked she was, as if God or fate would hear and realize an awful mistake had been made, pouring this all on one person.

And yet here was James, whose face proved that no one heard, no one cared, no one corrected this kind of mistake.

⊠

After Trisha brought him up to date, James folded his arms, leaned back in his black leather La-Z-Boy and squinted into the distance. "I don't mean to doubt you, but—I'm sure you've been told that a lot of this shit is curable with treatment."

"A lot of it is. Not mine. It's all over.... " She sighed. "And by that I mean not only that it's all over my body, but also that it's *all over*. Incurable. I'm terminal."

"Did the doctor actually say that?"

"I'm dying, and you're giving me the third degree?"

"Hold it." He raised his palms. "What exactly did he say?"

"*She*"—she paused to make the point—"said they'd do what they could 'to keep me around for as long as possible' with a 'good quality of life.'"

"Oh." He pursed his lips. "That does sound bad. That's what they told my mom at the end."

"God." Trisha began breathing loudly, like a bull ready to charge. "Nice knowing you."

"C'mon. You're obviously not dying *imminently*. Although, just in case: Will you leave me your couch? He paused. "And a word to the wise: I always thought sarcophagi were nice. Very vampiric." Seeing that the humor wasn't working, he added, more kindly: "Look it. Just tell me what you need from me, and I'll try to do it, and then you can leave or whatever you want."

"I don't know," she stammered. "I guess—I want advice." Actually, she was just realizing that she was *not* there for advice. She had no idea why she was there.

"About what? I never had cancer."

"Yeah, but you've been to hospitals."

He took a red rubber ball from his windowpane and tossed it at the wall, where it *thwaked* and bounced, loud and high, then fell back almost miraculously into his hand. He gained a rhythm at it. "Here's my advice about hospitals. They suck." *Thwak.* "The food's so bad you can't eat when you need it most, and you can't watch your favorite shows on TV 'cause they don't have good cable." *Thwak.* "Every time you start feeling almost okay, they come in and stick you for more blood." *Thwak.* "And you always get a crazy roommate who stays up all night screaming that he's pissing himself. And that's if you're lucky. Sometimes you get somebody who curses at you." *Thwak.* "And after a while, nobody comes to visit you, and there's this smell, *god* I hate that smell…." *Thwak.* "And they bug you to death about whether or not you had a bowel movement but heaven forbid you need something, like a pain pill; then you could ring the button for the nurse all day and they'd never come. They *never* get you the pain meds on time."

He stopped himself. "I'm sorry," he said. "I've lived with this shit for so long, I forget you don't know the drill. Maybe it's better you figure it out for yourself." *Thwak.*

"I just hope I have time to learn it."

"You will." He grabbed the ball and looked at her directly. "God, I'm fucking sorry. I'm sure everybody and their fucking dog is saying shit like that. 'You'll be fine.' 'You'll make it." "I have faith.' Bullshit! You need people to be real. To say, 'Yeah, you *should* be okay, buy you're gonna croak!' Well, I got news for them. We're *all* gonna croak. At least you know how you'll go—and everybody'll think you're really brave, like a fucking saint, and you'll have some pretty awesome painkillers, I bet. It's better than dying all alone in a fucking parking lot, all alone, bleeding to death after getting carjacked. Do I hear a 'fuck yeah?'"

"Fuck yeah!"

"Fuck yeah!"

They smiled at each other.

James got up to pour them some Coke. Trisha glanced out his living room window. The sun had gone down; it was black outside. She glanced at her watch. It was 4 p.m. How bleakly fitting, that the days should be growing short now.

The cola burned her throat. Trisha had dry-swallowed a Klonopin, for stress, twenty minutes before, and now felt its gentle fingers massaging the insides of her head. She let her eyes glaze over. Thought about offering James one, but was too selfish for that. She might need them.

"Can I be honest with you?"

James snorted.

"What?" asked Trisha.

"What if I said no? Would that stop you?"

Trisha chose to ignore the criticism. "The only thing that makes me feel better is the idea that I've got a medicine cabinet full of pills, and if things get too bad, I can make it end. And...I wonder sometimes—why not just end it now, and save myself and my loved ones a whole bunch of pain?"

There. She'd said it. She'd been afraid to tell her friends and family, sure they would take her pills away from her, put her on a suicide watch.

She waited for James to call her a pussy, to tell her how a strong bastard like himself had lived through so many years of abuse and she could, too.

"Well?"

"I guess this isn't the PC thing to say, but Trisha, I contemplate suicide every fucking *day*."

"*What*?"

"You know how I can't sleep? Lots of times I just pace the floor, trying to think of a reason not to do it."

"What do you come up with?"

He exhaled loudly, continuing to stare across the room.

"Use to be, I'd think about Ma. How she was worse off than I was and she could take it. How she'd be the one to find my body, and it would just kill her."

"Now?"

"Now? It's tough."

Trisha sat with the silence for a while. "I could tell you were feeling really down that time at the McNeill building," she said. "You know, when we were on the roof? Is it always that bad?" She felt guilty for not trying to help him, although she had no idea what she would have done.

He sighed. "It was especially bad right then. My mom was dying," he said, "but...yeah."

Trisha sat up straight. "Wait a minute. Your mom died while we were still in college? That's impossible! She seemed fine!"

"Not while we were there, but right after." James shrugged. "She was good at pretending she had energy," he said. "She took a turn for the worse." He looked down, opened his mouth to say something, closed it again. Then said, quietly, "She was really happy for you. About the job and all." He didn't look at her.

"God! Why didn't you tell me?"

James didn't say anything, but when Trisha thought back, she remembered what was going on at that time. James had caught her with Mitch, and then Trisha had disappeared for days.

"I'm so, so sorry, James," Trisha said.

He waved her off.

"So, how would you do it? When you think about it."

He shrugged cynically. "Throw myself under a bus. Whatever. If you really want to do it, it's easy enough."

They sat in silence. Like an amputee reaching for her lost limb, Trisha found herself wanting to tell him how important it was that he live, wanted to talk him out of it, but her reasons sounded hollow. "Well, now you can think about me," she said at last. "I mean—I know I don't mean that much to you. So maybe it won't work. But...I need you around while I go through this. You don't even have to be around. I just need to know there's someone else out there who knows what it's like to suffer. God, that sounds cruel, doesn't it? Like, I can't be happy so I don't want you to be."

"Misery loves company." James cracked a rare smile. "I swear, before long you'll be just like me: going out of your way to make others miserable."

Trisha laughed. "See? I need this. And I need someone who won't tell me they know what I'm going through when they have no idea. Who won't say, 'You could live for years and I could get hit by a bus tomorrow!' You have *no idea* how many people have said that. It's a tiny bit different when you're strapped to a ticking time bomb. And if *one more person* tells me that if Lance Armstrong can beat it, so can I, I'm going to go ballistic. *He had a different disease*, one that's curable. Mine? Like, no one in the history of the world has ever survived metastatic stage IV breast cancer that's this far gone. I'm going to die. It's a reality. They should deal with it." By now, tears—of anger? rage? relief?—flooded Trisha's face.

"Believe me, I would never 'Lance Armstrong' you," James said. "I want that fucker to die! Arrrrgh!" He raised a fist.

She smiled and joined along with him. "Death to Lance Armstrong!" she said.

"So, in all seriousness, do we have a pact?" Trisha asked. "You won't check out 'til after I do?"

"How exactly long have you got, again?" His crack fell on deaf ears. "No, seriously, I'm in," he said. "As long as you save me some pills."

"And...you're the only one I can ask. If I need help, you know, doing myself in? Will you help me? Get me pills? If I'm in pain?"

James raised his eyebrows. "Whoa," he said. "That's different."

"What the hell?" she said. "Breast cancer's, like, one of the most painful cancers to die from. My shrink—they gave me one at the hospital—she told me. She used to work at a hospice, and she said even just a couple years ago, they had no painkillers that could touch the pain, that euthanasia was the only humane thing to do. So don't let me lie there and *hurt*."

This was it, she realized. The reason she had come here. Nat—not Carly; she could be no one else now that life was too, too real—had already turned her down, had insisted that she fight to the end. "For me," if nothing else, Nat had said. Trisha needed someone who would be there for *her*. And most of all, she needed to know that she could exercise some control, even over the end. "I know there are still museums to visit and sunsets to see, and—I'm not depressed—I don't want to die," Trisha said. "I'm not like you. *I don't want to die.* But if I have to die, I want it to be...*okay*. I don't want to hold on for weeks in some stupid hospital bed, delirious with pain."

"I just don't want to be, you know, legally liable. Jail sucks."

"I thought you were going to be dead."

"Well, you know," he said, "you got to keep your options open."

James said he was hungry. Trisha followed him to a burger joint across the street. Now that she had *carte blanche* to eat whatever she wanted—who cared about fat and calories when you were dying?—she had no appetite. She felt it was almost a betrayal that *James* could eat, given her situation.

She'd heard before that the human mind can't fathom a world without itself. She was finding out just how self-centered her life really was, now that it was ending.

Over dinner, they talked about God, and the lack thereof. They both considered themselves agnostics. Trisha had been raised as a good Catholic and felt safe "just in case" the whole Christian thing panned out. "But I feel a real peace that it just...ends," she said. "I've had a good life. That's enough."

"I haven't," James retorted. "I want to be reincarnated. As the next Britney Spears."

"As a *woman*? That's a surprise."

"Course. I want to fondle my tits all day," he answered in utter seriousness.

"Can I ask you the truth?"

This, as they walked back to James's apartment. It drew time for Trisha to leave, to once again face reality, in the guise of her torn-apart loved ones, who probably thought she *had* jumped in front of a bus. She had left a note saying not to worry, but she saw, now, that that could be misinterpreted. But somehow the only one who tore at her heart was Baracus. When Nat had gone off to become famous, she had given Baracus to Trisha. Although Trisha had been reluctant to take on the responsibility—and Tom had never become a big fan—the dog had been a loving and faithful companion. What would he think, when she finally left him for good? How long would he wait, watching the door, for her to come back? Days? Weeks?

Suddenly, she wanted to go home.

"What did you want to know?" James asked.

"I suddenly feel the need to know the truth, the real truth, about everything. Did you ever think we could be together? Because I sometimes did. I wondered, if you hadn't…looked the way you looked, if we would have gotten together. Not that I didn't, don't, find you attractive, because I did. Do. I mean, obviously I did, I got totally drunk and made a pass at you. I just mean, I figured you didn't make a pass at me, or didn't take me up on it, because you were afraid. Nat and Glenn, they always said you were in love with me. I never really believed them, but…what do you think? Really."

She had gone too far. He looked as if he'd been slapped. It occurred to her then that in the same way she was in denial about dying—that she knew it and did not know it simultaneously—that he had not faced the complete truth about his appearance and how it put women off.

"I'm sorry," Trisha said. "I'm all screwed up right now. I don't know what I'm saying."

"I'm not in love with you," James said curtly. His voice was in marked contrast to how it had sounded earlier. It sounded serious. Perhaps angry.

"I didn't mean anything by it," Trisha said. "It's a compliment, really. Because sometimes I thought of you. And wondered. Like that time we got drunk. Like, *every* time we got drunk."

"Huh," he said. "That's nice."

"So, really? You never thought of it at all? Not even for one split second? I won't make a big deal of it; I know you think about *every* woman, or most of them, and wonder. You must have wondered about me."

"Trisha, don't take this the wrong way, because you're like one of the most feminine girls I know, but you were always just…one of the guys. I guess because you were Mitch's girl. And I hated you when we met. And then you always had a boyfriend. It was just never an option."

"You can honestly say that you never thought of me in that way?"

"I never thought of you in that way."

"Huh," she said, subconsciously mimicking him. "Good to know. Now I feel like an idiot." Who might at any moment start to cry.

"Don't feel like an idiot. Look at me." She did. "Don't feel like an idiot."

She sat back down on his couch but never got fully comfortable. She was just killing time now, waiting until that awful conversation passed over and she could leave without it being the main thing on their minds. "You mentioned…pain. What about it? What do you do when it's eleven on a scale to ten?"

"Have you had any yet?"

Trisha shook her head and coughed. "Only when I touch one of the tumors."

"Don't think about it until it happens. It just makes it worse," he said. "You've got my number, and when you start feeling it, give me a call and we'll talk."

"Okay." She got up to go. "So look. I know you don't want to hear it, but thanks."

James nodded, although he hardly seemed to register what she said. "I stay up real late," he told her. "You can call whenever."

She was halfway out the door when James called to her. "Oh and Trisha," he said, "Welcome to the club."

◻

Trisha's next week was as bad, if not worse, than the previous one. She had surgery to remove her breasts ("to reduce the cancer load," the doctor explained). Given the circumstances, the doctors advised that reconstruction put her too much at risk of infection (she nonetheless insisted on getting implants). Just four days later, right after leaving the hospital, she reported back to begin chemotherapy. A nurse inserted a strong chemical fluid into her veins, one that made her vomit repeatedly throughout the course of several days. Within weeks, it would make her lose her hair.

She didn't hear from James throughout that time, although neither did she take him up on his offer to call.

Of course, she was never alone. Nat insisted on leaving the scene of her first big-budget movie, in which she starred opposite Brad Pitt, for the week; she flew in with Glenn and her personal assistant, Jeffrey. Trisha's mother, Melinda, likewise appeared from out of town; she was never without a new box of Kleenex and her cell phone, with which she rang her friends to deliver the latest at the least appropriate times. Her new co-workers sent a huge fruit basket, and even Gresh stopped by the hospital momentarily, on his way to nearby tennis courts, to deliver her some Drum and rolling papers. "Thought you might want to take this up now," he cracked.

Tom had not been told. Trisha had briefly softened and called him, but when she got through on the phone, he snarkily asked why she hadn't signed and sent him the latest version of the divorce papers.

"I've been sick," she told him.

He scoffed and then said, "Stop trying to make me feel guilty, Trisha."

She hung up without further explanation.

Despite Trisha's attempts to discover the relative difficulty of each procedure, nothing was as she expected. Surgery involved no pain, and she woke up with so much gauze on her chest that she felt, for the first time in her life, like a C cup. (She *almost* looked like one, if she wore just the right type of bulky hooded sweater.) Life in the hospital was a little like a vacation. Jeffrey made sure she was never in want of movie mags, Häagen-Dazs, and pictures of Baracus. She even got to order up a free foot massage.

She'd been similarly afraid of chemotherapy, but the process itself was nothing; she could watch DVDs while the medicine drained into her. The nausea was bad, but not as bad as she expected. At least she was back home, with little pain and lots of painkillers—a beautiful combination. She didn't have to work. Baracus stayed by her side, thrilled to have his human companion around constantly. As long as she stayed relatively still, she had all the breath she needed.

If this is what my new life will be like, Trisha thought, I can handle it.

Then everyone went back to work.

During the divorce, and all that led up to it, Trisha realized how much she'd pulled away from the rest of the world—just like so many married women. Now she woke up to find herself with few sources of comfort.

She had known all along that Nat had to resume her normal life. Every time it came up, Trisha wanted to kick and scream that *her* life, the little that was left, would never be "normal" again, dammit, and how could they spend their hours doing their petty jobs if they truly loved her? But of course she didn't say it. Glenn, in an ill-guided attempt to make Trisha feel better, had the gall to say that Nat needed to work to keep *herself* sane, because she loved her friend so very much. He reiterated that any time Trisha needed them, they would be there.

I need you now, Trisha wanted to say. *And now and now and now….*

And to her credit, Nat knew this. Jeffrey let it slip that she'd turned down a role opposite Tom Cruise; she promised that just as soon as Brad had his way with her, she was all Trisha's. They'd once again lie around on the couch, watch *Oprah* and reruns of *Sabrina the Teenage Witch,* and talk about boys. *Until you die,* Trisha added silently.

But for now, Nat would have to go.

They had several heart-to-hearts about hair loss before she left. The very thing that had the doctors unconcerned was the most upsetting for Trisha.

"You know, it'd be hard to name a single Hollywood movie where both the stars have their real hair," Nat said, trying to be comforting. "Know how the starlets always have short hair one month, then Jennifer Aniston-style shit the next? Wigs! And extensions! And as for toupees—"

"It's different for the men," Trisha broke in. "And there's a big difference between having short hair and being *totally bald.* I mean, really: I don't hear anybody offering to shave their head in solidarity."

Nat gave her a woeful look. "Do you *really* want me to?" Earlier, she'd sworn up and down she'd do it if Glenn would let her, but he kept reminding her that Carly would be in violation of her contract. He also joked that he'd divorce her if she did it anyway. Even if he was joking, that hardly made Trisha feel better.

Reluctantly, Trisha said that Nat shaving her head would do no good: Nat was so beautiful, she'd look *great* bald, making Trisha look and feel even worse.

"I mean, really," Trisha said, "aren't my boobs and my life enough?" Actually, she had visions of overdosing before her hair started to go, but she didn't tell Nat this. "It's like, when I was being diagnosed, I was praying: Please, God, not the hair. Does that make me the vainest person on the planet? That I'd rather get my breasts cut off, throw up repeatedly, and die a slow, painful death than be *bald*?"

"No," Nat said. "It makes you a woman."

New York was home to dozens of wig shops. Although it would reportedly take Trisha's hair another two weeks to start its grand departure, on the day before Nat left, she accompanied Trisha to one of these shops: a salon-like space, all white, in an unmarked office building near Columbus Circle, hidden entirely from the street below. Once inside, a young blond man, gay as Sebastian, led them into a small cubbyhole housing a barber's chair. Trisha looked at the huge mirror and snorted. "I won't be needing *that*," she said, and turned her chair toward the wall instead of the mirror. Nat took a seat.

"Whatever makes you feel at home," the young man said. He introduced himself as Edward.

Trisha popped another Xanax as preparation for this experience, and perhaps as a result, she soon made the affable Edward her new best friend. It was a good choice: He sized her up, holding her head delicately, and then, handing Nat and Trisha copies of *Vogue* to peruse, promised to be right back. He returned seconds later with a wig that resembled Trisha's own hair except that it was ever so slightly blonder and much straighter. Although synthetic, it felt surprisingly real, if a bit overprocessed—like Barbie doll hair.

"Now, remember: You don't want to blow dry this baby, or stick your head in the oven to check on your meal—"

"Or to pull a Sylvia Plath," Trisha cracked.

"—or that, but otherwise, treat it like normal hair," he said. "Use hairspray and gel. Run your hands through it. And don't be afraid to get it wet." He instructed her to come back as soon as she was ready for him to shave her, in about two weeks.

Trisha's doctor, who had warned Trisha of hair loss and then never mentioned it again, had had one piece of advice: Buy only one wig, since that's all most people wear, and some patients don't like the way they feel on their heads anyway.

Trisha bought four, at $400 a pop.

And then Trisha was alone, waiting for the great exodus to begin.

Every night, she awoke and tiptoed to the bathroom, where, under the fluorescent lights, she got her fix. At the sink, she shook her head vigorously (but not *too* vigorously), and counted the strawberry blond hairs that fell out. At first she'd find three, or nine or seven; then twelve, and then, finally, more than she could count.

After *that*, she stopped shaking her head, or even touching it, so as not to disturb the precious strands.

Edward had said he would finish her off, but it was 4 a.m. when a huge chunk fell out, and he didn't work on Tuesdays. She would have to call James.

She was going to wait until after breakfast, but then tragedy struck: A clump fell into her Cheerios. She ran to the phone, leaving her cereal to go soggy.

It was clear from the sound of James's voice that when he'd said to "call anytime," he meant, "except morning."

"Mnnyeah?" he said.

"James," she said urgently. "Do you shave your head? Can I borrow your head shaver?"

"Aaahuh?"

"It's Trisha. A head shaver. I need a *head* shaver. A thing to shave your head with."

"Uh…yeah."

"I need to borrow it *right now. My hair is falling out.*" And according to Edward, she couldn't wear the wig until she removed her real hair, which made the wig look huge, fake, puffy.

"Uh…when do you want to come over?"

"How about *now*?"

"It's Tuesday morning," James said. Then he sighed. "Yeah, okay."

She hid her face on the subway all the way to Brooklyn, imagining that people were staring at her, belatedly concerned about the possibility of a bald patch in the back of her head, praying she wouldn't leave a mountain of blondness behind in her seat. She didn't relax in the slightest until had reached James's place and been waved in.

"Hey, Kojak," he greeted her, chuckling. He was dressed in a stained white t-shirt and white boxers, with a beige towel over his shoulder. He smelled like Irish Spring.

"Would you mind just giving me the razor? I want to get this over with." Trisha held out her hand.

"Oh no you don't," James said. "I get to watch this. Anyway, you ain't going to want to do this yourself," he said. "It gets kind of exhausting."

"Don't you need to get to work or something?"

"Nope," he said.

Trisha's gut instinct was to tell him to leave her, but then she considered. At least James had had lots of practice. She peered at him through increasingly sparse lashes. "All right," she said. "All right. But it's going to take me a while to get ready." She reached into her pocket and pulled out a medicine bottle. She dosed herself with one pain pill, one long-acting anxiety pill, and a short-acting "rescue" drug.

Then she went to sit on his couch and wait. He sat across from her, reading a cheesy mass-market paperback.

"You know, I hope you're going to get some kind of twisted pleasure out of this," Trisha declared. "Out of my misery."

James shooed her away. "It's not like that," he said, but he didn't say what it *was* like.

When the time came, he pointed her into his narrow kitchen and pulled out a rickety chair for her. He put the thinning brown towel over her shoulders. Before she had time to catch her breath, she heard the *bzzz*—an angry bumblebee coming for her, said her over-medicated brain. She did a mock Catholic blessing, and then covered her face with her hands completely as the cold razor touched the nape of her neck.

"All right, Meatball, you ready?"

Trisha jerked away. "What did you do, put that thing in the freezer when you knew I was coming?" she asked. She felt numb and hurt. When he didn't answer, she screamed, at the top of her voice, "When did *you* start balding?"

"Who's balding?"

He ran the razor up the center of her scalp. "What are you—"

"How would you look with a reverse mullet?" James chuckled.

"That's *not funny! What do you think you're—*"

"Might as well laugh about it!" James yelled over the loudness. "What else are you going to do?"

"But—"

The machine chugged…to a…halt.

"What the—"

"Uh-oh," James said. "It did this once before."

Trisha heard him shake it, blow on it. She refused to raise her hand to see where they were in the process, but things didn't feel good.

"You can't leave me like this." Trisha put up her hands to shield the top of her head from his sight. "You *can't*." She was getting increasingly hysterical. How much better it would have been if she had done this in the privacy of her own bathroom. Even as she told herself that, however, she knew that there, she would have crumpled and died. Like she might anyway. "I don't care if you have to walk from here to Manhattan to buy another one of those things," she said, "you're going to finish the job."

James laughed. "Don't worry," he said. "I'm just messing with you." He turned it back on to finish the job.

"Fuck you!"

She shivered every time the razor touched her scalp. She wanted to be home, curled up in bed. But then she imagined her cold head on her pillow.

"Are you almost done?" Blond chunks of all sizes fell into her lap.

"Yeah," James said. "Done." He turned the machine off. He walked around to the front to admire his work. There was a long silence.

"Well?"

He shrugged.

Now, when she tiptoed to the mirror in the middle of the

night, she forced herself to look. She saw a genderless freak, or, worse, someone with cancer. She wanted to hurt herself, or lock herself in the bathroom and never come out, or force everybody in the world to shave their heads, too. To think that just the previous month, she had fretted over whether to have Andrea, her stylist, take off two inches or three.

"How are you?" her mother asked her on the phone.

"I don't feel so good," she said, "and the wig makes my head sweat."

"Look, sweetie, you won't be bald forever," Melinda said. "Like the doctor said, your hair will grow back on some chemos."

"I don't believe him. I don't think I'll ever find a nice chemo that works."

She had already memorized the bleak statistics: Hair grew one-fourth to one-half inch a month. Six inches, at best, a year.

She was too afraid to look up the other statistics, the medical ones; about what it meant that her third chemo in a row wasn't working.

She cursed society for valuing those stupid dead cells in the first place. Why, *why*, did everyone pay heed to them, precisely cut and dye and twist them into sculptures? Why didn't anyone say *no*, I will not buy into that vanity, it's much easier to shave the shit off?

She took a hand mirror, held it up, turned around to gauge the patchiness of the stubble left behind. Sat on the vanity so she could get a closer look.

Why, after so many years of administering chemotherapy, had no one come up with a way to keep those damn follicles from giving up? *Because the doctors don't give a shit,* came the answer. *Screw them.*

Sometimes she walked in, looked in the mirror and sat, with her hands over her face in horror, for twenty or thirty minutes. She could understand, now, why James had removed the mirror from his medicine cabinet.

How did she look bald—objectively?

Her hair had always been the focus of her appearance. Now, her aquiline nose, long neck, and high cheekbones gained prominence.

That was okay. But given the lack of eyebrows and eyelashes, her face looked like a big toad.

She ran into an old acquaintance, a gallery owner who hadn't heard the news. "Your hair looks *great*," the woman said. "You changed it, right?"

It would have been easier to accept the compliment and go on her way, but that would be a lie.

"It's a wig," Trisha said. "Cancer."

"Oh my God. I'm so sorry," the woman said, holding her hand across her mouth. "Well if it's any consolation, I like it better than your real hair."

Trisha wasn't sure what to think about that.

When she walked down the street she felt like a fraud. She lived in fear that a spontaneous monsoon might arise and blow the hair off her head, despite the toupee tape she'd liberally applied to her scalp.

When she removed the wig at night, she felt, for the first time since her diagnosis, sick. Really sick. Now there was a visible manifestation of her illness.

She thought back to picture day in the second grade, when she developed a hideous cold sore *on her nose*. She "ran away," to 7-Eleven, but the teacher found her and forced her to have her picture taken anyway. Forever after, she would remember the girls whispering about how she was dirty and the boys pointing and yelling out, "Didja get into a fight?"

She was different, cootie-infested, weird.

She thought about the bad haircuts that made her look like a miniature housewife, an elf, a boy, that meant weeks and months of desperate wishing that she could turn back the clock and tell the barber to hold his scissors, that caused such burning shame she made herself physically ill.

She recalled standing in the bathroom for hours, trying on every hat her mother owned, experimenting with this barrette and that ponytail holder, with gel and mousse and styling liquid. She remembered accidentally singeing her hair with a curling iron, leaving her with fried frizzy hair. She relived the time she home-bleached her hair red, which turned a sallow orange-yellow.

Add together all of these tragedies, each of which seemed like the end of the world, and it didn't come close to losing her hair. Instead of making her seem ugly, or a little beauty challenged, she now felt like a *freak*, a leper.

Every morning she painted on her fake eyebrows and eyeliner. There was no need for mascara; she had no lashes.

She stared enviously at men with comb-overs or fringe around the sides. She wished, fervently, that she were a boy, so she could get away with being bald.

Her stomach burned constantly until the second she could get home and rip off the wig. She could understand why other sick people went without, showed their pasty white scalps to the world, wore bandanas—but she could not. She wanted to "pass," was not ready to admit to the world that she was Not Like Everyone Else.

She had told herself that it was worth being bald if the chemo added a year onto her life, but then she got the results of a CAT scan showing that for all her sacrifice, it was hopeless. The tumors, and there were many, grew fiercely. Her sacrifice was futile.

She called James in the middle of the night—his prime time, judging by his alertness upon picking up the phone. After exchanging pleasantries, she started in.

"How do you do it?" she blurted out.

"Do what?" he scoffed. "Be ugly?"

"No—I was going to say *be bald*—"

"Which is pretty much the same thing," he said. "I figure, people don't like the way they look, fuck 'em."

"So that's why you don't wear the eye patch." He grunted.

"And the dark glasses and loud music—that's to block people out." She sighed. "I have to say, I've gained a whole new respect for you. I can't handle this, and I can hide it under a wig. The idea of walking out without the wig, even for a second…. I couldn't do it. And add that to going blind, and for all I know you're in pain."

"Don't," he said. "Least I'm not dying of cancer."

"So how are you?" she asked. "How's the suicide watch?"

He sighed. "It's getting tougher," he said quietly. "The other night was really bad. But I was thinking it would be an affront to you. You know. You want to live and here I am, I'm perfectly healthy, and I don't even appreciate my life."

"Yeah, fuck you," she said.

"Watch your mouth."

"Anyway," she said, "for what it's worth, you're not ugly."

"Fine. But what I know is, people act different to me because of how I look. I can see right through their bullshit. And it sucks. Everybody feels sorry for you, I *hate* that, and people are trying to figure out what the fuck's wrong with you. And you can never, ever forget that you're different, even on the best fucking day of your life, not for a second."

He paused. "Did I ever tell you that I really used to like kids? I helped Cindy and her mom—they owned a child-care center. And after I got better, I went back, and all the little kids would take one look at me and start to cry."

"While me, I'm so shallow," she said. "If I get a *pimple*, I feel bad about myself. It must be like that, only magnified about a *million* times."

"No offense, Trisha, but you have no fucking idea what it's like. No one can understand me, and if they say they do, it's only because they've got their own selfish motivations."

"What are *my* reasons, then?"

"Guilt. You want to feel like a good person. That's why you hang out with me at all."

Trisha could hardly breathe. She'd *just* been feeling guilty. He read her too well. "What if I just *like* you?"

"You don't."

"How do you know?"

"Because I go out of my way to be unlikeable."

"What? *Why*?"

"Weeds out the phonies. I have far more respect for people who hate me," he said. "Of course, I hate them, too, so basically I have no friends."

"That's bullshit," she said. "You treated Cindy like a queen."

"Yeah, but—" He paused. "That's about manipulation. You can't be real friends with somebody you think is hot, 'cause then all you can think about is getting laid."

Trisha sighed. "You treat me okay." When James didn't say anything, she continued, "But you're probably using me in some way I don't know about, right?"

"Something like that."

"Or maybe you think of me as a real friend. I know that would be a first for you, but think about it. It just might be possible."

She paused. "Nah," they said, snickering in unison.

The chemotherapy made Trisha increasingly tired and nauseated. For the most part, she felt too depleted to call her friends and family to talk about her condition—what good would it do, anyway? But every night, she developed a depressed insomnia around 1 a.m., which more often than not resulted in a call to James (who apparently never slept). He would listen to her rant about how shitty life was treating her. Then his firm folded, rendering him as acutely miserable as she.

So James came up with a plan. "I'm usually the last one to try to make things *happy*," he jeered, "but I remember you saying you never been to Coney Island. It's a good time of year to go." And they didn't even have to wait for the weekend, since neither had anyplace to be.

Trisha broke away to wheeze for a minute and then returned to say yes, wondering if she had the strength.

She wondered even more when the day they chose, Thursday, dawned a little bit cold, a little bit wet.

"God, and it's freaking *May*," Trisha said to no one in particular as she walked, at a crawling pace, to the subway. Even so, she was out of breath; according to her latest CAT scan, she had at least a liter of fluid around one of her lungs. As an elderly black woman passed her, hearing the outburst, she mumbled, "Mmm-*hmm*."

Trisha made her way down to the large, dark wooden benches in the center of the subterranean station and caught a train that she rode deep into Brooklyn. When she got to his stop, she yelled James's name out the train door, some twenty-odd feet from where she saw him sitting.

"Yo!" she said, happy to see him. "Let's go."

Trisha smiled when she got a good look at him. He looked like a little kid dressed in his favorite articles of clothing: pulled-down Yankees cap, blue-mirrored sunglasses, a Nathan's Hot Dogs t-shirt covered by a thin jacket, jeans frayed at the bottoms, and flip-flops revealing gnarled, fungus-covered toenails.

He looks almost sexy, she mused. *What's wrong with me? Is it hormones?*

"Hey," he muttered and held out his hand for a high-five.

"So what's new?"

"Nothing," he replied. "Well. That's not true. Spent a while in the E.R. last night with Phil."

"Was he covered with red paint, or was it real blood this time?"

James replied, "He sort of…had an accident."

Trisha gave him a quizzical look.

James winced. "He set his clothes on fire. Lighting the bong."

Trisha just stared at him. "What was he—"

"I have *no idea*." James laughed.

"Is he hurt?"

James nodded—and pointed at his crotch.

"Oh my god!" Trisha raised her hands to her mouth.

"Don't laugh too hard," James said. "They said he's got, uh, like second- or third-degree burns. He's fried."

"He's got a 'hot dog?'"

James couldn't hold back on that one. "Girl, you are definitely losing it," he chortled.

"So what's there to see at this place, anyway, James?" Trisha asked.

"Oh god, like, a *ton*," he said. "There's the Cyclone—you

know the Cyclone, right?"

Trisha shook her head.

Then James had to shake *his*. "Dude, there's even a Brooklyn baseball team called the Cyclones. Didn't you ever wonder where that came from?"

Trisha shook her head slowly.

"This roller coaster's like, I don't know, maybe a hundred years old. It's wooden. It's a trip. There are other rides at Astroland, that's the amusement park part of it, and, like, arcades, and sometimes stuff like the Mermaid Parade, and, like, hot dog eating contests at Nathan's. But the Cyclone, that's the shit."

"Wow. You seem so happy."

James shrugged. "I love Da Isle," he said. "My pops, he always took me there." He looked down. In an instant, she imagined a bright-eyed kid, big for his age, worshipping the man beside him.

"I didn't know you knew your dad," Trisha said. "I guess I just assumed, because I never knew mine."

"That must have sucked," James said.

"I guess. I never thought about it."

Luckily for Trisha, who didn't feel like talking because of her increasing shortness of breath, James continued on in rare form. He loudly rehashed the lowlights of a gross-out movie he'd seen with Phil the previous week—unwittingly drawing the attention of an entire subway car full of people. Trisha nodded imperceptibly.

The car came above ground, and Trisha squinted into the sun to watch Brooklyn through the windows, smiling at dirt-caked signs and crumbling buildings straight out of a Seventies crime drama. A black boy in the next seat over peered out, too, whipping his head back and forth as he read "Avenue U. Avenue U. Avenue U." off the signs in a station. His younger brother, or friend or neighbor, hopped up to join him, repeating the phrase in unison without seeming to know what it meant. Then the car slowed and the boys jumped up to be first at the door, and Trisha knew they had reached Coney Island.

Trisha glanced at her watch. Eleven o'clock, as the sky could have told her, since it had finally reported to its job of baking the earth. She pulled down her sunglasses against the glare and zippered her purple fleece coat, then shivered and drew it to her.

They stepped onto the grimy wooden boardwalk and were at once bombarded with vendors hawking cotton candy and knock-off Yankees shirts to the off-season visitors. To their right, a few stragglers, looking for driftwood, walked the bottle- and bag-littered beach. Up on the wooden boardwalk, several deeply sunburned, shaggy-haired men with ballooning bellies—they might have been brothers—made little effort to restrain their hyperactive offspring. "Wow," Trisha muttered. Despite the biting ocean breeze, her cheeks burned. Something, sand maybe, stuck inside her lungs, and despite all the coughing, she couldn't get it out.

James happily inhaled the gritty air. "First things first," he said. "Dogs."

He made a beeline for Nathan's; Trisha lagged far behind. Up ahead, James stomped up and expertly pushed his way through the clamoring crowd, held up two fingers and yelled, "chili cheese"—winning his food as the cavemen once had, via intimidation. A profusely sweating employee obliged more quickly than seemed possible. Holding both plastic boats in one large paw, James pushed his way to the condiment bar and smothered the contents in ketchup and mustard, as Trisha tried to get in a word.

"Not so much ketchup for me," she said—too late.

"Oh." James turned, eyebrows raised. "Did you want one?"

"That's okay, I'll do it." Trisha blushed and started toward the counter. A moment later, she heard James call back that he was kidding. She joined him on a whitened wooden bench by the sea. Trisha picked up the overflowing, soggy bun. Some of the beany chili and then the dog itself slithered back into the paper cocoon. "Got a fork?" she asked, and James fished one out. "Don't say I never gave you nothin,'" he announced.

"Thanks." With a thin and therefore insufficient napkin, she gingerly brought the hot dog to her lips, careful to confine the sandwich to the area over the flimsy cardboard. "Mmm." She ate quickly, and listened, hypnotized, as a man with an Arabic accent attempted to sell a "real good bike" to everyone who passed—and occasionally to Trisha and James, who ignored him.

"So what is there to do now?" Trisha asked breathlessly, as she daintily ate her dog.

"That's it for you? One?"

"Girl's got to mind her figure," Trisha said. She'd lost twenty pounds lately that she couldn't afford. James raised his eyebrows at her.

James threw his left arm out from his side, inadvertently hitting Trisha as she brought the last chili-drenched bite to her face; simultaneously, the wind whipped at the polyester scarf she wore over her wig. She reached up reflexively, a tic she'd developed. She would never quite get used to the wig, or become comfortable *not* wearing it. "Goddamn it," she said.

"Why don't you just take the damn wig off?" James said.

"Hell no."

"I don't know *what* you're going to do at the Cyclone, then."

Trisha frowned, fretted, but decided she would figure that out later. They stood and walked, and the Arabic bike salesman followed. "Look at all this," Trisha said. "It *is* amazing." She looked up just as a more stationary salesperson, offering rusty saws and file cabinets and axes as well as dirty, naked Cabbage Patch Kids, feather boas, roasted nuts and a Seventies-era washer and dryer, yawned and reached into his pants to scratch his nether regions. To the right of his store, a stunningly obese woman in a muumuu—MADAME MARIA, said the sign above her head—lit a cigarette and waited for someone to approach her crystal ball. To *her* right, between stores and behind glass, sat a mechanized soothsayer labeled THE EYE KNOWS, so named for its single visible eyeball. Currently, it was unplugged (by MADAME MARIA, perhaps)?

Finally, to the left of the Five and Dime sat a building that left nothing (and everything) to the imagination: dozens of signs, in all fonts and sizes, proclaimed this a FREAK SHOW.

"God, I loved that shit as a kid." James chuckled. "Although sometimes, they just get real fugly women and call them mutants." He was halfway to the entrance.

"Fugly?" Trisha asked.

"Fucking ugly."

"I don't think that's very funny," Trisha said. "Can we get away from here? Now?"

"I'm going in," James said. "I want to see the half-man, half-monkey." He began to giggle uncontrollably.

"Suit yourself. I think it's really sad."

James actually did go in, for all of six or seven minutes, and came out admitting that he'd been taken. "But I had to do it for old times' sake," he said. "You know how it is when you're a kid: anything a little different and you think it's *weird*." He seemed wistful at the memories.

Trisha looked at him, searching for any hint of self-awareness. She found none. "What's next?" she asked.

They loitered on the boardwalk as a posse of pint-sized thugs in baggy pants and backwards caps ran to the freak show's entrance. The kids fidgeted and chatted—yelled, actually—waiting to be let in. They tried to jimmy the door, but it didn't budge. They finally started searching the entire boardwalk for the someone who could help, and then Trisha saw them hit upon the strangeness that was James.

"Look at *him*," one kid said. "*He* should be able to get us in."

"Yeah, but he might want our money. Maybe he's, like, a freelancer."

Trisha tensed. Loudly, she blurted the first thing that came to her mind, hoping to prevent James from overhearing their conversation.

"By the way, James," she said. "Do you ever hear from Cindy?"

The query caught him like a left hook. The right side of his mouth drooped, lengthening the gaps in his face like stretched holes in a block of soft cheese.

"Aaagh." He shrugged. "She was great when my mom was sick. Why, you talk to Mitch?"

"No way."

"There you go."

"Yeah, but you were *friends*. For a *long* time."

He shrugged. "What about Tom?"

She looked down and shook her head. She hadn't found it hard to be apart from him until she got sick. Then, she wanted someone who would go along to every doctor's appointment, every chemo treatment, share every trauma with her. She recognized that she really wanted someone she could bring down with her; so it was for the best, she always told herself, that she had no one. Dying alone was so hard. Although at least she had James.

"Have you even told him yet that you're sick?"

She shook her head.

James guffawed. "All that shit you say I should tell you about," he says, "and you don't even tell the person you dated for, like, five years, that you're sick."

"It was more like six or seven," Trisha said. "And…we were married."

She caught a glimpse of a man and woman swinging their little boy down the boardwalk with his arms; each had balloons tied around their wrists. She felt immeasurably sad. "What's next?" she asked.

"The Cyclone," James said. "Definitely the Cyclone."

Occupying a place of honor at the outskirts of the park sat the rickety wooden roller coaster, a patriotic landmark given its red, white and blue paint. Trisha eyed the slats and, when she thought no one was looking, dug her fingernails into the wood to test its sponginess. She was not reassured.

Above them, the giant creaked. James continually bounced up and down on the balls of his feet in anticipation. Ahead of them, in the good-sized line, several teenaged couples were making out. At first Trisha smiled at them, rooting for the guys and girls who probably never got the chance to do that during the week, until things turned grabby. "Kids these days," Trisha muttered under her breath. She felt old. And envious. Anger welled inside her, but James didn't notice the knuckles at her side, and as always, she willed herself to look at the bright side. She was here, alive, outside.

They reached the cashier, an old woman who took their money with a toothless grin. A sign behind her warned passengers to keep hold of all belongings, since things like sunglasses often fell off in flight. As James and Trisha made their way back and forth in a snaking line, like cows on their way to the slaughterhouse, Trisha wasn't sure why she was shivering. Was it the temperature or her dignity that had her upset?

Sighing, she pulled off her hair and then extremely quickly replaced the scarf on her scalp. She tied it tight, knotted it, and put her "hair" into her purse, which she promptly zipped up.

James clapped. "All right," he said loudly, making supportive hooting noises.

And then there was no escape: They had reached the front of the line. Trisha squeezed in first, and James followed her. When he got in, his leg touched hers. She scooted over but then fell forward as the car jolted and began to click-click-click its way up a very tall hill.

Even before it reached the top, Trisha screamed. The thought crossed her mind that maybe it was like watching a horror movie, that the anticipation might be worse than the fall. It had to be that way. Didn't it?

But that was not the case. When the car began its rapid descent, Trisha shrunk into James, looking for protection. She froze, barely aware of who or where she was at the moment, or how long this would take, or how it all would end.

James clamored to go again, but even he could see that Trisha was fading fast.

"Do you need food?" he asked her. "Maybe your blood-sugar level is low."

"Along with my white and red blood cells," Trisha said with a wry smile.

James offered to take her to Madame Mafarge's, a Russian restaurant best known for its vodka, but halfway there, Trisha got tired. As she sat on the bench, she changed her mind about dinner and insisted that she had no appetite.

James looked at her closely. "It's the nausea, isn't it?"

Trisha had told him that she was afraid to eat these days, because half the time she did, she threw up what went down.

"C'mere. I've got something for you. Top quality."

Miraculously, as the weather warmed, sitting on a board-walk bench was a viable option. James pulled out a small, flattened cigarette—unfiltered—and proceeded to light it up.

"But I've never smoked *anything*," Trisha said.

"Shhh," James said, looking around for undercover cops. "Take this."

Somehow, she did it right the first time, neither pulling too deeply nor nursing it. With James's instructions, she held it in as long as she could—which wasn't long, given her lack of breath. "Now you," she insisted, already paranoid.

They smoked almost the entire potent joint. James wanted to make a beeline for Madame Mafarge's—he had the munchies—but Trisha felt cozy, leaning up against him on a bench. She looked behind them, into the surf, while James sat face forward.

After a few minutes, however, trouble approached: "Sir, may I see a permit for that?" a loud, authoritative voice rang out.

Trisha's heart almost stopped—but James only laughed. He stood and gave a burly guy a huge bear hug. "How you been, man?" he asked, happily. "It's been forever."

He didn't bother to introduce Trisha, and she was surprised that he let her in on the guy's identity as he walked away. "Best guy I ever knew," James said. "Marc. That guy, he pulled me out of a burning building."

"*What?*"

Perhaps due to the pot, James had probably spoken without thinking. He sat for a very long time without answering.

"You might as well tell me," Trisha said. "As is obvious, I don't have long to live. Who am I going to tell? Besides, you owe it to me."

"How's that?"

"Because I told you so much."

He positively chuckled. "I had no choice," he said. "But good try." He paused and then took out a regular pack of cigarettes. Looked at it.

"Does it have something to do with your dad?" Trisha said softly.

"Okay," he finally said, "but we do this my way. No interruptions."

"O—" Trisha stopped midway and made the "okay" mark with her right hand.

"When I was nine or ten, I was, like, your average kid," he said. "Football was—" he harrumphed, shook his head, defensive, or angry, or both. "Art? Screw it. I couldn't wait to play on JV."

He kept his head tilted down the whole time, never looking at Trisha, but focusing on the distance somewhere, speaking quietly but with a mounting bitterness. He sighed deeply and continually, as if rolling a boulder up a hill, determined to end the task as quickly as possible.

"At some point, my ma enrolled me in art classes every Saturday. And I was just starting to like girls, and I really liked Cindy. She lived next door, so she rode to class with us. One time, on this field trip to the Met, she said she really liked abstract oil paintings, and she started talking about how stupid the watercolors were that our teacher made us do."

For two years, James said, he crammed football practice, art, and his mom's errands after school. It was tough on him.

"But look: it's simple," he said. "Ma had this shit in the basement where she let me work, like now. She let me use her acrylics. But Cindy didn't like that, so I started doing this painting for her—the *Junkyard* one." He shrugged. "I was going to give it to her on her birthday.

"One day my friends came over, and I didn't know they were coming and Ma told 'em where I was. I was so scared they'd think I was a pussy for what I was doing that I spilled all this turpentine and didn't fucking clean it up. And of course, they were smoking down there and threw their butts away and I didn't know it."

He paused to drag his own cigarette. Trisha imperceptibly scooted farther away from it. "You see where this is going. I got back from Chick's, and my house was—" He shook his head, unable to go on.

"I'm so—"

"What'd I tell you?" James said, angrily. "I'm not through. So my dad was missing, and I went in. That's it."

"The firemen *let* you?"

He snorted. "This was Bed-Stuy. They didn't get there for *hours*.

"Anyway, I find my pa in the basement, probably lookin' for *me*. I got, like, no clue smoke can kill you. He looked fine to me, just sleepin'. I keep tryin' to drag him out. I can't see shit, I just keep hittin' him to wake him up. And...I guess the roof just caved in and next thing I know, I'm in the hospital. And I didn't get out for a fucking *year*. No shit."

He shook his head.

After a good ten minutes of silence, he began again. "The thing is, I went back for the *picture*. Not my dad. I went in and I saw him and I moved him away from the flames and got the goddamn picture *out*. And *then* I went back for him. If I'd of got *us* out first...."

"People always say shit about tragedies, like, 'Oh, it's not your fault.' They're not always right. Sometimes, it is. And now I pay the price. I find it morally wrong to profit, in *any* way, from something that killed my family."

"*But you didn't know*," Trisha said. "You didn't know your father was in danger. You thought you *had* saved him, *before* you went for the painting. You moved him away from the fire."

James shrugged. "I remember right before the fire, in Catholic school, they taught us that *everything happens for a reason*. So when that shit went down, I was 100 percent convinced it was because I was a bad kid."

"But it wasn't—"

"I know that now," James interrupted.

"I don't think you do."

James glared at her.

And as she sat there, pensive, she had to own up to her own belief all these years that everything did happen for a reason. But if so, how to explain James and his tragic mistake? And her own cancer?

Destiny and karma had to be bullshit. It just had to be.

Or they were both, to quote James, fucking pricks.

They went on to the restaurant, where James ordered a great many plates of Russian food, and Trisha, thanks to the marijuana, ate a good deal of it.

She also had not one shot of vodka, but two. The waiter seemed *so* proud of the product of his homeland. "It'll cure what ails you," he said, and it did somehow seem to put the kibosh on her coughing spells. For just that one night, she felt wonderful. Halfway through dinner she realized she'd never replaced her wig on her head. But looking around, she saw a dozen babushkas and realized she had reached the perfect level of intoxication; everything in the world seemed good.

Well, almost.

"James," she said. She popped a tiny steroid into her mouth; it wasn't the first. James didn't notice. She coughed. "Know how we made that pact?"

He acted at first as if he didn't know what she was talking about.

"I want to call it off," she said. "I don't want you committing suicide. You have too much to offer."

"To offer *who*?"

"Everyone," she said. Then: "A woman. Like that assistant at my job—Rhonda." She paused for a minute. "Have you even ever been in love?"

He sighed, and when he spoke, his voice was hard. "I'll never be able to feel anything until I love someone and that person loves me back."

Trisha looked down at the table. "Well," she said, choking. "You have a lot to offer. Like this, for instance. It's the perfect date. You should be sharing it with someone else." Her eyes teared up but she willed the tears not to fall. She could clearly see what was behind what she was feeling right now. She wanted to scatter her seed as widely as possible, or some such evolutionary babble—to make as many people as possible love her, so that after she died she wouldn't be forgotten.

She saw the potential, too, for the kind of tragic unrequited love story, a sort of *Beauty and the Beast* meets *Romeo and Juliet*, that little girls like her had always dreamed of. And she wanted nothing more than to make it semi-requited—to be with him and then die. To live on through the melodrama.

Either way, she realized, she could do that. Either he wasn't in love with her, but loved her enough to say that he could have been, or he *did* love her but was too shy to say. Didn't that make it the most beautiful and pure of all?

"Anyway." Trisha cleared her throat. "I want you to do something for me. For a dying girl." She smiled grimly. "I want you to see a therapist. Tell him what you told me."

"Shrinks are for pussies."

"So what if they are? Go anyway. No one has to know."

"So let's pretend that I did, and I didn't tell you."

Trisha rolled her eyes. "James," she said, wheedling.

The look she gave him suggested that she needed more of an explanation, so he gave it, with a slight whine in his voice. "It's a big waste of time. I saw one before. After my father died. I was, like, fifteen years old and I was still smarter than him. Plus he treated me like a baby." He looked over toward the old man drying glasses behind the bar. "Nobody knows me better than I know myself and to be frank, nobody's smarter than me. Therapists are for the weak. For people who can't do it themselves."

It was on the tip of Trisha's tongue to say that that was him, but she stopped herself. "So you'll at least admit there's a problem? When somebody thinks about suicide all the time."

James flashed her a wry smile and nodded. "Yeah, I guess so."

"Well let's say you broke your arm. Would you think it was 'weak' to go to a doctor to have him set it?"

James looked taken aback, for once. "Your point," James said, holding up a hand. "I'll think about it, okay?" Then he smiled again, slyly. "But in the meantime, tell me more about this place where you asked Nat to spread your ashes."

⊠

"By the way, you owe me a painting," Trisha told James that very Saturday. To pay him back for giving her such a great time at Coney Island and to reward him for escorting her home that night—which meant a long trip to Manhattan and back to Brooklyn—she'd invited herself over on the weekend. At the time, she had no plan in mind, but on the way in she suddenly wanted a painting of his for her room. Right away. "You owe me a painting," she said, "and I'm not feeling very well, and I want it *now*."

James stepped back from the door and guffawed. "What, just like that? You're asking for a load of crap. An artist has got to be inspired. You can't just sit down and *do* it."

"Sure you can," she said. "That's what your mom always did to put food on the table before she came to the States."

James didn't look convinced. They stood on the porch; they could still enter the studio instead of the house.

"Let me ask you something: If you hate what painting has done to you so much, why do you paint at all?"

"So I don't kill anyone."

That silenced her, but not for long.

"So you're going to refuse a dying woman?" Trisha said. "What's your excuse now? You can't tell me it's the fire. That was twenty years ago. As you would tell me if I were in your shoes: Get over it. Stop worrying about what your dead relatives would think. Do this for me; I'm *alive*. I can't leave a baby behind, I can't make a work of art—I'm a terrible painter—so if you don't do it, who will?" she asked. "What will I leave? Damn it." She felt the tears coming, and she didn't want to cry. "No, *fuck* it. I'd ask you to do a straightforward portrait but you'd never do it. So. This is it. Payback time. For the essays." Which gave her an idea. "Maybe you could paint *me*," she said. "I've got nothing better to do than pose, and I need to be remembered for posterity."

"I ain't touching that one," he said. "You'd hate what I made you look like."

"Oh, but that's what I mean. Just do my chest. The cancer ate it up already. I look *shitty*. I'm finally twisted enough for you now."

He stopped and looked at her in what could have been interest—or actual concern. "You serious?" he said.

She nodded. "I have open, pustulating wounds and everything. You'd love it."

"Trisha…." He shook his head, but as it turned out, that meant *yes*.

Only then did it occur to her that this meant baring herself. *Stripping.*

"How should we do this?" Trisha asked. "If this was *Titanic* and you were Leonardo DiCaprio, you'd have a cozy little couch all set up for me downstairs." She struck a fake dramatic pose.

"Uh, I got a feather bed on top of my mattress," he said. "We could take that down there."

"Can I fall asleep on it?"

"Sure."

They migrated to the basement. Trisha sat at a stool beside one of the tables and surreptitiously put her left hand beneath her shirt. She had not exaggerated; her entire body, from her underarm to a good five inches below what was left of her breasts, was a sheet of bumpy redness, where the cancer had spread to the skin. As was her back.

Three dime-sized areas on the breast had opened up where the cancer broke through the skin to reveal a spongy yellowness.

James, who'd gone back upstairs for the feather bed, re-entered the basement with it and tossed it on the floor.

"You ever paint from a nude model before?" Trisha asked. "Not that I'm going to be nude," she hastily continued. "Make that *live* model."

"Sure. Nude or live, same thing."

She fell to her knees, kicked off her shoes. Took off her button-down shirt. With his eyes diverted, Trisha peeled off her undershirt and lay to her side, hands over her head as far as she could take them, revealing the sheet of red that had overtaken her. Then, she simply decided to take off all her clothes. When she smelled the paint and heard his brush, she knew he had raised his eyes to her. At that moment, she lost her breath completely, and sat there wheezing for a good two or three minutes. She refused to look at James, who remained silent. He didn't move at all until she had recovered.

She reminded herself that there was nothing sexual here. She didn't have breasts or even nipples. Her chest was less sensual, less sexual, than even his. But of course this seemed far more personal, felt far more vulnerable, than she had ever imagined.

"Do you need me to move?" she called out. "Let me know if you need me to move or anything."

"Thanks."

They said nothing.

At first she was too stunned to feel anything but mortified—and deeply mournful. She got over it. Then it was as if she were at the doctor's office, waiting for something to happen.

Then something did. He came to a break. He cleaned his brush and then simply stared at her, as all artists stare at their subjects. She felt his eyes roam her body.

She was in a compromising pose. Weight on her elbow, feet toward him, vagina where he could stare at it. Cancer, almost hidden.

He made his way up her body—and then his eyes met hers, and somehow conveyed to her that for him, too, this was personal, she wasn't just an art model, and this wasn't just a posing session, although what it was who could say.

By the time she left that day, she felt as if she'd run a marathon. She hadn't slept as she had intended; she was too on guard for that. Even hours later, as she was putting her shirt back on, she was shaking.

She returned two days later. Without speaking, he moved one canvas aside and began another. Once again, she removed all of her clothes. This time, she turned her back to him.

In the middle of the third day, James asked her to try another pose, this one seated. Days later, a third. She hadn't seen even one of them—although she could have looked whenever he happened to leave the room—but could tell by his palette that he used a variety of flesh- and earth-toned paints. No old canvases, not this time.

Trisha had sat for people before, although not in the nude. She had never had much desire to see the work in progress. There was an unspoken vow not to look; the model's feelings might affect the artist's work. How could James experiment if he had Trisha's feelings in mind?

Increasingly, she wanted to break this vow. She had to will herself to stay in her pose. She wanted to see how James saw her, how she moved him, and not only because of their personal connection. Knowing there existed a

Picasso of yourself, how could you not look? And how could you not be disappointed in what you saw?

After his first several works, she still felt vulnerable every time she loosened her shirt. One day, grasping for something to say at a moment that felt especially awkward, she blurted: "Turnabout is fair play. If I'm going to keep doing this, how about *I* paint *you*?"

She meant his face, only his face, and was beginning a preparatory sketch when he pulled off his shirt and revealed his own scars: no less gnarled than hers, in fact, more so; less red, but covering his entire chest. She gasped. "What—"

"They grafted skin," he said. "From the inner thigh, places like that." He eased off the rest of his clothing, show-ing her the graft sites, and then turned to lie on his side, with his back to her. He made such a stunning model, so muscular, like David—the sculpture—but completely marred, which only made him more beautiful. She realized right away that she could never do him justice.

She stood and stared at the blank canvas, breathing heavily, for several minutes. Then she put down her brush. "I'm sorry, it's not in me," she said. Her voice warbled. She could hardly stand, she felt so weak. "Let's get dressed."

The way he looked at her, and then looked at the can-vas—the transfer sometimes felt nothing short of divine.

Sometimes he attacked his painting with such fervor that Trisha was a little afraid.

"When can I see them?" she asked. It was all she thought about now, lying there cold, under the light. "And when can I collect my painting? I assume you'll let me choose?"

"Wha?" It took him a minute to readjust to a world in

which people spoke. He had been so deep in his own world.

"What are you going to do with the rest of them? Are you thinking of selling them? Giving them to Gresh for a show?"

"Maybe." He tossed it off in such a way that she knew he hadn't even heard her.

"It would mean a lot to me. It would be my legacy, you know." She said it lightly but didn't mean it. It sounded so ridiculously silly. "If you care about what I want, and I'm sure you don't, but if you did, I would want them to be seen."

Twenty or thirty minutes later he stopped, folded his arms over his chest, and said, "You know how I feel about that shit."

"You'd never have to work again. You could make so much money—" Somewhere, in the back of her head, she knew she was fighting this battle because she didn't want to face her own. As long as they had unfinished business, she never had to think about the *real* problem: She was rapidly dying. By now, she had to come to the studio with an oxygen tank that delivered fresh O2 to her. But that was Trisha, always one to dot her i's before she crossed her t's.

"I don't care about the money," James said.

"I don't *believe* you," she said. "And"—she smiled wanly—"if you showed your work, you could have any 'chick' you wanted."

"That doesn't matter either." He looked down.

She sat up and pulled her clothes to her. "Well, the painting does. I see how you are when you paint: happy. You think I don't wish I could paint? I would give anything, *anything*, for one iota of the talent you're frittering away.

That you're not even using it just kills me."

"I'm using it," he declared. "I'm just not whoring it out."

"You're good, and you're *original*, and—do you even know how rare that is? They say that those who can't paint become critics, and that's what the hell I am. *Was*. I can't even do *that* now."

"Even if I did 'use it,' as you say, it wouldn't make a bit of difference to you. Don't you get that?" he said. "It's like—if I finish eating what's on my plate, none of those starving children in China get fed."

"It would make a difference to *me*," she said. "To *me*." She put on her clothes and left for the last time.

◻

She didn't stay away out of anger, but because the next day, she woke up with a 103-degree fever: a high temperature for anyone, much less someone with a compromised immune system. She burned, and shivered, and could hardly catch her breath to tell the 911 operator she needed help. She almost cursed herself for having refused her mother's offer to stay with her. But she had fought for these last days of independence, of solitude, of her old life. Of *life*.

After seven hours in an overlit, understaffed emergency room, she landed in a semi-private room with a woman as loud as James had predicted, with a husband permanently attached to the phone—even at 11 p.m. Trisha was too delirious to notice. By the time a group of doctors came around for 11:30 a.m. rounds, they had a preliminary diagnosis: pneumonia. Which, given the cancer in her lungs, could be serious—*very* serious, as their somber tones suggested. She felt like death. When she wasn't in a fitful sleep, she hallucinated, telling anyone who would listen that she was ready to go, saying that slipping away in her sleep would be a blessing. Or she was crying. Or coughing. Mostly, gasping for air.

The doctors had little luck breaking her fever. Trisha reverted to the semi-conscious state she'd inhabited as a young child, when she drowsed on museum benches surrounded by color and form, free-associating, dissociating—this time from her condition instead of her discreetly drunk mother. In these fevered daydreams, she indulged all sorts of maudlin scenarios, in which after her death, Tom and especially James and even Mitch broke down, and found themselves forever unable to perform sexually, due to their mourning. Their wives learned to despise Trisha for owning a portion of their husbands' hearts, a place no one living could hope to touch. They thought of her, and regretted, for years and years, until they, too, might as well be on their deathbeds.

Not that it was clear that this was *it*. She had pneumonia, simple as that. Sicker people pulled out of these things every day, and lived to play another round of golf. But it *felt* like the end. Trisha slept round the clock, waking only to eat and eliminate and complain about the pain. Lucky for her, the nurses, young women just like her (except for the obvious), liked her. In vain attempts to purge the guilty thoughts that barraged them because it was she instead of them, they had her moved to a private, sunlit corner room. There was even room for her loved ones to sleep in her room on cots on the floor.

For instance: Several days in, Thomas arrived, looking worse than she did, if that were possible. Gaunt, red-eyed, crazy-haired. (Actually, *Tom* arrived; he'd given up the pretentious name change.) "Why didn't you *tell* me," he groaned. He knelt at the edge of her bed, grasping her hand so hard she had to tell him it hurt her, crying as she'd never seen anyone cry.

"Why?" she got out. She was on oxygen; a thin seethrough wire ran to her nose to deliver her breath. "What would it have changed?"

"Nothing, and *everything*," he said. "Don't you see? I *love* you."

"You *love* Sondra," she said, and turned away.

"I *love you*, but Sondra needed me, and you never did.

You never *let* yourself need me. You always had to be in control."

"And so did you."

"And so did I."

"Well, we can't control anything now," Trisha said, and laughed almost in hysteria.

James showed up just minutes later, carrying something which quickly trumped all the orchids and gardenias in the room: "I think I'll call it *Phoenix*," James said, as he pulled down the garden-variety landscape that the hospital had put on the wall and replaced it with his own work.

"Rising from the ashes," Tom cited, as if no one else got the reference.

It did look like a phoenix, to Trisha's mind: The center of his typical rough-and-tumble abstraction appeared to be a beautiful, unmarred woman's back. Only the wings were missing.

Trisha loved it.

"So have you decided?" she asked him, when they got a rare moment alone. "Who are you going to leave all your paintings to when *you* croak, Mr. Suicide? Or have you decided that 'life is too beautiful?' Taken up watching soap operas, maybe?"

James shook his head. "No such luck—but not a bad idea," he said. "I never tried that. Anyway," he said, "my paintings are going out with me: in a blaze of glory."

Others arrived. Mitch, who was working in the city for the next several months, brought over an expensive minia-ture Bose stereo, a perk of working on the Bose account, apparently. It was a loaner—but for as long as she needed it. Later, he'd sent over an underling with music, Sarah

MacLachlan, Aimee Mann, and Shawn Colvin—all the happy, mellow chick music she'd loved way back when they dated.

"Who tamed you?" Trisha croaked after thanking him. "I'd like to meet her."

"What?"

"This is a damn thoughtful gift you've come up with, mister." She smiled.

Mitch had had nothing to say. For the duration of his visit, he had futzed with the stereo, and he told her three times which CDs he had chosen, always promising he would bring more. By the time he left her with James, it was a relief.

"I'm just so sick of how everyone acts," Trisha gasping. "Like I'm a goddamn *saint*."

James raised his forefinger to her and shook it back and forth. "No way. I don't think you can be Saint Trisha unless you wash your mouth out with soap, young lady," he said, riffing on the overly earnest chaplain who came by four times a day to see if Trisha would pray with him. "You've certainly become quite a *headen* in your old age."

Trisha cracked up, although it hurt her to laugh. Just like it hurt her to lie on her back, or sit on her back, or lie on her stomach, given the blocks of cancer everywhere. "It's *heathen*, you sinner!" she said. "You go down five points in God's book just for that!"

"Oh, lord, do they really have a book?"

"I'll ask him. Anyway," Trisha said, "if *one more person* tells me I'm the bravest person they know, I'm going to kick them in the balls. Or the breasts."

"That'll get 'em," James said. "Especially the breast thing. Can you imagine? How can they complain—or retaliate, for that matter?"

They both laughed.

"Seriously, though, I know what you mean about the 'bravery' thing," he said. "What else are you going to do? You have *no choice*. It's not like you *decided* to have cancer. Your only other option is to kill yourself." His volume dropped precipitously when he mentioned the 'k' word.

⊠

Trisha was beginning to correct a lot of misperceptions she'd always had about The End. She found it nothing less than tragic that she would die without the world sharing in her knowledge. But for the most part, she was too damned tired to share it.

For instance. She had always planned that as The End approached, she would look up old friends and boyfriends, to find out the truth now that no one had anything to lose. Was her old high school friend Tina *really* in the CIA, as everyone had suspected? Had Nat had an abortion? Why had David *really* broken up with her? Had James slept with Doreen?

Only, now she couldn't care less about any of it. David could have walked through the door to declare his everlasting love, and she wouldn't have wanted to waste the energy to talk to him.

Some people had assumed that she would want to travel to Paris at last, or to read the great novels. Instead, she enjoyed nothing more than staying at home and watching *Dr. Phil* on television.

And she would have thought that as The End approached, she would stop hoping, and stop looking forward. But Trisha was incapable of imagining a world without herself in it. And her doctors encouraged this, always pointing out—to herself and, she assumed, her family— that despite the infection's resistance to the antibiotics they had tried, she might well be back in chemotherapy the following week.

If she made it to chemo, they would point out that there

was always a chance that *this* one would work—for a year, maybe, which was time enough for a new drug to enter the picture.

Of course, they all knew the truth, which is why the doctor wasn't *quite* as chipper as usual. "Tell me, doc," Trisha asked one day, "is it time for me to tell my mother that she's really my adoptive daughter?"

"Well, I always—oh, that's funny," the doctor said, although it wasn't and she didn't laugh. "I think it's *always* a good idea for us to tell people what they mean to us, and to tell them things that are important, and that goes for *everyone*. I'm serious. I could leave the hospital tonight and get hit by a bus."

Trisha nodded and tried to force herself not to roll her eyes. She noticed, though, that the doctor omitted the second part of the cliché: "and *you* could live to be eighty."

So she took that as a sign that whether she took a turn for the better or the worse, she should start saying goodbyes.

Tom first. That night, he had scrunched up next to her in her twin bed when someone knocked at the door. It was a young man with a violin who said he was a Juilliard student who would like to play for them. He started with a few Gershwin tunes and then broke into "Besame Mucho," a song they had danced to, once, under the stars in Puerto Rico. As the violin cried, Trisha nestled in Tom's arms with the lights dimmed. She felt there was no place she would rather be, and told him so; and although it was probably the morphine talking, it was a nice way to end their unfortunate romance. The last several days, with him back in her life, had been among their best: They'd been able to spend long, leisurely days laughing and shaking their heads about this ridiculous situation, and even watching a little bad television—all things they'd never had the chance to do before.

"Whatever happens, or I should say, *when* this happens," Trisha said, "I want you to take the time to *live*, and to share yourself with someone, because although you have your quirks, you are a beautiful person. And I can see how this has opened up your heart." The tears were flowing from him at such a rate that Trisha was almost alarmed. "You have to promise me, *promise* me, that you won't let it close again."

He nodded, and held her until she fell asleep.

When James came in the next day, Trisha had just had an excruciating procedure; the doctor stuck a foot-long needle (or so it seemed) into the sac around her right lung, so that he could draw out much of the two liters or more of fluid there. She lay in bed, not really wanting to move, but desperate for company.

"What was it like when you were in the hospital?" Trisha asked.

It was a topic James had always shunned in the past, but he must have decided that these circumstances made it appropriate. "It sucked," he said. "I was in a coma at first. And then when I woke up they wouldn't let me see my body. Gauze was *all* over, and every several days they had to change it and"—he sucked in some air, reliving the excruciating pain. "I can't *tell* you how much it hurt. But unlike the shit you're going through, every time it got just a tiny bit better."

"Okay, that doesn't make me feel good," Trisha said. "What else?"

"I found out later my skin sloughed off in sheets. Eventually I saw shit that no twelve-year-old, no *person*, should see. I saw it sometimes—it just...*came off*. I had *nothing* on the whole right half of my face. They kept saying they'd do these operations to make it look normal, but I was scared to death they'd never really do them. And it took, like, a year for them to do anything at all.

"One time this stupid intern was there, and I knew I was smarter than him, and I convinced him to let me look...." James shook his head. "You know, up until then, I had this idea that I was just going to get better and look exactly the same and go back to playing football with my friends, and get Cindy to love me, because she came to the hospital every week. After that I knew: Nothing, *nothing, would* ever *be the same*. Nothing. Like it wasn't bad enough just to lose my dad?

"That's when I started wanting to kill myself."

Trisha rang the nurse and asked for pain medication. "Go on," she said.

"And then...I found out what I looked like, which was *shitty,* and how no hair would grow all over half my head, so I'd be bald, and I could hardly see, which they made worse, because then I went in and out of the hospital having eye operations, where these doctors poked these long needles into my eye and couldn't anesthetize me because they had to watch me blink, and I had to be awake the whole fucking time. And I *still* can't really see. Is this good enough for you?"

"I take it back," Trisha said. "Cancer's nothing."

"That's the worst part," James said. "You got it worse than me. So I can't even be proud that I'm the toughest bastard around anymore."

"Sure you can, after I kill myself and you don't."

He shook his head and rolled his eyes.

"Don't worry," Trisha said. "I still think you're Most

Fucked. Although...."

"What?"

"I guess I...always thought my life would amount to something," she said slowly. Even given the steroids the doctors were feeding her now, it took her an entire minute to eke out every painful sentence. "How can I die when I've done nothing yet? I'm going to die and not only did I never do *anything*, I didn't even stay married and or have a child. And look at you: You can do it all. Get married, have kids, you've *already* fulfilled yourself creatively, and you get to be rich and famous if you want to be." She shook her head. "That's messed up. I'm kind of pissed with you, to tell you the truth."

"Why?"

"You went through all that when you were a kid, but you got to live. Screw you. It's like you said to me: 'Look at you and look at me and tell me who's fucked.'" She sighed. "I came to you because I wanted someone who would understand. Well, you can't. You're just a big fat poseur. Get out of my face."

She put her hands over her head then and started to cry. "I'm so sorry," she said. "I know you hate those words, and now I know *why*, but I am. Don't take it personally. I hate everyone now. Why does it hurt so much that everyone else gets to live?"

James sighed. He put out his hand, as if to comfort the bed. "The reason you care is, you have a sense of entitlement. I don't mean that to sound harsh. You just went through your life believing you'd look pretty and get married and live forever. Someone like me never thought *any* of that, so anything that happens is a big surprise. It's not that either way is right or wrong. But really, you ought to feel *lucky* you ever got to feel that way in the first place. Some people never do."

"You're a pretty frank bastard, you know that?"

"That's what they tell me."

"So does this mean you're happy now?"

"Are you kidding?" James laughed heartily. "I'm god-damn miserable. We're still on, Juliet. Now get some beauty sleep." He kissed her on the head.

"And by the way: You didn't do nothing. You helped *me*," James said after a while.

"Do what?"

He shrugged. "Kill myself if nothing else."

She didn't laugh, but she did say, "One less dick in the world. Goodie." Then she struggled for a deep breath. "You know I didn't mean that. It's just….

"I…guess I always really truly believed that things happened for a reason. I don't know that I believed that *people* were here for a reason, but…*I thought* I *was*. And when I met you, I don't know, I thought—I thought you had something to do with it. You were supposed to be the poignant one. But this"—she gestured toward her shriveled body. "I don't see the reason for this."

She coughed and reached for a tissue, which she used to blow her nose. She dabbed her eyes; she cried all the time now, from the unrelenting pain. "I was seeing this therapist, and she said, it's not that things happen for a reason, it's that the people who are most successful in life are those who *find* a reason for the shit that happens to them. And that makes sense. But what am I doing with it?

"I thought, then, that maybe I was here to keep you from committing suicide. I thought, maybe *that*'s the reason I'm sick. And I thought maybe…the reason you went through…what you went through, all that time ago, was…so you could be there for me.

"But I can't—I can see you're not happy, and you're not getting help, you refuse to see a therapist, and if you want to kill yourself it's not like *I* can stop you. So just go ahead." She struggled for breath.

And finally found it.

"Which brings us full circle," she said. "When I met you, I always knew you would go psychotic and kill someone, and now we know who: me." She told him, then, what she wanted. She directed him to her jacket, where he found the keys to her apartment. She described where he could find her pills, and which containers to bring.

"In return, I can only offer you good karma, although I don't think that exists anymore," she said, "as well as enough pills to keep in reserve for those lonely nights ahead. So go ahead; if you want to use them to commit suicide, go ahead. But I'm not letting them allow you into heaven unless you do *something* with those paintings.

"So there's nothing else." She paused. "Unless…"She said it quietly, almost in a whisper.

"Unless what?"

She took a deep breath, or tried to, although it didn't reach her lungs. Trisha could hear the wheeze. She whispered: "Unless you want to tell me that you were always in love with me. Or unless you want to get over this thing you have about your work and let the gallery have it. If you don't want it, give it to Gresh's assistant, Rhonda. Just don't burn it. Please." She got some air. "At least then I'd have made a difference. And been immortalized." She once again gestured to the sheet. "Yes, this beautiful body, preserved for the world."

She shook her head. "But even if you don't, there's a reason that *you* were here, and it's not to paint, although you're a brilliant artist. And that's to help me. Because without you, I swear, I wouldn't have made it this far."

More was supposed to follow. Trisha wanted to tell Nat she expected to be remembered in her Oscar speech someday because she knew Nat, or, well, Carly, would milk this death for a lifetime of crying scenes. More important, she wanted to tell Glenn to take care of Carly *and* Nat. She meant to tell James to take care of Baracus, who was apparently set to become a Brooklyn pit bull. She wanted to thank her mother for being both a mother and father to her over the years, whether or not that was true. She wanted to thank Rhonda for all the Jolly Ranchers. But then she took a turn for the worse, and the doctor barred all visitors except for immediate family, which meant Melinda.

"There's still a good chance that she will pull out of this," the doctor told those gathered. "Her fever could break while she sleeps, and she could be out of here in a week, taking Baracus for long walks." Trisha's doctor liked dogs, had always asked about the little guy during Trisha's visits. "It's just too soon to tell."

One day, Trisha awoke to find that James had somehow slipped past the "guards"—her nurses. She also sensed that she'd been moved—to another private room? Well. One with too many beeps. And the lights—could somebody dim the damn lights?

"I brought you something," he said. He looked different, somehow—*excited*. As he'd looked on that day they'd gone to Coney Island, which now seemed so long ago.

"What is it?" Trisha mouthed weakly.

"They wouldn't let me hang the painting in here," James said. "No nails. It's over there on the floor. But I got these."

James pulled up a stack of three shoe boxes. It took a minute, but then Trisha recognized them for what they were: the bins in which she'd kept the postcards she'd bought every single time she went to a museum, a lifetime of her favorite art.

"Where—?"

"Save your breath," he said. "And be still." Carefully, he stood atop her hospital bed and for the next fifteen minutes—until a nurse came in and asked him to leave—he rapidly tacked as many as he could to the ceiling over her bed. Trisha watched in wonder as Manets, Monets, Klees, Mondrians, Calder mobiles, Brancusi statues—all appeared above her. And of course, there was *The Death of Marat*, the martyr in his bath. Given the amount of morphine she was on, they almost came to life. She didn't even complain when an occasional tack fell and hit her in the head.

"Will you do me a favor?" Trisha asked after he'd been busted, but before he left.

He nodded somberly.

"Hold me," she said.

He hesitated, and then reached out his arms.

"Gotcha." She smiled weakly. "I must be really bad off if you're falling for that." It took her a while to say this, but he hung in there, and then shook his head, chagrined.

She reached up to wipe the sweat from her face. "I feel like one of those poor dying kids on TV. I'm pathetic."

"No you're not."

"I am. But seriously, a favor. Got any music?"

"Always. You know that."

"Can you loan me your music? It's *boring* in here."

"Uh, the only thing is, um, you may not like what I've got—"

"It'll be fine," she whispered. "Just fine."

"And the doctors—"

"When," she wheezed, "have you *ever* let the rules stop you?"

"Okay then," James said. "It's going to take me a while to get it set up—I got to go get Mitch's stereo—but I'll bring you some Metallica, going out to Miss Trisha Portman in the ICU."

James was back. She thought. She weakly whispered to him, asking if he was back to do 'his job,' as they had taken to calling the euthanasia.

Or maybe she was hallucinating. The morphine made her so groggy. Maybe this was just some male nurse.

"What job is that?"

She wanted to respond, "To Kervorkian me," but the word was too long, and what if it *was* a nurse? The last thing she needed was one of those hospital chaplains they were always pushing on you.

"Are you hurting?" James/Nurse asked quietly, looking toward the door. "I've got something that can take care of that."

"Go ahead: I'm ready," she got out. "Please." She hardly knew what she was saying, but she knew that she meant it.

"Okay, Trisha. Shhh, shhh. It's all right."

"Don't fucking shhhh me." She smiled. She started to say something, but then she couldn't stop coughing. Anyway, he knew what she meant. He gave her the pills and watched to make sure she swallowed them all.

And somewhere in there she fell asleep, or *almost* asleep, into her wonderful daydreamy state.

In her mind, she returned to James's house, wearing old jeans and a long-sleeved flannel shirt. She signaled for him to sit next to her on the feather bed. She noticed some overly sincere heavy metal ballad, playing low on the radio.

He caught the look on her face, and appeared puzzled. "What's—?"

"Shh!" She put her finger to her lips and then beckoned with it, as if she had a surprise for him.

And she did. When he sat, she touched her hands to his face and pressed her lips onto his. It didn't feel like any other kiss she'd ever had—in part because she initiated it. At first, he didn't kiss back. She felt like she'd just invaded his personal space. Like she was smushing her face against a glass.

Then he opened his mouth wide and kissed back. She thought, *I'm kissing James,* and the bizarreness of it hit her.

She couldn't let go because she couldn't stop analyzing what was happening.

After the initial twist of contact, she came up for air, making a noise that sounded like a gasp of passion and might well have been.

Words flooded Trisha's mind, as if she looked at flash cards.

Strange.

Confusing.

Complicated.

Wow.

"You know," she said as he approached her on the bed, "I know it could never work with us.…"

He caressed her arm. His movement felt stilted, like it was something he'd seen on the movies but never performed. "Why wouldn't it?"

"We'd drive each other crazy," she said. And then realized, as he stared at her, that he would take that as a *stop.* "But I don't know.… Maybe.…"

He sighed. Drew close and kissed her again. She was thinking this wasn't the way she had imagined it—she would have imagined a whirlwind of action, of body-slamming against a wall, of him *using* his strength—and only then realized that she *had* imagined it, a million times, in the level of consciousness just below thought.

They fell onto the feather bed.

"We have to stop," she said as she let him touch her.

"Shhh."

"Don't shhh me!" It came out angry. "Sorry. See? This is what I mean! *Crazy!*"

"Shhh—" he stopped himself. "I mean, don't say that," he whispered.

"I can't believe *you're* shushing *me*."

"What do you mean?"

"You're so *loud*."

"Shut up, Trisha," he said, and kissed her.

Because he had turned out the light it was all about touch. Any place he touched her tingled. Knowing it would never happen again, she worried about her performance, knew it was coming off badly. Her head tilted back and lifted, hovered above the earth, and she wanted to stop time and stay there forever frozen.

She was well, cured, and she would always exist, and she understood the *why* of it all, that now she would exist forever. He held her, cradled her, there was no doubt in her head that he loved her. There was no reason to say it. She rose, rose, rose, and took flight, up and away, exploding from her body, understanding for the first time that this must be where tales of a heaven in the sky came from. Nothing could keep her earthbound anymore. She was a phoenix.

She tasted tears, hers and his, and they were manna, a

panacea, homeopathy as it was meant to be practiced. She lay on top of him and covered his wounds, filling in the crevices. They fit together like an ancient puzzle.

Later, as she lay beside him and stroked his bare chest, she said, "You know, I know you've got this tough-guy thing going for you, but you're actually really sweet. You should let more people know that."

"Don't make me kill you," he said with a dark laugh.

The dream mutated again. It was dark now. She had been asleep and now her ears filled with ominous, foreboding music, backed by tick-tick-ticking drums and the crunch of electric guitars.

She wanted to whisper for water. A figure—James?—put a glass in her hand. She spilled it, but moments later, a straw poked the corner of her mouth. It felt like a stab.

"Open."

There might have been twenty pills or only two. They grated her dry mouth and she struggled to swallow them. And almost instantly felt better.

"Are you crying?" she murmured.

"No," he said. "It's raining out there."

"Now I lay me down to sleep," the singer rasped, bellowing out to the entire dorm room floor, *"I pray the lord my soul to keep."*

She closed her eyes. The music came through the walls. She wished the dick would turn it town. Wait! Ha! Rhett was coming to shush him. Rhett would take care of it....Wait....Something was wrong. She struggled to figure out what. For a split second she knew, and it broke her heart.

"Taaaaake my hand," the singer kept saying. *"We're off to never-never land."*

Someone must have left the stereo on too loud. Her head hurt. She hated that jerk next door.

A weird thought occurred to her. Maybe she was half in love with him.

Whatever. She babbled something about a bathtub. But she was too tired to figure it out.

Acknowledgments

On a sad day in June 2002, as I faced spending the next month in a post-operative sickbed, an old college friend came to visit. Like me, he had always dreamed of writing a novel, and he encouraged me to use my "month off" to start making my own dream come true. "I'll make a pact with you," I told him. "I'll write every day if *you* will." Who would have believed back then that our pact would lead to two kick-ass first novels? He did. I can honestly say without the encouragement from Adam Fawer (author of *The Improbable*, forthcoming from William Morrow), this book would not have been written. Put another way: King of the YYMF, I salute you.

In many ways, it has been a tough several years, and I would like to say a heartfelt thank you to those who have nurtured me both physically and emotionally. In addition to my angelic mother, Faye Williams, and spirit-lifting sister, Laurie Williams, these include Daniel Spirn and his own ever-generous family; my father, Larry, the original "big dog of Middagh;" Sonia Stoszek; Allis Marion; Erin Hennicke; the dog park gang (in particular, novelist Aaron Coe); and, of course, my loyal dog, Gus, who is always by my side. I'd also like to thank Gabriella D'Andrea, Kathleen Ferris, and Austen Hayes for keeping me alive and optimistic. And here's a "howdy, y'all" for my extended family in Texas; you may be far away, but you are never out of my heart.

As a small girl growing up in what is truly the middle of nowhere, I never thought it possible that I would get to do what I loved when I grew up, much less make a living at it.

I would like to thank just a few of the teachers and editors who taught me the craft, and, more important, encouraged me over the years. These include William Gilchriest, the late Nora Magid, Steven Reddicliffe, Amy Paulsen, Rick Schindler, and Pete Finch.

When it came time to put this project together, so many people came out of the woodwork to help. I'd particularly like to thank Anne Heller, Don Wallace, Maggie McComas, and Susan Dooley for their valuable editorial advice, as well as George Tripp at Camden Printing for expediting this book.

But first and foremost on this list is Ellie McGrath, who, in the past twelve years, has been my boss, mentor, surrogate mother, lunch buddy, great friend, and, now, publisher. I can never repay the massive debt I have accrued to her over the years. And now, she has provided the most remarkable gift anyone could possibly give me: the joy and peace that comes from knowing I will go to my deathbed a published novelist.

About the Printing

It normally takes months, even a year or more, for a manuscript to leave a writer's hands and be transformed into a finished, hardbound book. Because of the author's declining health, this book was produced in a matter of weeks. Four weeks and three days after the manuscript was transmitted to Camden Printing, Inc. in Rockport, Maine, a finished copy of the book was ready for the author to hold.

Although meeting deadlines is a daily routine for printing companies, binderies, and suppliers, the completion of this particular book involved very special cooperation—not to mention acts of kindness and good will—among dozens of people in all phases of production. George Tripp, president of Camden Printing, put together a team of suppliers, pressmen, customer service representatives, assistants, and bindery personnel, who worked overtime to finish the project. Spectrum Printing and Graphics Inc. of Portland, Maine provided high-speed presses to meet the accelerated deadline. The people at New Hampshire Bindery cleared their schedule to bind the book as soon as it was off the presses.

The text was composed in Book Antiqua and printed on acid-free Cougar Opaque text. The jacket was printed on Anthem Gloss Text. The finished product is a team effort by people who cared about a young writer, whom most had never met, with terminal cancer. The author and publisher thank them all.

About the Author

Stephanie Williams is a journalist whose work has been published in more than a dozen major magazines, including *New York*, *Men's Health* and *Glamour*. She is a former writer at *Self* and *TV Guide*, senior writer at *SmartMoney*, and contributing editor at *Teen People*. In 2002, the National Headliner Awards named her runner up for Magazine Feature Writing for her narratives in *SmartMoney*.

A native of Texas, she graduated from the University of Pennsylvania and has made her home in Brooklyn, near Prospect Park, with her dog, Gus. This is her first novel.